Ten Days in August

Books by Kate McMurray

Such a Dance

Ten Days in August

Published by Kensington Publishing Corporation

Ten Days in August

Kate McMurray

LYRICAL PRESS
Kensington Publishing Corp.
www.kensingtonbooks.com

LYRICAL PRESS BOOKS are published by

Kensington Publishing Corp.
119 West 40th Street
New York, NY 10018

All Kensington titles, imprints, and distributed lines are available at special quantity discounts for bulk purchases for sales promotion, premiums, fund-raising, educational, or institutional use.

Special book excerpts or customized printings can also be created to fit specific needs. For details, write or phone the office of the Kensington Sales Manager: Kensington Publishing Corp., 119 West 40th Street, New York, NY 10018. Attn. Sales Department. Phone: 1-800-221-2647.

Lyrical Press and the Lyrical Press logo Reg. U.S. Pat. & TM Off.

First Electronic Edition: March 2016
eISBN-13: 978-1-61650-801-2
eISBN-10: 1-61650-801-9

First Print Edition: March 2016
ISBN-13: 978-1-61650-802-9
ISBN-10: 1-61650-802-7

Printed in the United States of America

Day 1

New York City
Wednesday, August 5, 1896
Temperature: 89°F

Chapter 1

A small black dog with wild eyes ran up Broadway, snapping and snarling at passersby. As women shrieked and men hopped out of the way, a cry of "Mad dog!" echoed through the crowds out strolling, trying to find relief on a hot day.

The saloonkeepers and police officers from City Hall to Houston Street knew Jerry the dog; he would wag his tail and beg for scraps and get a head pat before jogging from one saloon to the next. Most considered him a harmless little tramp. But today, something was wrong. He ran for the open front door of a bank, alternately panting and growling. When the attendant tried to kick Jerry out of the way, Jerry bit his foot and ran inside. Someone said, "Look out, Mac! He may be mad!"

The panic inside the bank caught the attention of bulky Officer Giblin, who hauled out his gun and eyed the little dog. Jerry's gaze darted around the room as he slobbered all over the floor.

Officer Giblin brandished his gun, but didn't want to do anything rash. He poked at the dog with his nightstick, trying to ascertain if he really was mad. The dog snapped and lunged for the nightstick. That was all the evidence Giblin needed. He aimed his gun.

"Not in here!" one of the clerks shouted. "Think of the ladies present!"

Giblin nodded. "All right, you mangy rascal." He chased Jerry out of the bank. Once they reached the street, Giblin aimed his gun and fired. The little dog rolled over dead instantly. The crowd cheered.

Hank Brandt watched from a few feet away with some amusement as Officer Lewis ran across the street. He fired his own gun into the dog's head.

"Thank you, Lewis," said Hank, pulling off his hat and wiping the sweat from his brow with his handkerchief. "He was just as dead before you fired, but we appreciate your attention to detail."

Lewis thrust out his chest. "I just dispatched with a mad dog in *my* *precinct.*"

"So you did." Hank wasn't completely convinced the little dog was mad so much as suffering from the effects of the day's extreme heat, even more relentless than it had been the day before. "Congratulations, Lewis. You killed a dead dog."

Lewis muttered an oath and walked away from Hank, so Hank decided to continue on his way to the precinct house.

"Extra, extra! Heat wave taking over the city!" crowed a newsboy, thrusting a paper at Hank.

"I'm living it, kid," Hank said. Still, he tossed a nickel at the newsie and took a paper. The unbearable heat dominated the headlines, although a story below the fold complained about Police Commissioner Roosevelt blustering about saloons being open on Sundays again and gave an update on the trial of a woman accused of chopping her husband into bits before dumping the remains in the East River. *The World* had no qualms about declaring her guilty.

Hank had some doubts, given that he'd worked the case. He still suspected her lover, a married man who delivered ice. Maybe the city had decided the ice was too valuable to spare him for trial.

Hank was sympathetic. Dear Lord, it was hot. The air around him was thick and rancid. Simply being outside was like walking around with eight blankets draped over his shoulders. The street smelled of rotting food and horse manure.

Ah, New York in the summer.

He arrived at the precinct house on East Fifth Street, where the whir of the overhead electric fans drowned out all other noise, and still the fans weren't doing much beyond blowing papers around. It smelled slightly better inside, but it wasn't any cooler.

"Brandt."

Hank wasn't even at his desk yet and already someone was trying to get his attention.

He sighed and turned his attention toward his colleague and sometime partner, Stephens, who stood there with his arms crossed.

"Would you *like* for Roosevelt to give you a lecture?" said Stephens, glaring at Hank's bare forearms.

Hank had forsaken a jacket and rolled up his shirtsleeves in an attempt to escape the oppressive heat. Not that it worked. Stephens, of course, wore his full uniform. The collar of his coat was soaked with sweat. Hank wondered what Stephens hoped to achieve by suffocating under all that wool.

"It's amusing to me that Commissioner Roosevelt thinks any man could wear a coat in this weather. If he wants to discuss proper attire, he can do so when the weather cools off." Hank pulled his handkerchief out of his pockets and mopped his brow again.

Stephens balked, but recovered quickly and said, "We have a new investigation. That is, now that you've decided to grace us with your presence."

"It is too hot for sarcasm, Stephens. What is the case?"

Stephens puffed out his chest and made a show of pulling a wad of crumpled paper from his jacket pocket. He consulted his notes. "Murder at a resort on the Bowery."

Hank glanced back toward the front entrance to the precinct house. Taking on a case would mean investigating, which meant going back outside. The last thing Hank wanted to do was go outside. Not that the precinct house was cool and comfortable as such, but Hank reasoned if he sat very still, he might be all right. He turned back to Stephens. "Which resort?"

Stephens looked at his tattered papers. "Club Bulgaria."

Hank schooled his features. He wondered if Stephens knew of the reputation of this particular club. Not that Hank had ever been there. He'd merely been tempted.

"Any other information?" Hank asked.

"Not much. Officers who arrived at the scene first talked to the club owner briefly, but he didn't seem to know anything. The body is still there. A few of the staff from the club have been made to wait there for our arrival."

Hank could only imagine how putrid the body must smell in this heat. "Well," he said. "No sense standing around here dripping. Let's go."

Nicholas Sharp—stage name Paulina Clodhopper—stood outside Club Bulgaria in his street clothes, smoking the last of a cigarillo. It was doing nothing to calm his nerves. He tossed the butt of it toward the street and rearranged the red scarf draped around his neck. It was too hot for such frippery, but he had an image to maintain, and besides, the police were on their way. He wanted to look somewhat respectable. Really, though, Nicky would have much preferred a long soak in an ice bath while wearing nothing at all.

The sun blared down on the Bowery and it smelled like someone had died—which, Nicky acknowledged, had happened in truth—and it was nearly unbearable, but he couldn't stand inside any longer. Not with Edward laid out on the floor like . . . well. Nicky didn't want to think of it.

A man in rolled-up shirtsleeves and an ugly brown waistcoat, his hands shoved in his pockets, walked down the street toward Nicky. The man beside him must have been boiling inside his crisp police uniform.

The man in uniform looked Nicky up and down with an expression of deep skepticism on his face. "Are you Mr. Juel?" His tone indicated his real question was, *Are you even a real man?*

Nicky bristled. "No, darling. He's inside."

The man in shirtsleeves said, "You work here?"

"Yes."

This man was really quite attractive, in a sweaty, disheveled way, although Nicky supposed there was no way around that in this weather. The man pulled a handkerchief from his pocket and then pulled the dusty bowler hat off his head, revealing dark brown hair, cut short. He wiped his whole face from his damp forehead to his thick mustache before he dropped the hat back on his head. There seemed to be a strong body under the wrinkled clothing, but it was hard to tell. Still, this man intrigued Nicky. His companion in the uniform was blond and bearded and looked considerably more polished, but in a bland way. The disheveled man was far more interesting.

"I'll take you in to see Mr. Juel," Nicky said. "That is, if I could have your names."

"I'm Detective Stephens," said the uniformed man briskly.

"Hank Brandt," said the man in shirtsleeves.

"Acting Inspector Henry Brandt," Stephens said. "Honestly, Brandt, there are protocols."

Brandt grunted and waved his hand dismissively at Stephens. To Nicky, he said, "And you are?"

"Nicholas Sharp. Come with me." He led the police officers inside.

Julie waited in front of the door to the ballroom. He stepped forward and introduced himself, standing tall but fussing a bit more than necessary—"This is *such* a terrible tragedy, nothing like this has *ever* happened here before, I am still in such a state of shock!"—his voice growing increasingly shrill as he spoke. Nicky might have believed him if this had been the first act of violence perpetrated at Club Bulgaria.

"Can you tell us what transpired, Mr. Juel?" asked Detective Stephens, the picture of proper politeness, although it was Brandt who pulled a pad of paper and a pencil from his pocket.

"I did not know the fate of poor Edward until I arrived this morning."

Nicky glanced at Brandt to ascertain his reaction. Julie was lying just as sure as he had a receding hairline; he rarely left the club. Nicky knew for a fact Julie had been sleeping in his office at the back of the club for nearly a week, ever since his lover had thrown him out of their Greenwich Village apartment. Nicky didn't know for certain, but he also suspected poor Edward had been lying on the floor of the ballroom for some time before Julie had deigned to notice him.

"And where were you through all this, Mr. Sharp?" asked Brandt.

Nicky adjusted his scarf. "I went home just after midnight last night. I arrived back at the club about an hour ago, where Mr. Juel confronted me with the news that poor Edward had departed the earth."

Brandt nodded. "What exactly is your occupation here?"

"I entertain the guests."

Brandt pursed his lips. "You entertain them."

"I sing," said Nicky.

Brandt's eyebrows shot up. "Right. So. This Edward, is he a friend of yours?"

Nicky kept hoping Julie would intervene, but he stayed resolutely quiet. Nicky wasn't quite sure what the best answer to these questions would be or how much information he should give away willingly. He said, "He also entertained the guests. In a somewhat different capacity."

Brandt turned toward Stephens and said, "Would you go take a look at the ballroom? I'll follow along in a moment."

Stephens nodded and proceeded into the ballroom. Julie trailed after him.

Nicky shivered, alarmed now that he was alone with Mr. Brandt, who removed his hat and took a step closer to Nicky.

"Tell me honestly," said Brandt. "Edward was a working boy."

Nicky sucked in a breath. Brandt stood close enough for Nicky to smell him, a sour, earthy scent, the fragrance of someone who had spent too much time stewing in his own sweat on a hot day.

"Yes," Nicky whispered.

"And you are as well?"

"No. I only sing."

Brandt grunted. "I'm not here from the vice squad. I do not wish to toss anyone in jail unless they killed your friend Edward. Do you understand me?"

"Yes. And I am being honest. Edward was a working boy. I sing on stage a few times a week." Nicky pointed toward the ballroom. "That's all."

"You sing."

"Yes. And to answer your next question, last I saw Edward was last night. He was entertaining a guest. They went to the back. I do not know what happened after."

Brandt must have been astute enough to discern Nicky's meaning, because he jotted something down on his pad. "What did this guest look like?"

Nicky closed his eyes to try to picture him. "He had dark hair. He was quite tall. Thick mustache. A very fine suit of clothes, much nicer than the sort the guests here usually wear."

Brandt scribbled in his notes. He said, "Would you recognize this man if you saw him again?"

"Yes, I believe so."

"They went to the back and never returned?"

Nicky didn't quite know what to make of these questions. Clearly, Brandt was worldly enough to know how a club like this worked, so he must have known the back rooms behind the ballroom at Club Bulgaria were where men went to have sex with each other. Edward would have sidled up to a man like the one Nicky had seen him with last night and seen the money dancing before his eyes. He would have taken the man in back for a . . . financial transaction. And then?

"I'll be honest and tell you I didn't think much about Edward hanging on the arm of some man from uptown. This fancy dressed man was slumming, which is hardly a novel occurrence. Usually the bourgeoisie come down here to gawk and feel superior, but occasionally one of the boys here does get his claws in one. It wasn't strange enough for me to take notice."

"Except for his clothes."

"Yes, well. I quite liked the cut of the man's jacket and spent a brief, wondrous moment imagining I could afford to purchase such a thing."

Brandt nodded. "In other words, Edward may just have emerged from the back room unscathed after entertaining this man, but if he did, you did not see it." He stepped toward the ballroom. "Come with me."

"Oh, no, darling. I couldn't possibly. I've spent far too much time with poor Edward today as it is."

"Fine. Stay here, then. Don't leave. I'm not done talking to you."

"Your wish is my command."

Brandt narrowed his eyes. He probably didn't appreciate Nicky acting flippant, but Nicky knew of no other way to manage such a situation.

Nicky watched Brandt walk into the ballroom. When the voices of the men inside rose, Nicky found a spare chair to sit in. There was nothing to do but wait.

For nearly a year, Police Commissioner Roosevelt had been trying to cure the city of vice. Standing in the middle of a tawdry ballroom, Hank could see his point. There was something particularly sad about this room. Hank glanced toward Stephens, who he knew thought cleaning up the city was a worthy goal, and maybe it was. Hank did not believe it was an achievable one. The city was too far gone, perhaps. And its residents liked their vices.

Hank imagined this ballroom had once been grand. There were the remnants of a forgotten era everywhere: sculptural touches carved into the ceiling and a series of murals painted on two of the walls. On the other hand, the murals were somewhat vulgar and depicted men in various states of undress lounging about in parks or, in the case of one of them, in the ruins of Ancient Rome. Hank supposed the murals were supposed to be titillating, but there was something strange about them. Hank was no art scholar, but these were not quite right, as if they were a parody of art and not art itself.

Artistry and architecture aside, though, the ballroom inside Club Bulgaria was worn and filthy. The wooden floor was stained and scratched, the stage curtains were threadbare, and the sculptures were chipped or broken.

Stephens stood frowning as he took in the room. They hadn't discussed it on the walk over to the club, but Stephens was no greenhorn. He had to have known to expect a dance hall or brothel at least—the residents of New York did not come to this neighborhood to see Shakespeare—but he might not have known that this was a fairy resort. This was precisely the sort of place that would send him into fits. If Stephens was trying to hide his revulsion, he failed badly.

Hank knelt and took a closer look at the body. There was something vulgar about the dead man, too, something that made him blend in with his sordid surroundings, and not just because he was dead. Hank recorded every visible detail in his notes. The dead man wore a stained shirt and black trousers. A smudge of some kind of grime stained his cheek. His hair was unruly. There was powder on his face and some sort of rouge on his cheeks, which kept the paleness of death at bay.

Not to mention, there was a knife wound in his chest.

Hank turned to Mr. Juel. "Mr. Sharp mentioned seeing this Edward go off with a wealthy-looking man. Did you happen to see this man?"

Juel shook his head. "No, Inspector. I wish I had. Do you know what it will do to my business if word gets out this kind of violence could be perpetrated at my club? If that man is responsible for this, I want him caught! I want—"

"No need for theatrics," said Hank.

"No need? Why, just three weeks past, a man was killed outside Paresis, and what did the police do? Nothing. One more dead prostitute, eh? The working boys who walk along the Bowery at night are inverted and less than human, are they not? Why should the police bother to investigate?"

Hank leveled his gaze at Juel. "I care not a whit what a corpse did when he lived. It wouldn't matter to me if Edward were a working boy or a banker. Murder is murder, and I intend to find the killer."

"That is some consolation," said Juel, looking mollified.

"We should shut this whole place down," said Stephens.

Juel and Hank both turned to gape at Stephens. Hank shook his head. "It's not worth it. I know you don't like . . . institutions like this one, but for every one you shut down, three more are built. Let it be for now. And keep in mind the occupation of the victim is not evidence he deserved to die."

"No, that is not how I think," said Stephens, although Hank suspected he did a little. Hank imagined they'd be having a discussion later about whether police resources were really well spent on dead working boys.

Of course, Stephens also knew Hank had a much looser view of how the police should be regulating human behavior. He'd told Stephens once that if a man wanted to seek out temporary companionship, why should the police intervene? Perhaps Hank operated under a different moral code from many other officers; he had no wife at home despite being well into his thirties, for example. Not that anyone knew it, but he'd sought out some of that temporary companionship himself. Stephens had likely resigned himself to his lot as far as working with Hank was concerned, but he didn't always agree with Hank's approach to cases.

Hank walked a circle around the body, studying carefully, wondering if he'd missed something obvious. Stephens hovered nearby but didn't speak. There wasn't much enlightening here beyond the body of a man who had probably been killed by a patron. Solving this case would be an uphill climb. If this had been a different day or a different officer called to the scene, perhaps nobody would have bothered to investigate.

However, Hank was here now.

He said, "We will have to send a squad down to transport the body to the morgue."

"Yes," said Stephens.

To Juel, Hank said, "Do you have any record of your guests last night?"

"We assure our guests of our complete discretion."

Hank nodded; he'd suspected this would be the case. "No, then. All right. Who was here last night? Any other employees? Regulars?"

Juel balked. "If I hand over names to the police, I will be out of business in a week."

Hank grunted. "You want this murder solved or not?" His tone had an edge to it. "Who *can* I speak with?"

"Nicky—Mr. Sharp—can help you in whatever way you require."

Juel put a hand on Hank's shoulder and steered him back out of the ballroom. Stephens took one last look around and then followed them. As Juel walked through the door, he repeated, "Mr. Sharp can get you any information you need."

Hank expected Stephens to object and give a lecture on police procedure—Hank and Stephens needed to speak with witnesses directly, Juel could not dictate terms of the investigation, Stephens wasn't interested in the financial fortunes of Club Bulgaria, and so forth—but instead, he stayed quiet. Hank couldn't figure out what that meant.

Not to mention, Hank was pretty sure Nicholas Sharp had exactly what he needed.

Chapter 2

The meeting room was as stuffy as a mausoleum, and Andrew Ritchley wondered if this would not be his final resting place after all, particularly with all the hot air coming from the mouths of the meeting's attendees.

Commissioner Roosevelt stood now, leaning forward and hopping a little as he spoke. The conversation had shifted from Sunday's troubling tailor's strike in the Lower East Side to the report from the Fourteenth Precinct's captain that some saloons were skirting the Sunday laws by opening rooms above the bars for rent and calling themselves hotels, thus becoming exempt from having to close on Sunday. Roosevelt was furious, his face red as he ranted. Andrew struggled to keep the meeting minutes, scribbling quickly but probably missing every third word. Andrew wondered how Roosevelt could sustain the energy to speak so vigorously in this heat, although sweat poured off the man's body.

Commissioner Parker sat, looking unfazed, but then, he had never been a supporter of the Sunday laws.

Commissioner Grant said, "If it please my distinguished colleagues, might I point out this new development is perhaps a return to old ways, and not in the way we intended. These rooms above saloons, they are not much preferred to the old brothels renting rooms near the taps."

"Pre-cise-ly!" bellowed Roosevelt, drawing out the first two syllables and putting a staccato emphasis on the third. "This exception to the law is no exception if this is the result."

Parker leaned back in his chair laconically and held out his hand. "With all due respect," he said in such a disdainful way Andrew knew he meant no respect at all, "if we were not so intent on closing every saloon on the isle of Manhattan on Sundays, the police department could turn its efforts toward more valiant pursuits. Real crimes, theft and violence, are occurring in the precincts adjacent to this building as we speak but we do not have the officers to curtail it because they're so busy arresting saloonkeepers for the crime of serving a drink to a thirsty man on Sunday."

"Crimes fueled by drink," Roosevelt pointed out. "Perhaps if men did not spend their hard-earned coins on spirits at the saloon they wouldn't have to steal more to feed their children."

Grant let out a long-suffering sigh. "I doubt we'll find any resolution today." He ran a hand over his beard and glanced around the room. "I wonder if we shouldn't adjourn this meeting until a time at which it is not so hot."

The captain from the Fourteenth Precinct stood and said, "Thank you, gentlemen. I must return to my precinct. My men have already been called to the scene of three different incidents today of men succumbing to the heat."

Roosevelt resumed his seat. "Succumbing to the heat?"

Andrew wondered if Roosevelt had even noticed how ghastly hot it was outside. Probably he kept cool through sheer force of will.

"Collapsing, sir, while working on a construction project on Mott Street. And there have been a number of reports of dogs gone mad from the heat. One of my officers shot one just a few hours ago."

"It may be worth considering some kind of temporary measure to keep men from working while the high temperatures persist," said Grant.

"Yes, I agree that would be wise," said Roosevelt. "Ritchley, write up a note on the matter to be distributed to all precinct houses in the city."

"Yes, sir," said Andrew.

"We'll adjourn for now," said Roosevelt, "but I want a solution to the saloon problem."

The meeting broke, and Andrew gathered his notes, intending to return to his desk to type up the memorandum on restricted work hours. Roosevelt walked over and clapped him on the back.

"Did you finish the paperwork on former officer O'Dwyer?" Roosevelt asked.

"Yes, sir. He packed up his desk on Monday."

"Let it be known around his precinct exactly why he was terminated. We want to set an example. The police department will not condone corruption. Not on my watch."

"Yes, sir."

Andrew's mind dwelled on O'Dwyer on his trip back to his desk. As far as Andrew could tell, O'Dwyer's chief sin was a relationship with the widow who owned the perfume shop on Bleecker Street while also supporting a wife and three children in a cramped apartment near Madison Square. Andrew himself was guilty of much greater crimes than adultery, although he would die a grisly death before disclosing any details to his boss. Commissioner Roosevelt was weeding undesirable officers—morally corrupt officers, according to Roosevelt—from the ranks of the police department, and thus anyone of questionable values was vulnerable.

Andrew spared a thought for his friend Hank Brandt in the Tenth Precinct. At least Hank had always been discreet in his affairs.

Andrew spent the next half hour or so typing up his notes, and then who should come into police headquarters but Hank Brandt himself, a pensive expression on his face when he stopped by Andrew's desk. He wasn't wearing a coat and his shirtsleeves were rolled up to his elbows, something that probably would have merited a comment from Commissioner Roosevelt on a day when it was not ninety degrees outside. Still, Hank looked even more disreputable than usual, his shirt and trousers wrinkled, the hair of his mustache slightly ruffled.

"Murder on the Bowery," Hank said by way of greeting, running his hand over his mustache to smooth it down.

Andrew nodded. "Are you sure it is a murder? From what I understand, the weather has become a violent felon this week."

"The knife wound in the man's chest was the biggest clue."

Andrew would have laughed if it hadn't been so morbid. "Dear god," he said instead.

"Club Bulgaria, Andrew," Hank said under his breath.

"Oh, dear." Andrew's mind reeled. He knew the nature of the club and suspected there might be a greater story unfolding.

Hank seemed to agree. "Two possibilities as I see them." He took off his old bowler and wiped his face with a handkerchief as he sat in the chair near Andrew's desk. "Either a wealthy man slumming it at the resorts on the Bowery has taken to killing boys after he finishes with them or the staff at this particular resort has made up an elaborate story to cover up their crime."

"Which do you think it is?"

Hank frowned. "I do not yet know. My gut says the former, but the men I spoke to today were keeping something from me."

"Unsavory characters die in New York every day."

"I know." Hank pocketed his handkerchief. "An officer shot Jerry the Tramp this morning."

"Oh, goodness." Jerry must have been the canine menace the captain of the Fourteenth Precinct had been crowing about. "Why?"

"The dog went mad suddenly, according to the eyewitnesses. I believe he simply suffered from some sickness from the heat, though he was acting wilder than usual. He did not deserve to be shot, but the people seem satisfied the police eradicated a public menace today."

"Poor Jerry."

"Anyway, I wanted to file my initial report." Hank pulled a folded sheaf of paper from his waistcoat pocket and went about smoothing it out on the corner of Andrew's desk. Then he picked it up but seemed reluctant to hand the papers over.

Having a hunch as to the cause of Hank's hesitation, Andrew asked, "Do you think the police department will try to shut down the resort?"

"I hope not, but this would seem to be all the excuse Roosevelt needs." Hank let out a heavy breath. "I have some theories but not a lot of evidence. I want to wait for the coroner's report before saying what occurred for certain. I mean to further investigate the staff at the club in the meantime."

"You may be in for a month of Sundays if you wait for the coroner's report before further investigation."

"What do you mean?"

Andrew gestured at the pile of paper on his desk. "Since yesterday, there have been reports of a significant number of deaths across the city. More than usual. I'm supposing most of these are due to the extreme heat we seem to be experiencing. There were over a hundred reported just yesterday. The coroner has his hands full."

Hank breathed out an expletive and tapped his fingers on Andrew's desk. "Be that as it may, I intend to get to the bottom of this case."

"Of course." Andrew glanced around and, seeing no one near enough to overhear, he said, "If you need any help, please let me know."

"Thank you."

"I will file your report in the meantime."

"Much obliged."

"I can't promise much haste, I'm afraid, since Mr. Roosevelt also has me processing personnel discharges. Did I tell you about O'Dwyer?"

"The fellow who was fired on Monday? Yes, you did."

"Be careful, Hank. Especially with this case. Roosevelt is determined to ensure his police force is composed of only the most morally forthright men."

"I'm always careful." Hank shook his head. "If Roosevelt carries out this plan, he'll have a police force of five men."

"I know." A rather unpleasant thought struck Andrew just then. "Do you think there is any danger toward . . . well, toward inverted men? Any evidence the killer targeted this man in particular because he . . . ?"

"I don't know yet." The way Hank pressed his lips together indicated to Andrew he'd had the same thought. "If there is a danger, I will do everything I can to put a stop to it."

All Andrew could do was nod in agreement.

Hank hopped off the Third Avenue elevated train at Fifty-Third Street and walked west toward Fifth Avenue. He felt some comfort in the fact that at least New York's wealthiest residents were suffering through the heat as much as its poorest. Well, perhaps not to the same degree; this far uptown, the citizens of New York could afford ice and had running water.

He walked up the steps of the Cooper mansion on Fifth Avenue, mere blocks from the palatial Vanderbilt estate, and knocked on the door. A butler in livery who looked displeased by Hank's presence greeted him at the door.

"Is Mrs. Cooper available to callers?" Hank asked.

The butler, named Graves if Hank's memory served, raised one neatly groomed eyebrow and folded his hands behind his back. "She is to men who are not dressed as pugilists."

Hank glanced at his bare arms. He grunted, but began to unroll his sleeves. He pulled cuff links from his pockets and buttoned up properly. When he finished, he held up his wrists for inspection. "Better?"

"It would be better if you had a coat, but it will do. Come. Mrs. Cooper is in the library."

Hank rubbed his sleeves as he followed Graves, trying to smooth out the wrinkles that seemed to be pressed permanently into his shirt. He'd been too hot all day to give a toss whether he was properly attired or not, but now that he was inside the grandiose Cooper manse, he felt self-conscious. The feeling intensified when he laid eyes on Amelia Cooper, resplendent in a bright blue gown that hugged her midsection and seemed to have a lot of flounce and frippery. Her hair was pinned up elaborately atop her head and decorated with pearls that sparkled in the waning daylight pouring in through the open window. When she turned, a gleaming diamond necklace at her throat caught the light and reflected it back toward Hank bright enough to blind him.

"Ah, Mr. Brandt, my old friend. So good to see you on this wretched evening." She smiled broadly. "Leave us, Graves. Let Mr. Cooper know I will join him and Mr. Knight in the parlor in short order."

"At your pleasure, madam." Graves bowed and left the room.

Hank still wasn't used to seeing Amelia this way, decorated so thoroughly in all this expensive finery, even though she'd been married to steel magnate Jonathan Cooper for nearly three years now.

"What brings you here, Hank?" she said when Graves left.

"Caught a case today."

"Well, naturally. It is a day ending in *y*, is it not? Are you calling on me to discuss it?"

He wanted to talk to her, his closest friend, because this case troubled him far more than any that had been tossed his way in quite some time, and Amelia had been the person with whom he could most easily sort through his thoughts. She'd helped him think through difficult cases in the past, even though discussing cases with civilians was improper. Still, Hank trusted Amelia like no other person in his life. More to the point, a wealthy man slumming as a possible suspect was reason enough to come uptown; perhaps Amelia had heard something. "I am interested in your insights. The last person seen alive with my victim seems to be a man of some means."

"You believe him to be one of the Four Hundred, then?"

"That remains a leap in logic I do not have the evidence to support, but one of the witnesses implied he'd seen a man who might have gone down to the Bowery for sport."

Amelia rolled her eyes. "Oh, yes. What a jolly good time may be had when the population of Fifth Avenue decides to sojourn downtown to see how the other half lives."

"For all I know, the description of this man is an elaborate lie made up by the real killer, but you know as well as I do people of your ilk visit the resorts along the Bowery to make themselves feel superior."

Amelia bristled. "Not of *my* ilk."

"No, not you, my dear, but not all of your husband's friends are fine, upstanding individuals all the time."

She shrugged. She pulled an escaped curl away from her face and tucked it behind her ear. "What aren't you telling me? Do you suspect one of Jonathan's friends?"

"I don't have any suspect at all. Perhaps I'm just asking if you knew of anyone who went to the Bowery resorts last night."

"How should I know, Hank? I'm just a hollow-headed woman. No one tells me anything."

"Oh, come now. Bitterness doesn't suit you."

She sighed. "Jonathan and I dined with Mr. and Mrs. Beekman last night. Mrs. Beekman implied Mrs. Astor herself would grace us with her presence, but alas, we continue to be beneath her notice."

Hank gazed at Amelia, from the curls atop her head to the delicate jewelry at her neck and wrists, to the intricate pattern of embroidery on the bodice of her gown, to the satin slippers peeking out from under her skirts. It was a marvel to him that Amelia had triumphed over their childhood as kids in Greenwich Village. They hadn't been poor, not like the immigrants in the tenements in his precinct, but they hadn't been rich, either. Both of their fathers had worked in factories off Washington Square Park before and after the War, and both had lost their jobs as factories moved to Brooklyn and other places outside of the city. Hank's mother had been a seamstress, and she'd worked her fingers to the bone to support them while his father had struggled to find work. Amelia's family hadn't fared much better.

That Amelia had caught the eye of Jonathan Cooper while out for a walk in Central Park one day would probably never cease to amaze

Hank. That Jonathan Cooper, who had made his fortune in steel and dabbled in architecture, had fallen for a girl like Amelia would never cease to amaze New York's elite, who had been reluctant to adopt her as one of their own at first. Some rationalized Cooper's actions as being those of a New Money man unused to having to conform to society's rules and so allowed a few eccentricities. By all accounts, Amelia had charmed the stockings off nearly everyone she met, though, so society quickly forgot the scandal. And now Amelia was this finely appointed creature who no longer had to worry about money and instead worried about whether or not she'd be invited to Mrs. Astor's next ball.

"What is really troubling you?" she asked. "You would not have come uptown just to put forward the idea your murderer might move in one of my circles."

Hank met her gaze. "Honestly, this case is getting to me."

"How so?"

"I'm not sure. Perhaps because the body was discovered at . . ." He trailed off, wondering if he should elaborate.

But, of course, Amelia was his oldest friend and she knew him better than he knew himself sometimes. "Do not be concerned with my delicate sensibilities. Tell me plain. What concerns you about the case?"

He let out a breath. "The victim was a working boy at a resort where men go to find the companionship of other men."

"Ah," she said. She lifted her skirts slightly and walked across the room to a side table where a bottle of whiskey sat proudly. She picked up a snifter and filled it with two fingers before handing it to Hank. Then she did the same for herself. Hank watched her take a sip and savor it on her tongue before swallowing. He mirrored her, letting the rich flavor fill his nostrils before he swallowed. It burned nicely on the way down. "So you're worried men of a certain type are being targeted? Has there been more than one murder?"

"I spent the afternoon studying the file for another murder committed a couple of months ago. I do believe the crimes are related."

"Dead working boys both?"

"Yes."

"Could be a coincidence."

"Which occurred to me." Hank sipped his whiskey.

"But you don't think it is."

"No. But I can't prove it yet. I will, but I don't have enough evidence. There's something else, though."

Amelia took a step toward him. "What is it?"

"Commissioner Roosevelt has been stamping out corruption, as you know." Hank used a mocking tone, hoping to convey what he thought of this endeavor. Amelia smiled faintly. Hank went on, "There are too many unknown outcomes. Perhaps I'll be left to find the murderer and be hailed a hero, but I doubt there is much heroism in finding the killer of a prostitute, particularly a male one. If anything, the murderer will be praised. Roosevelt may decide this resort is too depraved to be allowed to continue its existence and will shut it down, giving men like the victim one less place to go."

"Men like yourself, too."

Hank's heart pounded as he contemplated this possibility. "Yes, although I have not indulged in quite some time."

"Since Roosevelt took over as president of the police commission."

"Never let it be said you are hollow-headed. But really only since this damned appointment to Acting Inspector. One of these days, they're either going to fire me or officially promote me to a position in which more eyes will be on me all the time."

Amelia nodded. "This crime bothers you because it involves men like you, and you're worried investigating it further will put you into some places that will garner the attention of one blustery, mustachioed police commissioner, and therefore you are afraid to investigate lest it end your career even as your greatest desire is to find this killer. Have I got the right of it?"

"You could be Watson to my Holmes."

She grinned. "Try not to worry too much, Hank dearest. I believe things will turn out for the best in the end."

"I can only wish I had your faith."

"Well, in the meantime, you might want to practice your soapbox speeches, because the promotion is a bit of a political one, is it not?"

Hank felt grim about the prospect. "Indeed. I'd have some discretion over which cases I pursue, at least, but it is a much higher-profile position."

"You'll be fine. I've never met a smarter man. Aside from

Jonathan, of course. That is, you are both intelligent, but in different ways." She laughed and put her glass down. "Jonathan would, of course, excel at a position in which he had to give speeches. You, perhaps not, but I feel certain you will make the most of the opportunity."

"Or I'll get myself fired."

"Such an optimist." She approached him and took the snifter from his hand. "Please do stop by more often and talk to me if you need any help. You know I am always available to you."

"Thank you, I appreciate it. I should probably go now, though, and let you attend whatever business you have with your husband."

She waved her hand as she put the whiskey snifters on a side table, presumably to be collected by a servant. "Oh, it is just Jonathan's horrid friend Mr. Knight. He brought him home with him from the club this afternoon and now they are laughing together like old friends. Would you like to meet Mr. Knight?"

"Would I? Not if he's horrid."

Amelia clucked her tongue. Hank extended his arm to escort her and she tucked a hand into his elbow. "He has an unfortunate habit of commenting on my fair bosom whenever Jonathan is out of the room. I don't care for it. I mentioned it to Jonathan, but he laughed it off, calling Mr. Knight an eccentric."

"Men."

"Indeed. I'll let you make your own judgments before you depart for the evening. They're in the parlor down the hall."

Hank walked Amelia down the hall and entered a grandiosely decorated sitting room. Jonathan Cooper, who was thin and neat with wire-framed glasses sitting at the end of his nose, sat primly in a lushly upholstered chair. The other man in the room was burlier, with curly dark hair and a broad chest. He had a body that seemed better suited to cutting down trees than to being a captain of industry, as Hank assumed he was if he sat in Jonathan's parlor.

"Oh, Amelia, there you are. And Mr. Brandt," Jonathan said. "Nice to see you."

"Likewise," said Hank. He meant it; he'd always liked Jonathan.

Jonathan motioned toward the burly man. "Allow me to introduce you to Brigham Knight. He's an up-and-coming architect with Daniel Burnham's firm."

"A pleasure," said Hank.

"Mr. Brandt is a police inspector," said Jonathan.

"Are you?" said Knight, practically oozing with condescension.

Hank kept himself from rolling his eyes. He knew the moneyed residents of upper Fifth Avenue had little time for such vulgar professions as police work.

"Mr. Brandt is also a very dear friend of mine," Amelia cut in, sounding a bit defensive.

Hoping to diffuse the tension, Hank said, "I take it your acquaintance with Mr. Cooper is borne of your architectural background. I hope we have not intruded on a business discussion."

"Not at all," said Jonathan. "Although Mr. Knight does have some revolutionary ideas."

"We were discussing skyscrapers," Knight said. "Wave of the future."

"Skyscrapers?" said Hank.

"We live on an island with a finite amount of space. When we run out of space in which to build out, we must build up! Steel is the key, Mr. Brandt. It is the only material strong enough to support a sky-high building. The newspaper offices on Park Row are just the beginning."

"Now you've uncorked him," Amelia murmured.

"The firm has its eye on a plot of land near Madison Square. The owner won't sell, but I have a vision of an efficient office tower, rising up above the squat buildings below, with a view as far as the eye can see from the upper floors."

"Where is there left to build near Madison Square?" Hank asked.

"I want to tear down the electric signs on the flatiron-shaped piece of land across from the square, right at Broadway and Fifth Avenue. Imagine a building there, how majestic it would look."

"That little sliver?" said Hank. "It's barely wide enough to stand on. You want to put a building there?"

Knight stood tall and laughed, his voice booming. "I like the challenge of it."

"All right. You don't think—"

Amelia grabbed Hank's arm and pulled him back. "Well, Mr. Brandt was just leaving. He merely stopped by to give me a bit of news about one of our childhood pals."

"Oh. Yes," said Hank. "Nice to have met you, Mr. Knight. Nice to see you again, Jonathan."

Amelia practically pulled him from the room. Graves waited by the door and handed Hank his hat as they arrived.

"I'll not have you starting fights with my guests," Amelia said.

"I apologize. You're right, though. He is horrid. Of all the cocka-mamie ideas, a skyscraper!" Hank glanced back toward the parlor. "How tall do you think you could build a building before it toppled over?"

"I imagine that is something Mr. Knight wishes to discover for himself. Perhaps we should not ruin the surprise."

Hank was reluctant to leave the livable warmth of the Coopers' house for the boiling streets outside, but he donned his hat and bowed to Amelia. Perhaps it would not be so bad now the sun was setting. "Thank you for whatever help you could provide."

"Do update me when you find your criminal."

"I will."

"Oh, and do not forget about the charity ball next week!"

Hank suppressed a groan. "The charity ball?"

"Yes, dearest. I realize the mail has not been the most reliable of late, but surely you've received your engraved invitation by now." She raised an eyebrow and there was a gleam in her eye, which Hank found a little alarming.

"I have no business at a charity ball."

"Nonsense. You are my friend. Wear your best suit and you will blend right in. Besides, it is a noble cause. We are raising money to help the children suffering downtown. Think of the children, Hank."

Hank wished for a hasty departure now. He couldn't think of any-thing less enjoyable than a charity ball where he'd be forced to hob-nob with New York's elite. "I will consider it." He stepped through the door. "Goodnight, Amelia."

"Sweet dreams, Hank."

As the sun set on a day that had brought nothing but misery, Nicky sat in his dressing room and rouged his cheeks.

He'd thought about Inspector Brandt quite a bit as the day wore on. Brandt had a ruggedness about him Nicky found appealing. He could practically hear Julie or Charlie joking about his fondness for rough trade, but there was more than that to Brandt, something real.

Not that it mattered. Nicky intended never to see him again. It wouldn't be much of a challenge, give that it seemed likely the police wouldn't bother to try to solve the mystery of poor Edward's death.

By some miracle, Julie had acquired enough ice to put in front of fans so cool air blew around the ballroom, but back here in the dressing rooms, the performers' makeup dripped off as soon as they applied it. Nicky stared at his assembled melted cosmetics, feeling frustrated; singing and dancing were about the last things he wanted to do tonight. Edward was dead, the heat was oppressive, and any joy Nicky had for performing tonight was only for his paycheck.

Charlie knocked on the open dressing room door, so Nicky motioned him in. Charlie closed the door behind him. "I heard about Edward."

"Yes."

"Is it true you saw him?"

The mental image of Edward lying on the floor, covered in grime, mouth agape, blood pooling at his head, hit Nicky in the face. He wished he could push it aside, but he imagined it would be quite a while before he managed that feat. "I did."

Charlie seemed to cotton on to the fact Nicky didn't want to talk about it; he nodded and sat at the table beside Nicky. He reached for the makeup and leaned toward the mirror to apply it. Charlie was about ten years too old to really be called a "boy," so he painted his face to look younger. Nicky wasn't sure he was very convincing.

"Are you worried?" Charlie asked, his tone light, as if Edward's death were an idle concern.

"I don't know."

Charlie wiped his hands on a rag. "Do you know anything about what happened?"

"Are you the police?" Nicky snapped.

Charlie held up his hands. "No. I don't mean to be nosy. But how am I to know if . . . how am I to know if the man I sit with tonight wants me to end up like Edward?"

It was like Charlie had reached into Nicky's chest and squeezed his heart. "I do not know. You can't. But this profession was always a risk."

"Which is why you dance now."

Nicky reached up and finished pinning his wig in place. He said nothing.

Charlie examined himself in the mirror and stood back up. "I need to pay my rent. No one wants an aging working boy, but Julie still lets me work here, and sometimes I do find a man just desperate enough to overlook my advanced years."

"You're not old," said Nicky, although that wasn't quite accurate, at least not in the circles they moved.

"It's all the same in the dark, I suppose." Charlie took a deep breath and put his hand on the door frame. "If I don't see you tomorrow—"

"You will."

"Good luck tonight, Nicky." Then he was gone.

Day 2

Thursday, August 6

Temperature: 91°F

Chapter 3

Nicky's sister Brigid lived on Hester Street not far enough from where they'd grown up in a crowded tenement building with barely enough room for each person to move his elbows.

The rest of the Sharp children had gotten out of the tenth ward. Brigid had chosen to marry an Italian man who owned a little shop on Orchard Street, and so she'd stayed. Thus it had fallen upon her to take care of not only her five children but also the Sharp patriarch, who had fallen into a bottle upon the death of their mother.

The heat worried Nicky. As he walked through the clamor of pushcarts and other street vendors to get to Brigid's building, he could not help but notice how wretched it all felt, how hot and hopeless. The air smelled of fish slowly spoiling where they lay on display, of rotting fruit and rancid meat, of sweat and urine and decay. Nicky did not want to be so prissy as to cover his nose with his hand, but he did pull out a handkerchief to feign blowing his nose so he could get some respite.

A man had buckets of water that did not look clean, but he offered refreshment to anyone who needed a drink. Others huddled under the white awnings that had been stretched out from the storefronts on Hester Street, hoping to hide from the glaring sun. But there wasn't room enough to hide everyone, and it seemed as though every resident of the neighborhood gathered outside. People swarmed about on the street or hovered above it on the fire escapes and roofs of the narrow buildings.

Brigid lived on the third floor of her building in a three-room apartment. Nicky gazed up at it and saw her laundry hanging from the fire escape. The front door to the building stood open, and two of Brigid's kids were sitting on the stoop having what looked like an intense conversation. The girl, Lucy, grinned when she saw him.

"Uncle Nicky!"

The boy, William, looked up, too. He smiled but looked too exhausted to do much more than lift his hand.

"Is your mother upstairs?" Nicky asked.

"Yes," said Lucy. She was the oldest, nearly twelve. "It's too hot, so Mother told us to go outside, but it is not much better out here."

"No, I imagine it isn't."

"Why is it so hot, Uncle Nicky?" asked William, rubbing his face, clearly miserable.

"I do not know."

He left the children to their conversation on the stoop and walked up to the third floor. The apartment door was wide open, as were the windows at the back of the apartment, Brigid clearly trying in vain to get some sort of cross breeze to cool off the rooms. Nicky strongly suspected this was a futile endeavor.

He found Brigid in one of the bedrooms, sitting next to a bed. Her youngest, a girl named Edith, lay wheezing, her tiny body gasping for air.

Nicky went to their side. "Oh, Brigid."

"Edith is ill."

"Yes, I gathered."

Brigid looked up at Nicky. "Were Lucy and William outside?"

"Yes."

"David and Anthony are asleep in the other room. What can we do besides sleep? In all my years, I have never . . ." Brigid sniffed and shook her head. "Edith needs a doctor, but none will come here. I do not know what to do." Brigid reached into a large bowl full of water and pulled out a cloth. She draped the cloth over Edith's forehead. Edith sucked in a breath.

"Perhaps it is just the heat. Edith will recover when it cools down again. Surely it will be cooler soon."

"Perhaps," Brigid said.

Nicky would have offered to take the lot of them to his rooms up on Third Street, but he didn't have much more space than Brigid. It was in a nicer neighborhood, granted, but he had no place to put children. Besides, Brigid did not approve of the sort of company Nicky kept. She thought his whole neighborhood a den of sin.

Perhaps it was.

Then again, politicians said the same thing about Hester Street.

Nicky said, "I wanted to check on you and the children. Where is Antonio?"

Brigid had one red curl stuck to her forehead. She pushed it away with her hand. "He went to the shop. He thought if everyone milled about outside, he might sell some of his meat before it all spoils in the heat."

"And where is dear old Pa?"

"Your guess is as good as mine. He left yesterday afternoon to find an ale and never returned."

This was hardly unprecedented. "It is probably cooler at whatever saloon he found than it is here."

Edith sighed and seemed to fall asleep. Nicky and Brigid both watched her chest rise and fall for a few moments.

"Perhaps it is just the heat," Brigid said.

"It is really unbearable. But if you can get away, I heard they are giving away ice near City Hall at no cost."

"I may send Lucy."

"I can accompany her if you like."

Brigid looked up, relief on her face. "Oh, please do. Thank you, Nicholas."

Heavy silence fell over the room, punctuated only by the sudden ragged intakes of Edith's breath. Nicky considered the central problem here; he'd escaped this neighborhood but gone uptown to a place not much better. For years, he'd tried to make enough money selling his body and soul to the men of the Bowery to get his family out, but Brigid had refused his money and he'd been utterly miserable. He made a little more now singing and dancing across the stage at Bulgaria, but it still wasn't enough. If only there were a way to earn more, to get Brigid a larger space to fit her children and get out of this heat.

Perhaps if he earned money in another way. Nicky twisted his hat in his hands and said, "I know perhaps I am not the brother you would have hoped for."

"Nonsense. You are the only brother here."

It was true. Of the seven Sharp children, Nicky was the youngest boy, and his three older brothers had all found respectable employment. Nicky had been about Lucy's age when his mother had died, after which his family had left him largely on his own to find his way through the world.

He'd chosen the only path that had seemed available at the time.

His only regret, however, was that he could not do more for his family. Perhaps Brigid did not think there was much honor in entertaining guests at a club, but at least he was not selling his body any longer.

He let out a breath and said, "I'll take Lucy and William to get ice. We'll find a way to help little Edith."

Brigid nodded.

Hank had spent all morning doing paperwork. Nicholas Sharp was supposed to have come in and given a more formal statement, but he hadn't, which didn't surprise Hank much. Hank sensed that Sharp was hiding something—that he knew something about the case he wasn't telling—and Hank was determined to figure out what that was. It meant he'd have to track down Sharp.

His feelings on the matter were mixed. He wanted to see the man again, but perhaps not for the right reasons.

That all would have to wait, however, because Stephens breezed in with the coroner's report.

"Do you recall our Mr. Juel mentioned yesterday a man who was killed in front of Columbia Hall?" asked Stephens, brandishing the report.

Hank thought it curious Stephens called the Bowery resort by its official name, not by the more common Paresis Hall as it was known, at least in the circles in which Hank moved. Hank didn't know for certain where the name came from, but he suspected it had something to do with "paresis" meaning insanity.

"He was quite incensed we had done nothing to investigate the murder," Hank said.

"He was not correct. The police department did look into it. The coroner inspected the body and the detective on the case decided there was not enough evidence to make further investigation worthwhile. No one even came forward to claim the body."

Hank knew all this already, having pored over the report earlier. "The detective did not think investigating the murder of a prostitute was worth his time, in other words. What was the detective's name?"

Stephens held up the report. "Er, a Detective Carr? Do you know him?"

"Vaguely. Fourteenth Precinct, yes?"

"No longer. Last week, he was exiled to Goatville."

Hank laughed despite himself. To be reassigned to one of the precincts in upper Manhattan, where goats still roamed free, was only a step removed from being fired. "What did he do to deserve such an assignment?"

Stephens shrugged. "I asked. His colleagues were not forthcoming, but if I had to guess, I would say neglect of duty. He barely investigated this murder, Brandt. Although, heaven knows, he probably looked at Commissioner Roosevelt's sister in the wrong way or forgot to wear a hat or something."

It was such a rare moment of levity from Stephens it surprised Hank into laughing, which he covered with a cough. "So what happened at Paresis?"

"Yes, right." Stephens pulled some crinkly papers from his pocket and consulted them. "Three weeks ago Tuesday, in the early morning hours, an officer found the body while doing a routine patrol. The body's proximity to Columbia Hall made Detective Carr assume he was a working boy who'd had a transaction gone wrong."

Not the first time it had happened. "Not a bad assumption."

"No, and normally it would have sadly been unremarkable. But the coroner remembered inspecting the body and the similarities to our dead man were so striking he found it notable before I even mentioned we suspected the crimes were connected."

Hank hadn't remembered explicitly making that connection with Stephens, but he nodded. "In what way were they similar?"

Stephens was practically giddy now. He rose up on his toes before he said, "In both instances, the cause of death was a knife wound to the chest from which the victim bled profusely. The coroner determined the weapon in both cases was a knife approximately eight inches in length, possibly a folding knife. Both victims were, ah, rumored to be male prostitutes. I am not certain if two is enough to constitute a pattern, but if both victims fell to the same killer, he's escalating. Poor Edward had several other shallow knife wounds that escaped our attention at the scene."

It wasn't that they'd escaped Hank's attention so much as Edward's clothes had been so tattered and stained, the wounds were concealed. Edward was an interesting contrast to the men who worked at Paresis Hall, who, granted, were often not much more than boys, but who were always impeccably dressed. Club Bulgaria catered to a lower class of clientele.

So what was a man like Nicholas Sharp doing singing there?

Hank was reluctant to admit to even himself that he found Nicholas—Nicky—beautiful. Nicky had stood there on the street with a soulful pout as Hank and Stephens had approached the scene, and there was something about Nicky's sass and indifference—insouciance, perhaps—Hank found compelling. His blond hair had shone on his hatless head, his clothes were well tailored and fashionable, and Hank got the feeling this was a man who had seen a lot in his short life, though he still had something delicate about him.

Hank was intrigued, certainly. Attracted, perhaps.

Still, if the violence was escalating, and if Roosevelt really did start shutting down the resorts along the Bowery as he was forever threatening to do, getting caught frequenting a fairy club was the last thing Hank could be caught doing. Even just two years ago, it would not have mattered. Now Roosevelt dismissed officers for far more minor offenses than frequenting a fairy resort. Hank's would-be promotion to Inspector was now victim to the bureaucratic infighting on the police commission, but one compromising situation could end the proceedings before his confirmation came up for a vote again.

"I need to talk to Nicholas Sharp," he said, certain now the man had to know something about what was really going on. Perhaps he knew more about the slumming aristocrat than he had disclosed.

Stephens sat on a stray chair and pulled off his cap. Sweat peppered his brow. "Sharp didn't come in this morning?" Stephens's tone indicated he was not surprised.

"No, but if anything, this confirms he knows something he does not wish to share."

"So you intend to find him?"

"It can't hurt to drop by Club Bulgaria again. I suppose I can go to Paresis, too. Ask a few discreet questions."

Stephens's eyes went wide. "I'm not sure that's a good idea."

"Probably not, but how else do you propose we find information?"

Stephens frowned. "You want to go today? You do not wish me to accompany you, do you?"

"No. Go home to your family tonight. I'll be all right on my own."

"Yes. Thank you. As long as you're certain."

Hank was certain. It would be easier to get the information he needed without Stephens tittering about how scandalized he was by the very existence of a house catering to men who sought the company of men. Hank took the now-crumpled coroner's reports from Stephens and started to read them more closely. Stephens leaned back in the chair he'd claimed and let his head loll about on his shoulders. He unbuttoned his coat and the top of his shirt, sure signs the heat had surpassed propriety.

The report didn't have much new information, but there was a note penciled in to indicate both dead boys had endured a number of injuries before succumbing to the knife wound. And not recent injuries; Edward had some old bruises on his chest and legs. Hank knew full well the men who worked the clubs like Paresis and Bulgaria probably saw a fair amount of violence. It wasn't unusual for a john to assert his power and masculinity with his fists, even if the prostitute in question was a woman, but Hank wondered now if Edward's wealthy client was a regular or if the bruises were a coincidence.

He needed more information.

"This is all inconclusive," Hank said.

"Indeed," said Stephens, fanning himself with his hands.

Officer Polk dragged a middle-aged, mustachioed man through the secretary pool at Police Headquarters and stopped at Andrew's desk.

"I apologize for interrupting your afternoon, Andrew, but this is Mr. Hines and he intends to start a riot."

Andrew felt suddenly weary, not particularly thrilled about having to deal with whatever the next crisis was. He rubbed his forehead and said, "All right. What is the issue, Mr. Hines?"

"This police department should be ashamed of how poor a job they are doing to keep crime away from the citizens of this city. I saw the article in this morning's paper about the murder on the Bowery. A dead man was found inside a . . . well, I cannot even say it."

Polk, who stood behind Hines now, said, "He's with the SPC."

Lord. The Society for the Prevention of Crime was essentially a vigilante group run by Reverend Charles Parkhurst. Parkhurst had recently made a fuss by declaring Commissioner Roosevelt was not doing *enough* to fight vice in the city, while the newspapers were daily publishing editorials arguing he was doing *too much.*

"The Society will not stand idly by while the police department looks away from the immorality plaguing our city! Why, you can't walk anywhere in Greenwich Village these days without colliding with a prostitute! Under the auspices of this allegedly great police commissioner, the world's oldest institution has been allowed to flourish!"

Polk sighed heavily. "The SPC is planning a raid of a few of the Bowery resorts this evening."

This was not good news. While it was true prostitution was perhaps more visible than it had been previously, and the areas around the Bowery and along Bleecker Street in the Village seemed particularly plagued by it, groups like the SPC rushing in would only cause more problems. "Mr. Hines, crime on the Bowery is clearly within the police department's jurisdiction."

"That's what I told him," said Polk. "He insisted on seeing a representative from the police department when I told him if he didn't stop yelling at passersby on Broome Street, I'd arrest him. So . . ."

Andrew was beginning to regret some of his social activity outside of the job. Becoming friendly with people like Hank and Adam Polk sometimes brought him more trouble than it was worth to maintain those friendships. Or else he was just having a really bad day.

"Well, Mr. Hines," Andrew said. "As a representative of the police department, I will remind you the last time the SPC decided to conduct a raid—on a theater off Delancey Street if I recall correctly—they illegally searched and arrested several innocent people. If your society is really for the prevention of crime, you might have a stronger argument if you did not break the law while carrying out your mission."

Mr. Hines bristled. "We were merely doing the work this department refuses to do."

Andrew stood. "As it happens, an inspector has taken charge of the Bowery case and intends to investigate the murder and perhaps shut the club down." Andrew doubted this was actually the case—Hank, who had little interest in shutting down vice when there were bigger crimes to solve, was as likely to shut down a club as he was to grow a second head—but the statement seemed to mollify Hines. "If the SPC raids the resorts tonight, it's only going to interfere with a legitimate investigation. It could destroy valuable evidence that would assist the police in eliminating some of the crime on the Bowery. Eliminating crime is your end, is it not?"

Hines frowned. "It is, yes."

"Give the police time to do their jobs, all right? In the meantime, if you'd like to report an actual crime, please see Mr. Thornton at the front desk."

Hines blustered a bit before turning and walking out of the room. Andrew turned to give his attention to the piles of paper that awaited his sign-off. Polk lingered for a moment. "You put an end to him swiftly."

"Yes, well. Not the first time one of the SPC members has shown up to tell me about how no one in the police department is doing his job. And if it's not them, it's somebody who thinks we ought to shut down every theater and dance hall in the city because they are the root causes of so much immoral behavior, or some such nonsense."

Polk laughed softly. "I'm sorry to have added to the pile, Andrew."

"It's fine. I'm glad I was able to defuse Mr. Hines."

"It's not my precinct, but it might be a good idea to talk to the captain there about putting a few extra men on patrol tonight to keep away any trouble. And by trouble, I mean the SPC."

Andrew nodded. "Probably a smart idea. Under the circumstances, it seems good to have a few extra patrolmen about to prevent a recidivist criminal."

"You think this murderer will strike again?"

"I do not know, but given he has yet to be apprehended, I would not rule out the possibility."

Polk pursed his lips. "All right. I'll talk to my captain." He glanced at the wall clock. "I should be going. Take care of yourself, Ritchley."

Chapter 4

As the sun set over the Hudson, Hank walked from the precinct house a few blocks west to the Bowery. He'd stripped to his shirtsleeves again before leaving the precinct, and he'd borrowed a tie and hat from another detective. He thought he looked fairly nondescript and hopefully unrecognizable as a police officer.

The heat was still unrelenting.

Hank knew a request had come down from headquarters to put a few extra men on patrol in this part of the neighborhood, and Hank understood the wisdom of doing so, although he was worried about being recognized. Logically, he knew there was a reasonable explanation for his presence—he was tracking down a witness to the crime he was investigating—and as Inspector, he had some discretion over how he conducted his business. But tonight was not a night he wanted to be spotted, and he worried the increased presence would make him much more conspicuous. All it would take would be a friendly officer from his precinct saying hello too loudly, and Hank's cover would be blown.

Not that it mattered, since the *lack* of a police presence was palpable. Not seeing any officers on patrol was alarming in its own way; if there was indeed a serial killer, there was not enough muscle here to act as a deterrent. Where were the extra men? Hank saw a few uniforms in his peripheral vision near the corner of the Bowery and East Third Street, but they were chatting with each other and not paying attention to their surroundings. Hank recognized one of the officers and made a mental note to write him up when he got back to the office in the morning.

In the meantime, he had more important concerns.

He considered going to Paresis Hall first, but he wasn't sure he'd find anything there in the end. He'd go tomorrow if tonight's mission proved inconclusive. His greater concern now was finding Nicholas Sharp.

Women hung out of windows and called to him as he walked along Bleecker and then turned onto the Bowery. One woman with an ample bosom eyed a police officer who crossed the street, which Hank thought quite brazen of her. Then a scandalously undressed woman snagged his arm. "Oh, you're a handsome one," she purred.

"Not interested," Hank said.

"On a night like tonight, when it's so hot, I bet I could find ways to cool you off." She reached over and ran her hands down the front of Hank's shirt.

"I'm sure you could, but I'm not interested."

"Aw, why the rush, handsome? There ain't no other girls on the Bowery who can do what I can."

Hank wanted to flash his badge at her, but he thought that might bring too much undue attention, so instead he said, "You aren't my type, sweetheart." Then he gestured toward his destination.

She seemed to get it. "I see. Well, I hope you find what you're looking for." She winked and moved on to talk to the next man walking down the street. Hank watched her, feeling a little ridiculous. He took a deep breath and continued on his path.

There was a man at the door at Club Bulgaria, but he didn't seem to be doing much beyond waving guests inside. He barely looked at Hank.

So Hank went in, following the other guests into the ballroom. Tables were scattered around the room with men seated at each, many of them quite young. There was no sign of Nicky.

Hank took a deep breath and thought about how to blend in. He acknowledged to himself that some of this subterfuge was a pretense, because he was tempted by this crowd. The air of it seemed to lure him in, the promise of sex and male companionship laid out before him like a fine dinner.

He slid into a chair at a table occupied only by a man who looked to be about twenty. The man had neatly combed blond hair and rouge on his cheeks.

"Hello, sir," the man said. "I hope I can make your night a little more enjoyable."

"I hope so, too," said Hank.

The man smiled and leaned closer. He reached over and touched Hank's tie. So Hank put an arm around him and took a moment to feel the warmth of another man near him. It had been quite a while since he'd done this. There was too much scrutiny from Roosevelt now. He supposed if he managed to get himself arrested this night, he could argue he was there to investigate. A reasonable explanation. Even though the room smelled of sex and desire.

This would not be an easy investigation.

"Do you have a name?" Hank asked the man in his arms.

"My friends call me Charlie."

"All right, Charlie. What is the entertainment tonight?"

"Oh, would you like to see the show? I would, too. Paulina Clodhopper is singing. I just adore her."

"Paulina Clodhopper?" What a name!

"Oh, she's delightful. Have you never seen her before?"

"No, I can't say I have."

"She should be starting in a few minutes. Unless you want to go to the back?"

Charlie was handsome, but so very young. Not that it would have been the first time Hank had let himself be enticed into a back room or closet or compartment for a tryst with a handsome man, even one this young, but he had a greater agenda. More to the point, there was something unseemly about allowing himself to be propositioned while he was technically on the job.

And there was still no sign of Nicky. If he really did sing here, perhaps he came on after Paulina Clodhopper.

"Let's see the show," said Hank.

Charlie slid his hand over Hank's thigh. "Thank you, sir. Then after, for three dollars, I can show you some other entertainment."

"Perhaps."

The lights on the stage came on suddenly. The tinkly notes of an old, out-of-tune piano wafted out into the audience. Hank was curious, though his sweat seemed to act as a glue wherever his body touched Charlie's, which was distracting. It was too hot for affection, even in a darkened ballroom with iced air being blown by mechanical fans.

Off stage, someone sang out the first few bars of "The Sidewalks of New York." Then a woman walked onto the stage in a stunning green dress, tight around her narrow waist with a large bustle in the back. There seemed to be jewels sewn into the fabric, or something shiny that caused the stage lights to reflect off of it. She had blond hair piled high on her head, big eyes, and rosy cheeks. She was beautiful, frankly, and had a seductive air about her. Every movement of her body was intended to pull the audience in. Everyone seemed to collectively lean toward her.

She gently crescendoed until her voice rang out over the audience. There was something husky and androgynous about her voice. Something sexy. Hank was captivated.

It took him a moment to realize Paulina Clodhopper was a female impersonator, as if the name hadn't been enough of a clue. Then he realized he recognized those big eyes.

Nicholas Sharp.

On stage, Paulina finished the song and launched into a second, sauntering across the stage as she sang. Everything around her seemed to sparkle. She was mesmerizing.

When the set ended and Paulina left the stage, Charlie pulled away gently and said, "I'm afraid I've lost your interest."

"She's amazing," Hank said, still in a daze.

"She is. I do adore Paulina."

"I've never seen a show like this." Realizing he had an opportunity here, Hank added, "I'd love to meet her."

Charlie glanced toward the stage and then smiled at Hank. "Come, I'll introduce you."

"You would? Really?" Hank sighed. His enthusiasm was downright embarrassing, and unfortunately not at all fake. "I'm sorry. I don't know what came over me."

Charlie smiled sadly. "It's Paulina. She has that effect on people. I will take you to meet her. As long as you understand, she never takes men home. If you came here looking to satisfy some desire, I'm a better bet."

"I came here looking for Paulina."

Charlie nodded as if he understood. "I imagine you did. Come along."

Hank followed Charlie to a door near the stage. Charlie knocked and said, "It's Charlie. There's a guest of the club who would like to meet you."

There was a long hesitation. Then, "Yes, come in."

Hank doffed his hat as he walked through the door and could tell immediately Nicky recognized him. Even through the makeup, Nicky was still unmistakably the man Hank had met the day before. Hank wondered if they should pretend to be strangers for Charlie's sake. So he said, "It is a delight to meet you, ma'am. I enjoyed your show immensely."

Nicky—Paulina—smiled coquettishly and said, "Thank you, darling."

"May I speak with you for a few moments?"

Paulina glanced at Charlie. "Well, if you plan to regale me with compliments, I shan't say no."

"You are quite stunning."

Paulina preened. The gown was made of a shiny fabric the color of an evergreen tree, and Hank saw up close it was meticulously tailored with many fine details, including beading all over the bodice that caught the light like gemstones. He supposed the foofaraw about the gown's shoulders and waist had names, but Hank knew little about women's fashion. As a confirmed bachelor with no sisters, he'd never had need.

"I shall resume my post then," said Charlie.

Hank had nearly forgotten Charlie was there. "Er, I won't be but a few moments."

"It is all right, sir. I understand Paulina's allure."

And so Charlie left Hank alone in an anteroom off the stage with Nicholas Sharp, a man in a dress.

"I did tell you the truth, Inspector," said Nicky/Paulina.

The name conundrum was perplexing Hank, so he said, "Please. Call me Hank. What shall I call you?"

"My friends call me Nicky." Nicky walked to a side table and picked up a mirror. "I feel as though I've been ambushed."

"I apologize sincerely." Hank felt unmanned. Nicky's stunning beauty as Paulina, his unquestionable talent and stage presence, had taken Hank off-guard. "You missed your appointment."

"I had another more urgent matter to attend to."

"More urgent than solving the murder of one of your colleagues? Because if this crime proves to be part of a series, which I strongly suspect it is, everyone here could be in danger. Charlie could be next. Or you."

Nicky's eyebrows shot up, but then he shook his head. "This was not information I had this morning, darling, but yes, even my life was a trivial thing compared to what I had to attend to today, so you'll forgive me for not coming to your office. I can do so tomorrow if you insist."

"Or you can talk to me now."

Nicky glanced at Hank, his expression dubious. "How exactly did you charm Charlie into taking you to meet me?"

"To be honest, he saw how taken I was with you."

"Oh, sure, yes, it's all right for the police inspector to go slumming at the fairy resort as long as his lust is directed at the one person in the room who looks like a woman. Well, I hate to tell you, darling, but I am all male beneath my skirts."

"Yes. I know. It's part of your appeal."

Nicky made a few incoherent noises. Hank couldn't tell if he was befuddled or offended.

Hank leaned close and lowered his voice. "That is, I have never felt myself attracted to a female impersonator before. I usually like rougher trade. But you are just so astonishing."

"This is a trap, is it not? You are one sentence away from throwing me in the Tombs."

"Or perhaps we are exchanging secrets."

Nicky shook his head. He still looked startlingly like a woman, though of course, close up, the seams showed. The hair piled atop his head was a wig, and a pin stuck out above his left ear. The makeup had softened his face, but he still had a strong, masculine jaw line and an Adam's apple. His shoulders looked delicate beneath the puffed sleeves of the dress, but they were broad, too, wider than a woman's. He'd corseted his waist into a narrow curve, padded his hips, and created an elaborate illusion.

Still, Nicky paced and said, "I do not know what you want of me."

"Information, primarily."

"So why tell me you find me so fetching? Oh, you like rough trade. Indeed. You, of all the people in New York, a police inspector, come down here to ask me for information but instead confide in me you are secretly an invert. Next you'll tell me you wear lingerie and parade about at Paresis Hall on Sundays."

"No, not quite." Hank took a deep breath, trying to gather his wits. "I found your appearance on stage surprising, is all. You told me you sang, but somehow, I did not expect—"

"You expected me to be among the boys at the tables, not on the stage."

"Well."

Nicky proceeded to prance about a little, his skirts swishing as he did, the clack of his heels and the quiet *shh*-sound of fabric moving the only noise for the moment. He wore some sort of perfume on top of it all, something floral and sweet and feminine. Hank wondered if the scent was part of the act as well.

Hank said, "Perhaps it will be a comfort to you if I told you I chose to seek you out here and was comfortable with such an assignment because I am not exactly a stranger to clubs like this. I had never been to Club Bulgaria before yesterday, but I know how these places operate, and not just in my capacity as an investigator."

"Would it not be disadvantageous to be a member of Roosevelt's police and be caught with a working boy?"

"Which is why I have not been to the Bowery except in a professional capacity in nearly two years."

"And tonight is no exception because all you want from me is information."

Hank understood Nicky's reticence but still found it frustrating. "Yes. And I want you to trust me, which is why I am being so forthright."

"And your friend Detective Stephens has no idea you harbor inverted tendencies? That perhaps you have been guilty of the most heinous of crimes against nature?"

"No. He does not. I sent him home to his wife and children before I came here."

Nicky sat on the edge of a worn settee. His back was perfectly straight. He sat like a woman, really, but Hank imagined this was partly due to Nicky's clothing. "I don't understand," Nicky said at length.

"What should I tell you? The bald truth? Well, here it is. I'm a queer police detective. Or inspector, I suppose, should my promotion ever be approved by the police board. I am now investigating the murder of two working boys who operated out of resorts on the Bowery. The evidence these crimes are connected is scarce and circumstantial, but my gut tells me the same man is involved in both killings and he is becoming more violent. Perhaps another detective would leave it be. Perhaps he might determine no one will miss a nineteen-year-old boy who sells his body to men for unseemly purposes. But not this detective. A murder is a murder."

"And this detective has paid working boys for sex in the past, yes? This is what you are telling me?"

"It is not something of which I am proud."

Nicky nodded slowly. "I believe I am beginning to understand, love."

"I did not expect to find you so captivating done up as a woman, although I will admit to finding you quite captivating when we met yesterday."

"You have two separate problems, I believe." Nicky picked up a fan from the side table. He opened it with a flick of his wrist and began quickly fanning his face. "Lord, it is hot."

Hank had nearly stopped noticing it. He felt a heat of a different kind in Nicky's presence.

"While we're telling secrets," Nicky said, "I might as well tell you I was once among the boys on the floor. At times, the pay was not enough to afford more than a room over a saloon on Ludlow Street where I never slept for all the noise. So I worked to convince Mr. Juel I had other talents."

"You have nicer accommodations now, I trust."

"It's not the Waldorf, but yes."

The heat started to get to Hank to the point where he got a little dizzy. The air in this room was perfectly still, with no doors open and no windows. Beside the settee where Nicky perched, there was only a wooden chair in the corner. Hank grabbed it and sat across from Nicky. He pulled his notepad from his pocket.

"It was never my intention to cause trouble for you, if that is what you think of my purpose. I don't intend to call in a raiding party or cost anyone their jobs. I merely want to get to the bottom of this crime."

"Yes. Of course."

"Do you trust me?" Hank asked.

"Not really. Do I have a choice?"

"No."

Nicky rocked a bit in his seat. "Ask your questions then."

Hank looked at his notepad and gathered his thoughts. The spare room they were sitting in, Nicky's inherent beauty, the blasted heat, all of it was distracting.

"This man you saw with Edward. Had you seen him before?"

"Not that I recall, no. And he was remarkable to me because he seemed so well appointed. Most of the upper-class gents who come slumming in this neighborhood do so at the nicer clubs."

"How could you tell his clothes were expensive?"

Nicky leveled his gaze at Hank. He crossed his legs in a womanly way and rested his hands on his raised knee. "I know the difference between quality fabric and the cheap, ill-fitting trousers you wear. I have to have all my gowns custom made at considerable expense."

A valid point. "Have there been any other wealthy men here recently?"

"None that stood out to me like he did."

"Have there been any other violent acts committed here?"

Nicky leaned back a little, but clearly the boning in his corset kept him from sitting comfortably. He sighed and said, "The better question is whether we ever have a night when there is not a violent act committed."

"As I feared," said Hank.

"You think Edward's death may be tied to another, you said?"

"That boy who was killed in front of Paresis Hall a few weeks ago."

Nicky let out a quiet gasp. "The one the police ignored."

"The one ignored by an officer who has since been transferred to watch after goats in Harlem. It is no longer being ignored."

"Ah," said Nicky. "The gallant Inspector Brandt is on the case, eh?"

Hank chose to ignore the sarcasm. "Is there anything else you can think of?"

Nicky closed his eyes for a moment. "Well. Edward did mention a john of his who had gotten a little aggressive. But such is the way of men. Some of them hate us as much as they hate themselves."

Hank nodded. "So you found Edward mentioning this man unremarkable."

Nicky shrugged. "Once, maybe five years ago, I gave comfort to a man who afterward beat me so senseless I had to keep to my bed for nearly two weeks. Incidents like that are not rare."

"And of course you never reported it to the police because then you would get arrested."

"Do you have any idea what happens to a fairy when he is thrown in jail?"

"I do, actually." Hank rubbed his forehead. "I apologize if these questions seem inane. I had hoped you would be able to provide me with more insight. A direction to go in."

"I don't think I can help you."

Hank disagreed. On more than one front. "I think you can. I think you know more than you're telling me."

Between the corset, the heat, and the man sitting before him, Nicky could barely breathe.

"I've told you all I know. Edward disappeared with some man who may not even be your killer. I don't know anything more than that."

"Could you identify this man if you saw him again?"

"Perhaps. Are you plaguing me with these questions because you're interested in me for more than just information?"

That, at least, pulled a small smile from the police inspector. Hank then pursed his lips and echoed, "Perhaps."

"So how true was Charlie's introduction? You recognized me. You wanted to meet me."

"All true." Hank leaned back a little and ran a hand down his mustache, as if he were squeezing the excess moisture from it. His forehead was covered in droplets of sweat and he gave off a strong odor that was sweaty sourness and something raw. Nicky couldn't quite identify it, but he liked it. Hank went on, "I'll be honest with you, all right? If I want honesty from you, I should provide you with the same. So. The answer to your questions is yes. I came here tonight to find you because you missed your appointment today. I don't have enough clues to solve this crime and I was convinced you held the key to unlocking whatever the puzzle is here. Not to mix metaphors. Then I saw you perform." Hank shook his head. "I was already intrigued by you. Seeing you sing tonight was something else entirely."

"Some men try to rationalize it. I look enough like a woman all done up this way, so it's all right to lie with me."

"I don't need to rationalize anything."

Nicky could only hope that was true, or he'd be in a cell by the end of the week. "You'll understand my caution."

Hank leaned close again. Nicky couldn't lean either way, confined to his position by the corseting and the stiff fabric of his gown. He had to be content to let Hank steer this conversation. He still didn't trust Hank. And he wondered if Hank didn't find him as frivolous and shallow as he portrayed or if Hank could see through it.

"I do understand," Hank said. "But I want you to trust me."

Hank's face was so close. Nicky imagined if he leaned forward just a little, he'd be able to feel the bristles of Hank's mustache brushing against his lips. But it was all a fantasy. There was no way a man like Hank could realistically care anything for Nicky except as a sideshow freak.

"Well, darling," Nicky said. "It is my occupation to endeavor to make people happy. I'll tell you anything you want to hear."

Hank let out a disgruntled choking sound. "No, damn it all. I want you to tell me the truth."

"And I have told you I don't know anything. Men come and go here at all times of the day and night. I couldn't tell you who most of them are. The only piece of information is the one I keep telling you, that Edward was with some man in expensive clothing last night. You are a smart man. You can make a picture just as easily as I can. Likely Edward was picked up by a man from uptown who decided to reassert his dominance over the situation by hurting Edward. I think I would recognize him if I saw him again, but who is to say Edward didn't encounter someone else in the back room?"

"I want to solve this case."

"And I appreciate your conviction. But what can I do?"

It wasn't an expression of indifference so much as of fear and frustration because Nicky couldn't figure out how to help. Thinking back on his brief conversation with Charlie the night before, he also fretted there was nothing that could be done, that Hank could be as fierce and tenacious as he clearly intended to be, but he would never get anywhere. Other men would die. Such was the way of things.

"Nicky." Hank spoke softly.

Nicky looked at his lap, his hands crossed there, his fingers long and graceful, he supposed. He always thought it was his hands that betrayed him; they looked too square and masculine, not feminine enough.

But none of that mattered now because there was a different hand cupping his chin, lifting his face up. Nicky gazed into Hank's eyes and felt utterly bereft for a moment. In Hank he saw something that looked like hope. Hank would march in and solve all his problems. He'd rescue the boys trapped in this life. He'd offer a hand, a way out . . .

But of course, he would do none of those things.

"I *will* solve this case," Hank said, never looking away from Nicky's gaze.

Nicky felt trapped in the strength of that gaze, in that conviction. The greenish irises of Hank's eyes were so clear. They were like a cool pool in the desert.

"Perhaps solving one case is nothing but a quick fix. A bandage on a shallow cut."

"Perhaps. But I would be remiss in my duties if I let it go."

Nicky found Hank's gaze too intense and wanted to look away. Hank's hand held his chin still and his corset kept him from moving. So he was caged in, surrounded by Hank, by the sour sweaty smell of him, by his strength, by his conviction.

He wanted to kiss Hank suddenly. He wanted to bury his face in Hank's neck. He wanted Hank to carry him out of here as if he were a princess in need of rescuing from the dragon keeping him captive. Perhaps Julie was the dragon, or his family, or any number of things keeping him at a fairy resort in the Bowery instead of seeking some more respectable form of employment.

"I do not want to die," Nicky whispered.

"No."

"I don't want any of my friends to die, either. But even if you catch whoever did this to Edward, there will be someone else."

"I know. I want to do what I can to prevent such an outcome. I think I can help."

Nicky let out a breath. "You want to keep me safe, do you?"

Hank smiled faintly, but then his face went slack, serious. The mustache obscured his expression somewhat, the exact nature of his smile hidden, but his eyes said volumes. "I want to find out more about you before you meet your inevitable end, then, I suppose." Hank's tone held a joke.

"That was morbid," said Nicky.

"Yes. You smiled."

"Did I?"

"I wonder what your lips taste like."

Nicky started, jolting upright a bit, but not hard or far enough to pull out of Hank's grasp. He found now he wanted to taste Hank as well, to find out how that mustache would feel against his own lips. Nicky wanted to be wrapped in that scent, in that warmth, and it reminded him of the best kind of sex, sweaty and passionate and crazy, with no obligation and no money exchanged. He wondered if he could have that with Hank. He took a deep breath and put his hands, his clumsy masculine hands, on Hank's shoulders and looked into those eyes and he wondered.

But it was too much to hope for. The power imbalance was too great. And one wrong move would be Nicky's end. He knew full well he couldn't very well survive another night in the Tombs.

"Darling, I can't—"

"Do men still pay you to take you home?"

"No. I gave it up when I started singing. I only go home with men on my own terms."

"And when was the last time that happened?"

Nicky didn't know. It had been quite some time. He shook his head.

"Coyness?" Hank asked.

"A faulty memory."

"Indeed. My memory is similarly faulty. Or, rather, my boss does not condone fraternizing in the sorts of place at which I can find the men I'd like to fraternize with."

"So you'd like to fraternize with me?"

Hank shot him one of those enigmatic smiles again. "I would like to do a lot of things with you."

Nicky leaned forward, as far as he could in his confining clothes. He was close enough to breathe in Hank's breath. "I must say, darling, I am similarly intrigued, but I cannot imagine a more difficult situation."

"No, but just for a moment, don't you wonder . . ." Hank leaned forward.

Nicky straightened his elbows and kept Hank at a distance. "I'm sorry, but no."

"On your terms. Right."

"Honestly? I have to go on again in a few minutes and kissing you would wreck my makeup."

That seemed to break the tension. Hank burst into laughter. "Right. Of course. Wouldn't want that."

Nicky pushed on Hank's shoulders. "Help me up."

Hank stood and then held his hands out and helped Nicky to his feet. This effectively put them facing each other again, the heels of Nicky's shoes bringing him up close to Hank's height. They were close enough to kiss again.

But now was not the time for that. Nicky briefly entertained the fantasy of letting go and kissing Hank and seeing where things went, but he had to suppress it. Instead, he took a step back.

"Can I call on you again?" Hank asked. "If not here, then perhaps at your home?"

Nicky hesitated. He had learned years before not to trust a police officer, but an inverted police officer was another matter. Unless he was lying about that, too. But, no, Nicky trusted his instincts, and Hank was definitely attracted to him, as more than just a font of information.

"All right." Nicky grabbed a scrap of paper from a side table. "Do you have a pencil?"

Hank pulled one from his pocket. Unable to bend over to lean on the table, Nicky gestured for Hank to turn around and then used Hank's back to write out his address. He handed the paper to Hank. Hank looked it over.

"Thank you," he said softly. "I appreciate that you trust me enough for this. I'll call on you tomorrow afternoon."

"I'll be home."

Hank nodded slowly and glanced at the door. He opened his mouth to speak, but then Julie ran by and shouted, "You're on, Paulina!"

"You have to leave," Nicky told Hank.

"All right. Tomorrow?"

"Fine."

Hank met Nicky's gaze again, and then nodded and left.

Day 3

Friday, August 7
Temperature: 101°F

Chapter 5

According to the thermometer in front of the Herald building, it was already seventy-eight degrees at six a.m. when Andrew left his apartment. It felt even hotter inside the car of the elevated train he rode downtown. Bodies pressed together, the smell of sweat pungent and sour, and everyone on the train looked as abjectly miserable as Andrew felt. He wondered if his suit might suffocate him before he even got to his desk.

The newspaper he grabbed between the train station and police headquarters contained Department of Public Works Commissioner Collis's decree that work hours be changed to prevent workers from keeling over during the hottest times of the day. Andrew knew of six people who had collapsed on the job the previous day, and not all of them survived once they reached the hospital.

Perhaps New York City had finally sunk into Hell as so many had predicted.

Commissioner Roosevelt stood outside his office when Andrew arrived to check in for the day. He stroked his mustache absently a few times before hopping and coming to life suddenly. "Ritchley. Meeting."

"Yes, sir."

"I want the captain of the Eighteenth Precinct in my office by noon. We need to discuss the force necessary for William Jennings Bryan's visit on the twelfth."

"I'll see to it." Andrew considered just how much force would be necessary. Bryan was scheduled to make a campaign stop, giving a

speech at Madison Square Garden that would be his formal acceptance of the nomination as the Democratic candidate for President of
the United States. Roosevelt had no fondness for Bryan and had
made his displeasure about having to make policemen available to
act as security for the event known loud and clear ever since Bryan
had announced the speech.

"I'll be leaving for Oyster Bay in a few days. I intend to spend
time with my family."

"Of course, sir."

"Now what is next on my schedule?"

Andrew deserved a raise. "Well, sir, you're supposed to do a cere-
mony in a few minutes commending the officer who killed a mad dog
yesterday." It was nasty business, this particular commendation, but
Roosevelt had heard about it the day before and been enthralled. The
officer embodied the masculine energy Roosevelt seemed to want the
New York Police Department to emulate.

"Ah, yes," said Roosevelt. "I look forward to that."

And so, fifteen minutes later, Commissioner Theodore Roosevelt
gave Officer Charles Haas a commendation for beating a dog suffering
from heat sickness with a cane instead of just shooting it. Roosevelt
gave the man a cane made to commemorate the occasion. Andrew was
disgusted. But far be it from him to argue with Roosevelt about what
constituted masculine heroism.

After that bit of pomp, Roosevelt retired to his office, so Andrew
went back to his desk to try to catch up on the ever-growing pile of
paper. A report from an officer in the Seventeenth Precinct sat in the
pile: dead woman found on Third Street off the Bowery. The apparent
cause of death was a knife wound to the chest.

Andrew's memory was hooked. He sifted through the coroner's
reports he needed to sign off on. Nearly every person who had died in
New York City the day before had passed out from some heat-related
illness, but there was also the report Andrew wanted: woman with unknown identity dead of a knife wound to the chest. Except the woman
was actually a man in a dress. And the man's torso was covered in
shallow wounds.

Andrew ran to the telephone and asked the operator to put him
through to the Seventeenth Precinct. When Andrew got to the dis-
patcher, he said, "I need Hank Brandt."

* * *

A dead horse sat like a mound in the middle of East Fourth Street. Flies buzzed about its heavy body and the scent of flesh rotting permeated the air. Hank hurried past it, although it was the third such horse he'd seen since he'd left the precinct house. The smell was so putrid that if he saw one more dead animal in the middle of the street, he might vomit. As it was, he barely held on to his dignity in this heat.

Heat and death were everywhere. That was all this miserable week had brought him. He'd spent a significant portion of the morning at the home of a woman who was convinced her elderly husband had been poisoned, but it became clear quickly enough he'd simply expired in the heat. The hospitals had been swarmed with people flagging under the relentless, inescapable dread of August, and the morgues could not keep up with the demand.

Hank would be forever grateful to Andrew for pulling the one coroner's report out of the mess of others he'd surely had to sort through. Hank had worried briefly the dead man in the dress had been Nicky, but the body had been found before Hank had last seen Nicky. They couldn't have been the same man.

That report could easily have been lost because everyone was suffering under the heat. Stephens had said with some mixture of horror and detachment that children were dropping like flies in the tenements.

The heat would break, but the toll on the city once the dust cleared was unimaginable. Commissioner Roosevelt had compared it to a cholera outbreak in a meeting the day before.

Hank couldn't identify the sudden swooshing sound behind him, but then he realized someone had turned a hose on First Avenue. Children ran naked through the erupting water. Word had come through the precinct in the morning that the commissioner of public works had been instructed to "flush" the streets, but Hank wondered if this was merely a way for the city to help those suffering the worst effects of the horrific heat.

This had been going on for four straight days. How many more could they really take?

A few minutes later, Hank arrived at a nondescript building. The front door was wide open, as were all of the windows. Curtains from the third floor billowed out of the building as a gentle breeze moved through, but the breeze wasn't enough to do much more than furnish the citizens of New York with the memories of cooler days.

Hank pulled his handkerchief from his pocket and mopped some of the sweat off the back of his neck and his mustache. Trying to look presentable was likely a futile enterprise, but he wanted to try. He then climbed the stairs to the fourth floor, his lungs burning as he did so. He had to pause at the top of the stairs to mop his face again and catch his breath.

He would have jumped into the East River right then if it weren't so far away.

Huffing a bit, Hank walked across the hall and knocked on the door to apartment 4B.

It took a moment, but eventually Nicky opened the door. No wig or makeup adorned him this time. He wore only a flimsy, floral-printed dressing gown, one that looked like it was probably made for a woman. The top parted in a long V down the front of his chest and a thin sash was knotted at his waist. It wasn't doing enough to block Hank's imagination.

"Hello, Inspector," Nicky said, leaning on the doorframe.

He was beautiful. His hair was disheveled instead of carefully combed, which had the effect of making him look a little wild. His exposed chest was flat and strong and lightly dusted with hair. The opening of his dressing gown was like an arrow pointing toward the gentle rise below his belt. He wore no makeup now, no affectation. He was tall and thin with pouty lips and sparkling blue eyes. If Hank had ever seen a more beautiful man, he could not remember the occasion.

"And here you are, just as promised," Nicky said.

It took Hank an embarrassingly long moment to speak. He was dumbstruck, speechless in the wake of Nicky's beauty. But he swallowed and said, "I need some more information."

"So you said. But I don't know what further information I can provide."

"A man was killed not two blocks from here yesterday."

"A tragedy." Nicky sauntered away from the door, so Hank followed him into the apartment and let the door close. Nicky added, "Men die here all the time."

"This man wore a dress."

That brought Nicky up short. "The hell you say."

"The identity of the man remains unknown, but he was indeed found last night by an officer on patrol. The officer thought the man was a woman. The coroner unearthed the truth. This man also died of a knife wound to the chest, just like your friend Edward." Hank took a deep breath. "It could have been you, Nicky. Do you appreciate the kind of danger you're in?"

Nicky's eyes went wide. "You think the crimes are related. It's the same killer."

Hank nodded. "I can't prove it, but my instinct tells me this is a serial killer focused on the working boys of the Bowery. It seems unlikely a loved one will claim the man in the morgue. So many people are expiring from the heat he will likely get lost among the other deaths this week. But the way he died was similar to Edward and this other man who died a few weeks ago, and I believe the crimes are related. Which means you or any of your friends are at risk."

Nicky grunted. "Well, what do you propose I do about it?"

Hank could practically see the fear radiating off Nicky now. Nicky wasn't being flippant, as Hank had suspected at first. He was terrified.

"I don't suppose my telling you not to go to work until I solve this is an option."

Nicky balked. "Would you like to pay my rent, then?"

Hank looked around. Nicky's apartment was not the most glamorous of spaces—it was sparsely decorated and the walls and floors were scarred—but he seemed to have a reasonable amount of space and plenty of sunlight streaming in through the windows. "Do you live here alone?" Hank asked.

"Yes."

"By virtue of the fact you do not do favors for the men who patronize Club Bulgaria, I think you are probably safer than others, but I would take nothing for granted."

Nicky stood up straight and crossed his arms over his chest. "Never, darling."

"Did everyone report to work today? Was anyone missing?"

"No one was missing that I know of."

"So this victim might have been a fellow who worked at another resort. Or he was, er, independently employed."

"Yes." Nicky looked down. "I want to help, I do, but I have nothing left to say. I think perhaps you knew I could not share more with you than you already know. But then, you did not come here just for information, did you?"

Hank looked Nicky over, from his mussed hair to his bare chest to his graceful little toes. "Perhaps there was a bit of pretense to my wanting to see you."

Nicky looked straight at Hank and said, "I tell Charlie to convey to men who come into Bulgaria that I am not for sale. You were not the first to see me on stage and 'become enchanted' as Charlie described you."

"I *was* enchanted."

Nicky pressed his lips together. Then he said, "Occasionally my admirers come to that little room to greet me. When I first began dancing, I was still in the habit of letting men do as they wished to me. I no longer feel the obligation."

"So you turn them away."

"Who I allow in my home, in my bed, must be on my terms. For years, I survived because men paid me to do their bidding. Now I don't need their money. Now I dictate the rules."

Hank respected Nicky's wishes, but he couldn't overlook an obvious fact. "I am currently in your home."

Nicky's shoulders sagged. "Yes, well. It is not every day a handsome police inspector barges into your drawing room."

Hank smiled at that. "You think me handsome."

Nicky waved his hand dismissively. "Don't get a big head."

Hank stepped closer to Nicky. "I don't believe I'm misreading this situation. You are as intrigued by me as I am by you."

"Perhaps."

"If circumstances were different, if we merely met on the street, would you have invited me to your home?"

"Probably not. You are dreadfully overbearing."

"You can still say 'no.'"

Nicky took a step away from Hank and crossed his arms over his chest. "Perhaps it is time for some of that honesty you keep insisting on." He pressed his lips together again for a long moment. "I found myself drawn to you last night. It has been quite some time since any man has done that for me. It was nice to know I haven't died inside."

"You seem very much alive to me. And I intend to keep it that way."

"But why?" Nicky began to pace. "Why this insistence on finding a killer who I'm sure all of New York thinks is doing God's work?"

Hank didn't have a ready answer beyond that he felt he was acting in the right. He closed his eyes for a moment, tried to put himself in Nicky's shoes. "I was once on an aimless path. This was shortly after my mother died. I was not much older than Edward at the time." He'd been angry, frustrated, terrified. And lonely, so very lonely. "The first time I walked along the Bowery, I was barely a man. I got pulled into some dark place by a man I liked the look of. He wanted my money and I freely gave it for a few minutes of passion, so I wouldn't feel so alone anymore. I'd been fighting these feelings I had for years, you know. And I didn't think anyone felt how I did."

"I know how that is," Nicky whispered.

"Maybe it's strange, but I'm grateful to that man, even though I gave him more than I could afford to. And even after I joined the police, I kept an eye on your stretch of the Bowery, wanting to be sure the men there were all right." Hank tried to catch Nicky's gaze, but Nicky stared at the floor. Hank went on, "It has never been my aim to prosecute the men who work in resorts like yours. I have no interest in arresting working boys or prostitutes or even saloonkeepers who serve intoxicating beverages on Sundays. A little vice is good for a man. It keeps him from becoming too self-righteous."

"Look who's self-righteous," said Nicky.

"I do not think hunting down murderers is self-righteous. I think it is my duty as a police inspector."

"Theodore Roosevelt might have a different opinion."

Hank wanted to dispense with the nonsense here. By coming to Nicky's home, he'd made a clear decision, and he needed Nicky to know that. "You understand the considerable risk I'm taking by being here, then."

"I suppose I hadn't really considered it, darling. Where I come from, the police have the power and I have naught but the clothes on my back. And sometimes not even those."

"I became a police officer because I wanted to make the city safe."

Nicky nodded. "I began to sing because it kept me safe. Does that make me selfish?"

"No."

"I suppose you fancy yourself a hero."

Hank closed some of the distance between himself and Nicky,

stepping close enough to Nicky to smell him, to see the sweat beading at his hairline. "I'm no hero," Hank said.

"You're the first person to come along in a very long time who seemed interested at all in doing anything but beating or arresting me." Nicky finally looked up and met Hank's gaze. "That seems heroic to me."

Hank reached over and cupped Nicky's cheek. Nicky glanced down again, his surprisingly dark eyelashes fluttering, but then he looked into Hank's eyes.

"On my terms," Nicky said. "We do this my way."

"All right."

The expression on Nicky's face turned fierce. "I choose you. Money plays no part in this exchange."

"I understand." Hank's heart pounded now.

"Kiss me."

Hank did, bowing his head to at last banish the distance that separated them. He pressed his lips against Nicky's, gently at first, but then more forcefully as Nicky parted his lips and let Hank in. Nicky put his hands around Hank's neck and tugged him a little closer, so Hank felt like he wouldn't be overstepping if he put his hands on Nicky's waist.

Once Hank's hands met with the warmth of Nicky's skin, even through the flimsy fabric of the dressing gown, Hank didn't want to stop touching Nicky. He finally got a taste of Nicky's lips, found them oddly sweet, and he explored Nicky's mouth until he was convinced he could get lost there. When Nicky wrapped his arms more firmly around Hank's shoulders, Hank pulled him close, until their hips met.

It had been so long since Hank had been this close to a man. It had been so long since he'd felt the rush, the skin tingling, the burst of arousal that couldn't be replicated when he was alone deep in the night. His longing for Nicky was a palpable thing, and not only because he was a man and he was nearly naked. No, Hank wanted *this* man, the one in his arms, the most beautiful man he had ever laid eyes on.

And Nicky wanted him. Nicky had chosen him.

"I didn't come here for this," Hank said against Nicky's lips.

"It's all right, love." Nicky brushed kisses across Hank's cheek and then whispered in his ear, "You did, at least in part. But I want this, too."

"I believe you when you say you don't have more information about the case, but I sense there is something you are not telling me."

Nicky grasped onto Hank a little tighter and said, "There are many things I am not telling you. My consenting to this does not mean I trust you yet, not completely."

"And yet."

"And yet nothing. It's pleasure and sex. No more."

Hank sensed the lie, but let it be. Instead, he kissed Nicky again, but otherwise let Nicky lead him. When Nicky slid the dressing gown off his shoulders and stood nude before Hank, Hank looked his fill—and Nicky was striking, his body thin and perfectly formed—but made no further moves or gestures. He waited for Nicky to tell him what to do, although his heart raced and he longed to grab Nicky, to touch him, to drag him to the bedroom. Out of respect for Nicky, though, he waited. He was rewarded when Nicky turned and walked out of the room with a gesture to follow.

Hank trailed behind, watching the long length of Nicky's back and the soft rise of his buttocks. Nicky had the kind of beauty that artists likely would want to paint or sculpt.

As he walked, Hank loosened his tie and started to undo the buttons at his throat. Nicky reached the bed, then turned abruptly to face Hank, completely nude, hard, incredible.

"There are certain limitations," Nicky said.

Hank couldn't believe they were still talking when Nicky was so naked, but he nodded.

"I will not allow you to bugger me," Nicky said. "I will not allow you to spend near my face. If I say no to something, you must stop right away."

"All right." That still left Hank with a lot of options. He went about unbuttoning his shirt and undid the top button of his trousers.

"I did not intend to make this a contract negotiation, but you must understand—"

"I understand perfectly."

For a brief moment, Nicky's face went completely blank, and he looked sweet and innocent and closer to his actual age. Hank had him pegged as older than twenty-five but not yet thirty. His face showed signs of aging, though, from the crinkles at his eyes to a faint scar on his chin; Nicky had lived a difficult life and had seen more in his few years than some people saw in their whole long lifetimes. Hank knew this without knowing the particulars, because those lines of memory were engraved on Nicky's beautiful face. But here, for a fleeting moment, it all went away, and Nicky was soft and vulnerable.

The vulnerability went away almost as quickly as it appeared.

Hank continued to peel off his clothes—a relief in the stifling heat of the bedroom, where the cloth of his shirt stuck to his clammy skin—and met Nicky's now-defiant gaze.

"I imagine you do understand," Nicky said softly.

Nicky took a step toward Hank and grasped the button plackets of his open shirt. Nicky peeled the shirt off and dumped it on the floor, then made quick work of Hank's tie and cotton undershirt, letting them fall away. He grasped the waistband of Hank's trousers and yanked him close, pressing his naked cock against Hank's still-clothed one. Hank went rigid immediately, his whole body springing to life, and he groaned because he'd forgotten this. He'd forgotten the intensity of it, the smell of another man, the flush and tingle of skin, the softness of hair. He thrust his fingers into Nicky's hair and tugged his head until their lips met in a fierce kiss. Nicky groaned into his mouth, quivering, pressing his palms to Hank's shoulder blades.

Hank loved the feel of man in his arms, of slick skin under his palms, the hot press of a hard cock on his hips. He grasped Nicky's hips and brought them together, rubbed until Nicky cried out. Nicky hooked his thumbs into the waist of Hank's trousers and pushed them down. He shifted his hips so their bare cocks rubbed together, and Hank could do naught but surrender to it, thrusting his hips forward and throwing his head back, closing his eyes to just feel. He stepped out of his pants and kicked them away as Nicky tugged his arms and guided him toward the bed.

It was so overwhelmingly hot, the air in the room dense and heavy, dust clinging to the sweat of their skin. Hank didn't care. Nicky lay on his back and spread his legs wantonly, and there was nothing Hank could do but go to him, to hover above him, to guide their bodies together until they fit, cocks sliding together, bellies and chests touching.

Hank dipped his head and kissed Nicky, licking into his mouth, exploring all of his flavors lest he never taste this again. Nicky put his arms about Hank's shoulders, holding loosely. Hank could feel the moment when Nicky's whole body surrendered to him, became limp and receptive. It was a rush, Hank's head and heart overpowered by this man, until Hank himself wanted to surrender everything to Nicky, would have given anything to make this pleasure go on forever.

Nicky reached between them and took their cocks in his hand, his fingers clever and pressing just enough to tease until he grasped more firmly. Hank gasped, surprised by the magic of that. He moaned out Nicky's name.

"Yes," Nicky whispered. "Hank."

Nicky shook, his body moving jerkily, perhaps overwhelmed by the heat. Hank worried they'd die this way, suffocate together in the oppressive blanket of air around them, but he didn't care. This would be a marvelous way to go.

"So beautiful," he murmured in Nicky's ear.

Nicky jerked beneath him, groaning, digging his fingers into Hank's skin. "Too much," he whispered.

And Hank knew all about that, because pleasure pooled at his groin, powered over his chest and skin, started at his toes and zipped up through his body.

"Just like this," Nicky said, still stroking. "Just like—"

Then Nicky went stiff, his body bowing off the bed, his cock thrust up against Hank's and his hand, and Hank felt the wetness of Nicky's spend on his skin. Hank reached down and kissed him, pressed his cock against Nicky's hip as Nicky went limp, and then found his release as if he were being hit over the head with a mallet. He groaned and cried out Nicky's name and shot and shot until he thought his body completely empty. He still shook afterward, like aftershocks from an earthquake, and he pulled Nicky into his arms as he rode it out.

Then they lay tangled together, their skin sticking to each other as if it were glued. It was so miserably hot in that room, but Hank's mind swum in a pool of pleasure and relief.

Still, he asked, "Was that all right?"

"More than all right, darling," Nicky said.

Hank felt disappointed by Nicky's tone, so calm and cool as if he had not just had a life-changing experience. Hank wanted for Nicky to have achieved the same bliss Hank had.

"This was not what I came here for," Hank said.

"I know. That is why I allowed it."

They lay together for some length of time Hank could not determine. Hank mostly lay on his back and stared at the ceiling, lightly stroking Nicky's shoulder. He breathed deeply, relaxed, and sank into the old, saggy mattress.

Then he looked at the clock.

"I have a meeting," he announced.

Nicky sighed. "When, darling?"

"Twenty minutes. At the precinct house two blocks from here."

"Plenty of time." Nicky's voice sounded sleepy.

"Well, not really. I've already been gone long enough for Stephens and my other colleagues to notice."

With a long groan, Nicky rolled away from Hank. Hank watched, took in the long line of Nicky's spine, the curve of his hip, the subtle musculature on his arms and shoulders. He reached over and ran his hand over those muscles, but then forced himself to stand.

He kept an eye on Nicky as he dressed. Nicky rolled onto his back and stretched languorously, throwing his arms above his head and pointing his toes toward Hank.

"You really are the loveliest of creatures," Hank said. "I do not wish to leave."

"Thank you, love. But you must depart."

Hank considered. He did have to leave, and he would do so in minutes, but he did not wish this to be the end. Although he was still convinced Nicky was hiding something vital to his case, he also thought Nicky had told Hank all he would. Nicky's involvement in the case might as well be over, from an ethical perspective. Or so Hank told himself. As he finished buttoning his shirt, he said, "I would like to see you again. Socially."

"As long as you quit badgering me for information I do not possess." Nicky sat up, stretching his arms over his head and yawning. He was still naked as a newborn babe. "All right. When?"

"Tonight?"

Nicky laughed. "Now you've had a taste, you want the whole feast."

"Something like that." Hank considered his options. "Come to my house after your performance ends tonight. It is but a few blocks from Bulgaria."

"I will consider it. Write down the address on that pad of paper on the chest of drawers over there."

Nicky pointed at an ivory-colored chest of drawers with chubby cherubs painted on the faces of each drawer. It was . . . not a piece of furniture Hank would have chosen for himself. There was a sheaf of paper atop it, not a pad so much as mismatched scraps of paper held together with a clip. There was a pencil nearby as well, so Hank dutifully wrote his address. He wondered if he should really expect Nicky or if this was all for show.

On his way out of the room, he bent to give Nicky a quick peck on the lips. Nicky lifted his head and held onto the kiss, drawing it out, prolonging their connection.

Hank forced himself to pull away. "No more, or else I'll never leave."

"Good-bye, Hank."

Hank left, hoping it would not be forever.

Chapter 6

Brandt felt a bit like he'd set himself up as the punch line in a joke, as he strolled into the precinct house. No doubt he looked disheveled and disreputable after his midday encounter. Stephens stood as Hank reached his desk and opened his mouth, likely to point out how far away from the dress code Hank had wandered.

"Have you been outside?" Hank said in response, but he did tug on his waistcoat and run a hand down each sleeve to try to free them of wrinkles.

Andrew burst into the precinct house just then and looked around quickly. When he located Hank and Stephens, he headed right for them. "I have news, gentlemen."

Stephens held out his hand for the report. "Yes?"

Andrew glanced at Hank. Hank feverishly wished Stephens would disappear. Alas.

Andrew took a deep breath. "I went to the morgue to request a more thorough report, as you suggested. Even the coroner suspects we have a series of murders."

There was a bit of an edge to Andrew's voice, cynicism perhaps. The coroner held no medical degree and had indeed been a political appointment, so there was no telling what cockamamie ideas he had regarding these crimes.

Before Andrew could continue, Captain Leavy walked through the room, gathering those assembled for the afternoon meeting. Andrew handed Hank a folder, and then tipped his hat and left. Hank thumbed through the papers as he and Stephens walked to the meeting room, amused that Andrew had circumvented Stephens's request for the file.

The meeting was ostensibly about the police power needed for William Jennings Bryan's speech, and Stephens, who had earlier expressed that he didn't see the point in being there, looked bored senseless. Hank knew Stephens to be a Bryan supporter, but everything was political; Stephens, and Hank for that matter, worked hard to put himself into a position wherein he'd be promoted out of having to be glorified security. Stephens had taken a step further, and kissed up to Roosevelt regarding the Sunday laws. Hank figured even if one agreed the saloons were a scourge on New York society and Sunday was a day reserved for family, Hank had spent enough time on the streets to know how futile the enforcement of those laws really was. That Hank had been appointed Acting Inspector chafed at Stephens. Probably Stephens was better suited for it, but someone on the police board had likely recognized Stephens was a weasel, and so here they were.

Hank sat through the meeting, hoping Captain Leavy would appoint Stephens to be a glorified ticket taker at Madison Square Garden. Stephens let out an audible breath of relief when Leavy finished assigning people without mentioning him and moved on to the next topic.

Stephens gave his report, a just-the-facts run-down of the open cases, but he added a lot of, "code of conduct" this and "if it please the Captain" that.

Hank didn't have time to dwell on Stephens's political machinations, however, because it was now his turn to speak.

He stood and cleared his throat. "Good afternoon, officers. I thought some of you might be interested to know I testified in court on Monday in the matter of the Boresky trial. This morning, the jury found her not guilty."

"And you disagree with the verdict," Captain Leavy said.

"No. Her lover was the killer. I would have him tried for the crime, but the prosecutor seems to think the matter closed."

Captain Leavy grimaced.

"If nothing else, the outcome of this case illustrates the need to be thorough and collect evidence when investigating. Some of what happened was prosecutorial discretion and out of our hands, but I believe if we'd been more diligent in our efforts, the right man might be behind bars."

"Not much can be done about that now," said Stephens under his breath.

"Indeed. Moving on." Hank looked down at the folder in his hands. "Detective Stephens and I have been investigating the murder of a man found in the ballroom of a resort on the Bowery. Evidence indicates he may be one in a series of dead men."

"Dead prostitutes," Stephens added.

Hank shot him a look intended to quell further discussion, but Stephens ignored him. Hank said, "Yes, it seems likely, albeit unconfirmed, the dead men worked the streets, as it were. But a dead man is a dead man, and we are obliged to investigate, particularly if we have a serial killer on our hands."

"How many dead?" asked Captain Leavy.

"Three that I'm aware of."

Stephens was likely still not altogether sure these were crimes worth investigating, but he sat back and nodded. Hank was the ranking officer in the room, and pursuing this particular line of investigation fell under his purview.

Hank paused to consider how to phrase the next thing he wanted to say. "An hour or so ago, I spoke with a witness to one of the murders, and he believes he can identify the killer if he sees him again, although I have nothing but a description so far." Hank frowned at the folder and thought of the lack of police presence on the Bowery the night before. "I had hoped to have more information to report by now, but so far I only have coroner's reports linking the murders and one possible witness. But, given the circumstances, I'd like to request those officers who patrol the Bowery between Houston and Eighth Street be on alert. There may be a dangerous man about."

Stephens sat back in his chair and stared at Hank as if this surprised him. Hank pushed Stephens's reaction aside; he was the one in charge now.

Leavy nodded. "We can do that. I assume you still want additional officers on patrol?"

"Yes," said Hank. "I intend to pursue the matter, though I do not want to spread police resources too thin. For now, I'll keep Stephens on the case and keep up the increased patrol until we determine the people who frequent the clubs there are safe. In the meantime, I'll ask officers in this precinct to use caution."

After the meeting broke, Stephens tailed Hank back to his desk. "You really should keep me informed of your movements."

Hank looked at him, surprised. "You are upset I interviewed a witness without you. Need I remind you I outrank you? You report to me, not the other way around."

Stephens frowned. "This is still my case. You should tell me when you decide to conduct any interviews."

Hank crossed his arms. "I'm telling you now I interviewed Nicholas Sharp this afternoon and wasn't able to gather more than that he is a potential witness. At least I have that much. If I'd left the investigation to your discretion, we'd have nothing, given you barely think this case is worth investigating."

Stephens opened his mouth as if he intended to argue the point, but he was interrupted when a woman burst into the precinct house. "Help! Oh, please help me!"

Stephens was closest and ran to her, Hank on his heels. She led them out front and down the block a little ways to a man who had collapsed on the sidewalk.

"What happened?" Stephens asked.

"He collapsed."

"Is he your husband?" asked Hank, kneeling to check the man's vitals.

"Yes. He seemed fine as we walked down the street. Then he said he felt strange. Then he simply . . . fell."

"Where does he work?" Hank asked.

"What has that to do with anything?"

Hank felt for the man's pulse and pressed a hand to his forehead. The man was still alive, at least. "Does he have an occupation that would require heavy lifting? Manual labor?"

"He works as a carpenter. His shop is on Eighth Street."

Hank nodded. "I fear he may have succumbed to the heat. He is still alive, but he is very ill, possibly with heat stroke. We must get him to a hospital. They will be able to cool him off there."

"I'll fetch an ambulance," Stephens said.

"Yes," said Hank.

Hank stayed with the woman and her husband, and used his own handkerchief to wipe the man's face. Stephens stood there for a moment and pursed his lips before he went to find emergency personnel to secure an ambulance.

By the time Stephens returned to the scene, the collapsed man was awake, but stared unseeing into the distance. His wife was apoplectic, crying and screaming and generally making a scene. Hank worked not to let his agitation show. He helped the man into the ambulance. The driver hopped down and said, "Sixth time today."

"Where will you take him?" asked Stephens.

"Bellevue. Some hospitals are turning away patients because there are so many crumbling under the heat, but at Bellevue they will put him in an ice bath. I saw them do it not an hour ago. The man who they treated is now quite recovered."

Hank nodded.

"Or," the ambulance driver went on, "they're bleeding some patients because the heat causes high blood pressure. It offers some relief, from what I can tell. Either way, ma'am, your husband will be in good hands."

"Bleeding?" said Hank. "How barbaric."

"Yes, but if it helps . . ." said the driver. He then helped the wife into the ambulance.

Hank bid him to go, although Stephens held up a hand. "I am tempted to go along to make sure the man is all right. Sixth time today, you said?"

"Or the seventh." The ambulance driver made a nickering sound to his horse. "It's hard to keep track."

Stephens looked alarmed by this news. "All of them are all right, though."

"No." The driver dropped his voice, soft enough so as not to be heard by the wife. "Actually, most expire before we reach the hospital. One man had a seizure when he was placed in the ice bath."

"Oh dear," said Stephens.

"I'd better get going if this man is to have a chance. Good afternoon, gentlemen."

Hank and Stephens stood on the sidewalk and watched the ambulance go. Hank shook his head. "Perhaps the real crime is this infernal heat."

"It is difficult to argue with that." Stephens grunted. "You spoke with Nicholas Sharp this afternoon? Was he the funny little man with the red scarf? The one who failed to make his appointment yesterday?"

Hank nodded. "I tracked him down. He keeps rooms in a house not far from here."

"Why bother to put forth all that effort? I can't imagine he was forthcoming with the truth."

"I believe he's been honest with me. He thinks he could identify the man he saw with Edward if he saw him again, which is not an indictment, but it is something. I just need a suspect now."

"But you can see how this could be a waste of time. We don't have enough evidence, we have no way of even finding a suspect, there's not really enough manpower to patrol the Bowery at night unless the city is willing to pay for it, which they undoubtedly will not do—"

"I refuse to give up. Not yet, at any rate."

"Why do you care so much? Why bother with dead working boys at all?"

Hank glanced at Stephens, whose face betrayed his frustration with an unsolvable case. It didn't matter. Hank could solve this case himself if he had to. He said, "As I've said, a dead man is a dead man. This one died in this precinct. Three men died in this precinct. That makes them our responsibility."

"Yes, but it is morally reprehensible, what these men do. Do you not think we are better off without them?"

Hank pursed his lips and looked up First Avenue. The elevated train tracks above them at least blocked out the sun, so it was not nearly so oppressive right in this spot, although the heat seemed inescapable even here. Stephens took off his hat and a hint of a breeze moved his hair.

But Hank was angry now. "I suppose next you'll want to set fire to the tenements and watch them all burn. Good riddance, right?" He went back inside without waiting for a response.

"Ritchley!"

Commissioner Roosevelt burst out of his office. Andrew eyed him warily. It had been a long day and didn't appear to be ending soon. Andrew had agreed to stay late at his boss's request, but he suspected Roosevelt's appearance at his desk meant not that he would be dismissed but instead that a parade was about to take place.

"Tell me, Ritchley," Roosevelt said. "In your intense study of the crime reports of the day, where would you say the most attention is needed in terms of police protection?"

Andrew suppressed a reaction, even though he knew precisely where this was about to go. "Probably the Bowery, sir. The tenements as always. Eight arrests for theft on Orchard Street alone. The Seventeenth Precinct has seen quite a bit of crime today as well, although some of the violence was due more to the heat than anything else. Ten men at a construction site near Cooper Union collapsed this afternoon."

"Let us take a walk, Ritchley."

Naturally.

They exited Police Headquarters onto Mulberry Street. It was well after dark, but Andrew didn't have a sense for the time. Probably close to midnight. Roosevelt was fond of these late-night constitutionals to check on his patrolmen. He was never completely satisfied with reports and insisted on periodically checking for himself that his police were doing their jobs.

So Andrew accompanied Roosevelt on a walk around the neighborhood, looping south to Canal Street and then east into the Tenth Ward. Here was the heart of the tenements, and nearly everyone was still on the street. From his vantage point at street level, Andrew could see people gathered on fire escapes, on stoops, and likely also on the roof, anything to escape the heat in their buildings. There was even a child asleep alone on the steps in front of a tall, crumbling tenement building. Andrew thought perhaps Roosevelt would wake her up and tell her to go home, but he only spared her a glance before continuing to walk.

The temperature was still high despite the late hour, the darkness providing no relief from the thick warmth in the air. Andrew removed his hat, feeling daring, but the air stood still and did nothing to relieve him.

"Where are the patrolmen?" Roosevelt said. "Caspar and O'Sullivan are usually walking around these parts."

Andrew looked around. He spotted two uniformed police officers in the distance, walking up Christie Street. "There, sir," said Andrew.

"Capital! Come along, then."

Both officers shot Andrew a wary look when Roosevelt met them. "I believe, sir," said Caspar, "there has been little crime tonight because everyone is too hot to move. The only person we've encountered tonight flaunting the law was a twelve-year-old boy who stole a moldy loaf of bread from a man on Forsyth when he closed down his pushcart for the day. Then the man let the boy have the bread."

"Hear that, Ritchley? What an orderly night!"

Andrew did not believe their luck would last, and indeed, when they crossed Houston some time later, they were almost immediately accosted by a woman who hiked her skirts up to show off her shapely calves.

"Put that away, madam," Roosevelt told her. "Or I'll have you arrested."

Andrew was tired by then from the heat and the exertion of walking quickly to keep up with Roosevelt, but Roosevelt seemed to have an unending tap of energy, gallivanting over toward the Bowery.

Andrew was aware of Hank's reports and of the other news of the day filtering in. "Sir, I believe this neighborhood has been the site of some recent violence. You would do well to be cautious."

"Finnegan patrols this area, yes? And his partner's name is . . . De-Lauria."

"Yes, sir. I believe so." It had been Finnegan who had found the dead female impersonator the night before, in fact.

They crossed under the elevated tracks, and Andrew couldn't help but notice just how many people were about even here, just like those in the tenements trying to escape the extreme heat indoors.

They encountered a young man at the corner of Bowery and Second Street who stood with a cigarillo in his hand, the smoke billowing up into the night. The man was quite striking, young with tousled blond hair and an insouciant expression, his dark suit neatly tailored although a bit threadbare, as if it had been made for him years ago but was now well-worn. Andrew thought this might have been the one nice suit this man owned and so probably got a fair amount of use, but then, this man was probably standing here in case a man such as Andrew happened to be strolling by. Of course, with Roosevelt at his side, Andrew could not be tempted by this bait.

"You there, young man!" Roosevelt said. The man looked startled for a moment. He dropped his cigarillo and put it out with the heel of his shoe.

"Do not fear us," Andrew said, attempting to defuse the situation. "We are merely on a late stroll. If you are just out here to smoke, you are doing nothing wrong."

The man nodded. Up close, Andrew could see his youth was manufactured with makeup and the man was quite a bit older than Andrew had first supposed.

"Do you know who I am?" Roosevelt asked.

"I have a notion," said the young man. "Police Commissioner Roosevelt, yes? I've seen your photo in the papers."

"No doubt next to an article excoriating me for caring too much about the Sunday laws. It is good policy, though, regardless of what Mr. Hearst or Mr. Pulitzer may print in their papers. What is your name, son?"

"Charles Evans, sir. Most people call me Charlie." The poor man had a look in his eyes like a boy who had just been caught with his hand in the sweets jar.

"Have you seen anything interesting tonight?" Roosevelt asked.

"No, sir."

Even Roosevelt could tell the response came too quick.

"You should know," Andrew said, searching for the right language. "This row has seen a bit of violent crime of late."

"Yes," Charlie said. He met Andrew's gaze, but Andrew only saw fear there, not real understanding.

"Have you seen my men on patrol?" Roosevelt asked.

"A pair of officers walked by not five minutes ago," said Charlie.

"That is good," Andrew said, trying to catch Charlie's gaze again. He wanted to convey that he was friendly. He noticed little tells, signs this man was just what Andrew suspected he was: his hair looked like it had been brightened with peroxide and he'd tucked a red handkerchief into the pocket of his jacket. To someone who knew the signs, this man was practically waving a flag saying he was available for purchase to any man interested. "Be mindful of the officers on duty."

Charlie worried his fingers together and looked off in the distance. He opened his mouth as if about to speak a few times and then clamped it shut. Then he seemed to think better of silence and said, "I heard about the boy killed here two nights ago."

"Yes," said Andrew. "The detective on the case is a friend of mine. He has sworn to investigate the matter with his full capacity."

"Which inspector?" Roosevelt asked.

"Henry Brandt, sir. Acting Inspector Brandt, I should say." Andrew quite deliberately failed to name George Stephens, whom he disliked intensely. Stephens wanted the glory of solving a crime to get a promotion, but had no interest in solving crimes that involved anyone poor or queer. Which was most crime in his jurisdiction; Stephens would have been better suited to an uptown precinct. Andrew hoped he'd soon be minding goats instead of the wallets of Mrs. Astor's Four Hundred uptown, although at least if Stephens got his wish, he'd be mostly out of Andrew's and Hank's hair.

"Oh, yes, Brandt. Of course," said Roosevelt. "Bit of a rebel our Brandt. Saw him without his coat yesterday."

"It was rather hot, sir," said Andrew. "Still is."

Charlie looked between them as if he didn't know what to make of this. "How much danger do you think there is?"

"Enough," said Andrew. "Do you work around here?"

"A resort on the next block. I needed to take a few minutes to myself. Er, do not tell my boss."

"Perish the thought," said Roosevelt. "Though it would be the responsible thing for a young man such as yourself to return to his work and leave the patrolling of the streets to the professionals."

"Yes, sir," said Charlie.

Roosevelt turned and bounded up the block. Andrew fished into his pocket for his card and handed it to Charlie. "Listen," Andrew said quietly. "Hank Brandt is a good man and he will find the man who is terrorizing this neighborhood. My greatest hope is you will soon have nothing to fear. But if you need anything, that is where you will find me. I work as a secretary at Police Headquarters."

Charlie's eyes went wide. "But, sir . . . do you know . . ." He looked worried.

"I know what you are. I do not judge you for it. Neither will Hank Brandt."

Charlie met Andrew's gaze. He was a handsome man, that did not escape Andrew's attention, and it was a shame he was rotting down here, an aging working boy who would likely die on this street. Andrew wanted to rescue him but knew he could not.

Or could he?

"If you see anything, know anything, fear anything, need anything, please come ask for me at Police Headquarters."

Charlie nodded.

"I must go catch up with the Commissioner. Please, Charlie. I want to help you."

"I do not know if I can be helped." But he pocketed the card instead of throwing it away.

Andrew reached over and briefly squeezed Charlie's hand. Then he darted up the block to catch up with Roosevelt.

Chapter 7

As Nicky peeled off the last vestiges of Paulina, someone knocked on the door of his dressing room.

"Come," said Nicky.

Charlie came through the door, a dazed expression on his face. "You will never believe what just happened."

"Likely not," said Nicky. He hung his gown in the closet and then shrugged into a white cotton shirt.

"I needed a few minutes away. A man got rough with me tonight, and I worried he was . . . well, you can imagine."

"Yes."

Charlie walked into the room and ran a finger over the edge of Nicky's makeup chair. "So I was outside. And who should come up but the police commissioner! Mr. Roosevelt, I think is his name."

Nicky dropped the suspenders in his hand. He clucked his tongue and then bent to pick them up. "The hell you say."

"The very man! He was with a fellow who claimed to be a secretary at police headquarters."

"Out on some patrol, no doubt," Nicky said as he fastened his suspenders to his trousers. "I read somewhere Commissioner Roosevelt does that sometimes. Just decides to check on his patrols at odd hours of the night. I cannot believe you actually met him, though."

"The secretary gave me a card." He pulled it from his pocket and showed it to Nicky. It said, "Andrew Ritchley" in fine script across the middle, then "Secretary, Special Assistant to the Commissioner, New York City Police Department." The address of police headquarters was below it. Charlie went on, "He said the detective on the case to solve Edward's death was friendly to us. He"—Charlie looked around the room—"I am not sure what to say, but there was something about him."

"What about him?" Nicky handed the card back to Charlie.

"I thought at first he was interested in, ah, procuring my services, but he left with Roosevelt. Now I think on it, I wonder if he wasn't . . . a man of our kind."

"Ah."

Charlie pocketed the card again and then put a hand over his pocket as if its cargo were precious. Maybe it was. "Anyway, I believe he may have been trying to tell me the detective investigating the murders was tenacious. This Ritchley fellow essentially told me our profession mattered not, that the detective would still find the killer."

"The detective on the case?"

"Someone named Brandt?"

Nicky let out the breath he'd been holding. "Yes, I do believe Brandt to be friendly. I have spoken to him."

"I was terrified I'd be arrested. But I did not solicit them. I was merely smoking outside."

"And no arrest was forthcoming, so you'll be all right."

Charlie seemed exasperated, waving his hands. "The secretary told me to go to Police Headquarters if I needed anything."

"Maybe he was sweet on you."

Charlie wrinkled his nose. "I think that unlikely."

Nicky looked in the mirror as he pulled his suspenders on over his shoulders. He picked his waistcoat up from the table and briefly lamented the fact he'd have to put on clothes, further insulating his body despite the heat.

"This Brandt. Do you trust him?" Charlie asked.

Probably more than he should have, particularly considering he was seriously considering walking to the address written on the scrap of paper now in his trousers pocket. "As much as I trust anyone."

Charlie frowned. "Not at all, in other words."

Nicky laughed, despite himself. "Well. I trust him a little more than that. However, he is still a police officer. As ever, I believe we should be cautious."

Charlie reached into his pocket, likely to touch Ritchley's card. Nicky knew the feeling. It was all he could do to keep from reaching for Hank's address, tidily written on that piece of paper.

He looked back at the mirror. He'd successfully transformed back into a man, or done a sufficient enough job to walk about in public. He grabbed his coat and pulled it on reluctantly, already feeling the lining sticking to his shirt.

"Do you really think the police will catch the man who killed Edward?" Charlie asked.

"No, but Inspector Brandt certainly seems determined to try." And that Nicky did believe. He hadn't quite overcome the sense Brandt would turn on him and throw him in jail at any moment—and certainly anyone with half a brain would take the word of a police inspector over the word of a man who wore dresses when he performed, so Nicky was at a disadvantage—but he believed Brandt genuinely wanted to solve this crime.

Charlie glanced out the door. "I do not want to go back to the ballroom tonight, but I need the money."

Nicky's heart broke for Charlie. He looked so unhappy. "I could lend you—"

"No. It is my problem to solve." Charlie smiled, but it didn't go to his eyes. "I'll be all right."

Nicky knew about pride, but he said, "If you need something . . ."

"I know, Nicky, and I love you for it, but I have to make my own way. The days I'll be able to make money are numbered, and then I don't know what I'll do, but for now, I can close my eyes and pretend I'm something else."

Nicky's chest tightened, but he nodded. "Well. I must be going."

"Of course. Good night, Nicky. Be careful."

Nicky sometimes felt the same way about Charlie as he did about his sister Brigid; if he could afford to move the lot of them out of their situations and into safer environs, he would do it in a heartbeat. As it was, keeping his own roof over his head was a struggle on a singer's salary.

As he walked out of the club and onto the Bowery, he fingered the slip of paper in his pocket and entertained the fantasy this liaison with Hank Brandt was his ticket out of this life. But that was utter nonsense.

Nicky walked up the Bowery toward the Cooper Institute, but instead of turning right toward his apartment, he went left toward West Tenth Street.

It wasn't a great distance to walk, although in this weather, it felt interminable. There was a heavy haze hanging over the night, making the electric lights look like they had auras. Nicky had been a teenager when most of these lights had been installed, and he had no nostalgic feelings toward the old gaslights, but the way these lights flickered tonight cast a pall over West Fourth Street as he walked across town. There was something ghostly about the night, although it was too hot to be anything but alive. People were gathered in Washington Square, likely because it was an outdoor space, and it was at least cooler outside than it was in many indoor locations.

It was a dreary night. It smelled more of death and decay the closer Nicky got to Sixth Avenue. A man lay unconscious—Nicky hoped he was unconscious—on the sidewalk, hidden in the shadows from the elevated trains above. There was a dog howling somewhere in the distance. The clop of horse hooves echoed in the canyon created by the buildings on the avenue. Nicky crossed over to the other side of Sixth Avenue and not for the first time entertained fantasies of leaving this whole city behind. What did it have to offer anyone but hopelessness?

Well, except for a certain man who lived on West Tenth Street.

Nicky found the address without any trouble and was surprised to see it was a squat, three-story brick house. The wide front door was painted dark green, or so it looked in the sickly electric lights from the street, and there was a brass knocker below the house number. Did Hank really live in this house? Did he rent rooms here? Only one way to find out.

Nicky lifted and banged the knocker against the door a few times. He wondered as he waited whether to expect a mistress of the house or a butler or another man or what, but then Hank himself answered the door with a smile.

"You came."

Hank stood there wearing just a white shirt with his sleeves rolled to his elbows and the first few buttons at his collar undone. He had a couple of days of beard growth shadowing his face and his dark brown hair was carelessly tousled. He had on the same trousers he'd been wearing earlier in the day, but Nicky hadn't noticed earlier how nicely fitted they were. Hank had the sort of body that had seen violence or defended himself from same—strong and muscular but not boxy. Without a waistcoat, it was clear how trim his waist was, how well formed his buttocks and thighs were, and Nicky vowed then and there if he ever saw Hank naked again he would take the time to savor him instead of rushing.

"Nicky?"

Nicky came back to himself. He lowered his eyelids and cocked his hips. "Apparently you are irresistible, darling."

Hank ushered Nicky inside, and again Nicky was struck by how nice the house looked. It was modestly furnished but clean, from what Nicky could see. "Do you live here alone?" Nicky asked.

"Yes. It was my family's home, but I'm all the family I have now."

The foyer was all dark wood with a grand staircase that presumably went to the second floor. There was a large room off the foyer that had a threadbare settee and more dark wood. The furniture was scratched and worn at the edges, from what Nicky could see, but there was something comforting about that. This house was worn and lived in. It was well-loved and cared for, despite Hank's modest means, or so Nicky imagined. He had no real sense for what money a police inspector made.

"Can I find you something to eat?"

Nicky looked at Hank, feeling astonished. "You want to feed me?"

"If you're hungry. When was your last meal?"

Nicky couldn't remember. His indecision seemed to push Hank into action and he walked to the back of the house. Nicky followed into a small kitchen. There was an ice box in the corner—an ice box!—from which Hank pulled a block of cheese.

"I think this is still good. I couldn't get ice delivered today, but the box stays cool for a long time." He sniffed the cheese. "Seems all right. Sit at the table."

Nicky sat and watched as Hank put out cheese and bread and fetched a knife from a drawer.

"I apologize for not having more. I have not been home much of late."

"This is wonderful." And it was. The cheese was cool and tangy and the bread was hearty.

Hank excused himself and came back with a pitcher of water. That was remarkable, too, and the water was clear and cool and refreshing.

Nicky gulped down a glass full and then poured a second. His apartment had running water most of the time, which he couldn't say for Brigid's family—the pipes were forever clogged and water rarely came out of the taps clean if it was working—and that weighed on Nicky's mind. He was so hot and thirsty, though, that he was thankful for this.

He wanted to do more for Brigid and decided he'd go see her in the morning. He felt guilty pushing thoughts of her and little Edith away, but there was nothing he could do for them in waning hours of the night.

"Did you eat?" Nicky asked.

"Yes. Really, eat as much as you want. I wish I could give you more."

That gave Nicky pause. "You aren't just doing this because you feel sorry for me, are you? Because of my lot in life and all that?"

Hank balked. "No. I just know what it's like to work long hours, so I figured you might have missed a meal."

Nicky believed him and saw the compassion in Hank's actions. In that moment, they'd crossed a threshold, when they went from strangers who stumbled into each other's lives to something like friends. Hank didn't care about Nicky merely as a witness or as a warm body in his bed, but rather he cared enough to make sure Nicky ate.

"Any progress with the case?" Nicky asked.

"Not since I saw you last. It was . . . a difficult afternoon."

"How so?"

Hank reached over and nabbed a bit of bread. He chewed on it and then said, "This heat is a terrible villain to contend with, because there's nothing to be done for it. There's no escape from it unless you're wealthy enough to buy ice or leave the city."

"People have died," Nicky said.

"Yes." He stared off into the distance. "Among others, an officer who had spent all day on patrol passed out in the precinct house this evening. We took him to Bellevue, but he may not survive."

How much was the heat making Edith's illness worse? There was no way to know, but Nicky assumed it was a factor.

"Are you all right?" Hank asked.

"Better now I've eaten."

"You looked so sad just then."

Nicky felt a little thrill that Hank was paying enough attention to detect his moods, though he was a detective, so it was probably habit. "I was thinking about my family."

"Do they live in the city?"

"Mostly, yes. I have six siblings. We all kind of scattered once we became adults."

"It was just me when I was a child. Although my friend Amelia was like a sister to me." Hank looked wistful for a moment, but then his whole face changed. "Amelia. She's having a party next week."

Nicky couldn't imagine what that had to do with anything, so he said, "I'm sure it will be lovely."

"Not just a party." Hank sounded disgruntled. "Her husband is Jonathan Cooper."

"Should that name mean something to me?"

"Steel. He owns a steel production plant in Pennsylvania. Worked for Andrew Carnegie ten years ago. He's become something of a magnate. He's made more money than you or I will ever see in our lives. He and Amelia have been rising up through New York society for the last few years."

"Well, love, that is impressive."

Hank narrowed his eyes. "You start dropping nicknames on me when you want to build walls. I explain about Amelia not to show off some connection I have, because believe me, Jonathan Cooper is nice to me but thinks I'm worth about as much as the dirt beneath his butler's shoes. I mention it merely to show how Amelia has changed. We grew up like siblings, but she lives in another world now."

Nicky was surprised to have been so easily deciphered. "All right," he said softly. "My brother George owns a horse stable up in Longacre Square. That is the extent of the glamour in my family."

Hank looked at Nicky and met his gaze. "To get back to my point, you told me you would know the man you saw with Edward if you saw him again. If our theory is correct that he's of the uptown elite and he was slumming downtown, he might be at Amelia's charity ball. It is set for this Monday evening."

"I'm afraid I don't follow."

"You could come with me to the charity ball and perhaps see the man there. Most of the Four Hundred are off at their summer homes, but anyone who is anyone and still in the city will very likely be there."

Of all things, a charity ball. Nicky had never been to anything like that, and he wasn't sure how well he could blend in. "Are you sure?"

"I think it is the best idea I've had for breaking this case open. I believe if we put you in some sort of disguise, you could act well enough to blend in. All I would need you to do is point out the man in question should you see him."

Nicky could picture himself strolling into a ball like that on Hank's arm, so to speak, mingling with high society, dressed to the nines. He liked the image, even if he was not entirely convinced he was that good of an actor. "All right, I will think on it."

"Naturally. No need to decide right at this moment."

Nicky polished off the last of the cheese and felt a great deal better than he had just minutes before. "Well, darling, just as you did not come to my apartment this morning with the intention of ending up in my bed, I did not come here with the intention of eating dinner. Not that I do not appreciate the gesture immensely."

"Perhaps I should show you the rest of my home."

"Perhaps."

Hank took the plates away and put them in a basin. Then he doused the light and helped Nicky stand. Hank took Nicky's hand and led him to the staircase. Hank put his foot on the first step, but Nicky stopped him.

"Hank?"

"What is it?"

"I just want to say thank you."

Nicky leaned up and pressed a kiss to Hank's lips. When he pulled away, Hank smiled.

"If no other good comes of this wretched week," Hank said, "I will always have these memories of you."

How could it be a man as gruff as Hank could be this sweet? "Take me to bed, darling."

The large mechanical fan over Hank's bed ineffectively blew hot air around, but at least they were naked as Hank took Nicky's cock into his mouth.

Nicky writhed beneath Hank. This intimacy was surprising. There had been a few dalliances over the years, mostly with the aging working boys who worked at Bulgaria looking for reminders their customers were not the beginning and the end, but nothing quite like this. Hank was enthusiastic, his lips moving up and down the shaft of Nicky's cock, his mouth hot and wet, the groan in the back of his throat genuine and not a performance. Hank's mustachioed upper lip sliding over Nicky's cock made for a scene that was unmistakably masculine and unbelievably arousing. Hank wrapped his hand around the base of Nicky's cock and stroked it as he licked the tip, and every now and then he'd look up toward Nicky and meet his gaze. Every time Nicky saw those big eyes, greenish in the dim light of the bedroom, a part of him melted.

This was not a quick fumble in the dark to relieve stress and pressure or to be reminded he was a man and not an object. There was something genuine here.

Nicky arched off the bed, thrusting his hips up so his cock slid into Hank's waiting mouth and he went hot and flush everywhere as pleasure and arousal coursed through him.

Hank sucked and licked and then pulled away slowly. He crawled up Nicky's body and kissed him hard. Nicky kissed him back, happy for the touch, the intimacy, the way this moment made him feel like himself in his own body. He'd gotten into the habit of floating out somewhere else when someone he didn't truly desire was all over him, but he wanted Hank. Hank was rugged and handsome and gruff and sweet and a whole pile of tiny contradictions. Nicky would have chosen him over and over again.

He thrust his fingers into the skin of Hank's bottom and pulled him close so that their hips lined up, so that their cocks slid together. Hank groaned into Nicky's mouth, and Nicky moved his hands up to tug on Hank's hair. Hank broke the kiss to sigh and then plunged back in, moving his hips rhythmically against Nicky's.

"God," Hank said. "You will be my undoing."

"Spend against me, Hank. Come apart for me. I want you to be desperate for me."

"I am. I am so desperate for you. I want you all the time. I've been thinking about you ceaselessly for two days. And now you're under me and you're so . . ." Hank pressed his lips against Nicky's and thrust again, perhaps finding purchase, because he groaned again.

Nicky felt the tingles, the boiling inside, and he knew it was just a matter of moments before the crash.

Hank's obvious hunger made something wake up inside of Nicky, flipping on like an electric light bulb. When he fetched, it was like the pop of that bulb exploding. He clung onto Hank, throwing his arms around Hank's shoulders, and he pumped his hips up as Hank bit his earlobe, and he felt himself fly to pieces. Hank murmured something incomprehensible and then spent as well. Their sticky spend spread on Nicky's belly. When Hank dipped his head to lick some of it up, Nicky thought he would die from the fierce pleasure of it.

Hank rolled over and lay on his back, panting. "There may come a time when we simply concede to the fact we are attracted to each other."

Nicky laughed breathlessly. "Oh, darling, that moment passed for me half an hour ago."

"I'm glad." Hank stretched, his long body taut as he threw his arms up. "Seemed silly to argue otherwise."

Nicky wanted to ask Hank what he intended to happen here, but he was afraid to make more of this than it was. Perhaps this was just two men who found mutual pleasure in each other and nothing more. Nicky certainly couldn't afford to take more than that. He still had a career to think of, his own apartment, a life that needed to be away from the curious eyes of the police or the prying intentions of other spectators.

Though if anyone understood the need for privacy, it was Hank.

Nicky let his body relax, melting into the mattress. He was sweaty and sticky and a little uncomfortable, but he didn't have the where-withal to move. He took a deep breath, then another, trying to decide if he should leave or talk Hank into letting him stay the night. He was not particularly eager to walk back across town in the wee hours of the morning—Nicky had no delusions he was the picture of mas-culinity, and as such, he tended to get harassed by drunken toughs when he was out late, which was not to mention the killer apparently on the loose—nor did he want to overstay his welcome.

But then Hank said, "Please stay with me tonight."

And Nicky couldn't say no.

Day 4

Saturday, August 8
Temperature: 103°F

Chapter 8

Hank woke up sweaty and overheated and thought at first he'd somehow pulled his quilt over his body despite the heat. Then he realized the "quilt" in question was actually Nicky, draped over his chest and snoozing softly.

That was . . . lovely.

It was also far too hot.

Hank tried to nudge Nicky toward the other side of the bed, but Nicky woke up with a start. He jerked up into a sitting position and then looked around. "Hank."

"You're all right," Hank said, cupping his hand over Nicky's shoulder and easing him back down on the bed. "Sorry to wake you, but you were lying on top of me like a down quilt. On a winter night, I would have left you, but as I believe the temperature in this room is already well above eighty degrees . . ."

Nicky lay on his back beside Hank and pressed a hand to his forehead. "I apologize."

"Don't. To be clear, I only minded because it is so hot this morning. Otherwise, I quite liked you on top of me."

"I should not have stayed this late. I did not intend to."

"You were tired."

"Your bed is comfortable." Nicky yawned.

Hank reached over and trailed a finger from Nicky's Adam's apple to his navel. Nicky had yards of skin that now glistened with sweat and sparkled in the sunlight. The effect was quite magical, as if there were something otherworldly about him.

"Pardon me for a moment." Nicky got out of bed and left the room.

The washroom was down the hall, so Hank figured that was where Nicky was headed. Hank lay back on the mattress and kicked the bedding onto the floor. He was naked but it was too hot not to be. He was starting to drift back to sleep when Nicky returned, also naked. He still had lines near his eyes from last night's makeup, still had rouge on his cheeks.

"I like your house," Nicky said.

"Thanks. My parents bought it just after I was born. My father's pension. He was in the war."

"Ah." Nicky settled beside Hank, though they stayed about an inch apart on the mattress. That was a shame, but just as well. Holding each other probably would have cause them both to melt.

"Took a minie ball to the leg," Hank said. "His shin was shattered and had to be amputated. As a kid, I thought it was amazing to have a father with a peg leg, but I didn't appreciate until I was much older how much pain he must have been in all the time. My parents actually lived in the room on the first floor for a time because he could not climb the stairs."

"So your father was a war hero." Nicky rolled onto his stomach and propped himself up on his elbows.

"I suppose. I never knew him well. I was about twelve when he passed."

Nicky nodded. "Well, darling, my father is still among the living, at least when he deems it reasonable to climb out of his bottle. When he is not intoxicated, he lives with my sister Brigid."

Nicky was doing the nickname thing again, so this was a topic with which he was uncomfortable. Hank reached over and cupped Nicky's face with his palm. Nicky's gaze met his. They stared at each other for a long moment, and Hank imagined some silent communication passed between them. They understood each other despite their differences. Hank certainly had a clearer picture of what Nicky was about now.

Or that was his imagination.

"I should be leaving," Nicky said, rolling away. "Things to do today."

Deliberately flippant, Hank said, "What does a singer who works nights have to do so early in the morning?"

Nicky began to gather his clothes. He stopped to aim a sardonic look at Hank before he pulled them on. "Well, you know, darling, I have many things to attend to. You'll just have to use your imagination. Maybe I'll fritter away the day on frilly things at the department stores on Ladies' Mile. Or I've got another lover to see to."

A deflection. Which meant Nicky didn't want Hank to know where he planned to go. That Hank cared so much was problematic, but he said, "I'll bet I made you shoot more last night than your other lover could in a month."

Nicky let out a surprised laugh. "You think a great deal of yourself, love."

Hank got out of bed and walked to his own wardrobe. He stood there, pretending to be indecisive about what to wear, probably longer than was necessary, but he felt Nicky's gaze on him. Nicky was attracted, all right. That was all to the good, since Hank intended to have him again.

"Have you given any thought to my proposition about the charity ball?"

Nicky walked to Hank's mirror and tied his tie. He pilfered a handkerchief from the little stack Hank kept on the dresser and wiped at his face, removing the last vestiges of the makeup. "Lord almighty, but I look a fright in the morning."

"You're beautiful," Hank said. "One of the most striking men I have ever laid eyes on."

Nicky turned around. Were his cheeks pink from the rouge, from the exertion of removing the rouge, or from embarrassment at the compliment? Nicky said, "I believe I have just the disguise for your charity ball. Two days hence?"

"Monday evening, yes." Hank started pulling on his clothes, an idea forming in his mind.

"Come to my apartment an hour prior to when you'd like to arrive." Nicky glanced at the clock. "I really must be going, but if you need to find me, leave word for me at Bulgaria. Presumably you could use the pretense of your investigation to do so."

"All right. I believe I can manage that." He made a show of buttoning his shirt and pulling on his suspenders. "I should leave as well. Criminals to catch and all."

"Of course, darling. Crime does not take off for the Sabbath, I imagine."

"Usually not, no."

Nicky smiled and walked over to Hank. He gave Hank a slow kiss, sexy and drawn out, but more affectionate than a prelude to anything.

"I will see you Monday," Hank said.

"If not sooner," said Nicky.

Hank quite liked the sound of that.

He gave Nicky a moment's lead and then locked up and bounded down the front steps. He saw Nicky round the corner onto Sixth Avenue, so he followed at a distance. He was good at keeping to shadows and dark places, even on sunny days, and it was not difficult as Nicky seemed to be following the elevated train path.

This decision was foolish, perhaps, but Hank's nagging sense Nicky was up to something and hiding an important element of the case would not let go. So Hank followed Nicky east along Houston Street and then, somewhat to Hank's chagrin, Nicky turned into the Tenth Ward.

At first Hank suspected Nicky knew he was following and had deliberately turned into a crowded neighborhood teeming with people in order to lose the tail, but Hank stuck with him and soon realized Nicky walked with the determination of someone with a specific destination. Indeed, Nicky walked up to a tenement on Hester Street, but rather than going inside, he paused to talk to the children gathered on the stoop.

"Where is your sister?" Nicky asked a boy who was maybe five or six.

"Mama can't work, so Lucy went in her place."

From Hank's current vantage point behind a pushcart—he'd pulled his hat over his eyes and pretended to browse the fruit on display with the intention of purchasing it, even though most of it was already spoiling in the hot sun—he couldn't see Nicky's face, but there was displeasure in his body language.

"Why can't your mother work?"

"Edith is sick," the boy said.

Nicky's shoulders rose and fell. "Is your grandfather home?"

"Yes. He's sleeping."

Nicky put his hands on his hips and looked around him. Hank ducked behind the vendor selling the rotting fruit. Nicky didn't seem to see him.

Hank felt guilty suddenly. Nicky knew these children clearly, and Hank couldn't imagine how they'd be tied to his case. That Nicky had business outside Club Bulgaria was obvious, and, given Hank and Nicky had only known each other for four days, there was no reason for Nicky to confide in Hank. Hank was now witnessing what was probably a family moment.

But just as Hank was about to sneak away and leave Nicky to his family, Nicky said, "Is Edith improved?"

"No, Uncle Nicky," the boy said.

Nicky immediately went into the building. Hank considered following to be sure everything was all right, but suddenly his feet were lead. He waited instead, keeping to the shadows, watching the Lower East Side come to life around him. People moved about on the sidewalks, pushcart vendors fought for land ownership, and conversations bloomed in a dozen different languages.

The kids sitting on the stoop of the building Nicky had gone into were half-heartedly playing, tossing a small ball back and forth. Hank felt a pang as he realized there wasn't really anyone to watch out for these children. He walked up the sidewalk, past them, hoping to get a better look. Their clothes were stained and their hair was damp with sweat. Hank walked to the end of the block, trying to decide what to do. Really, he should leave. He should let Nicky have his privacy and he should walk uptown to his precinct house. Instead, before he was even conscious he was doing anything, he turned and walked back toward the building in question.

The boy Nicky had spoken with now sat on the top step. He pushed his hair away from his face with the palms of his hands.

"Do you live here?" Hank asked.

The boy nodded but eyed Hank warily.

Hank fished his police badge from his pocket and showed it to the boy. "I'm a police officer. I just want to make sure everything here is all right."

"My sister's sick."

"What is your name?"

"Anthony."

Hank was about to ask more when a blood-curdling scream sounded through the building.

"Mama!" Anthony said, turning back toward the open door.

"How many floors up is your apartment?" Hank asked.

Anthony held up three fingers but said, "Four."

Delightful.

Hank bounded up the first flight of stairs and glanced in the open doors on the second floor. An old woman wearing an alarmed expression looked back at him. He ran up the third floor . . . and there was Nicky on the landing.

Nicky's eyes went wide and his face white. Hank knew his presence would not be a welcome surprise, but he wanted to dispense with the awkwardness.

"What in the name of the devil are you doing here?" Nicky hissed.

"I followed you, all right? I wanted to know what you were up to."

"It is none of your concern." Nicky's shoulders went tense.

"I realize that now, but I heard someone scream, and in my capacity as an officer of the law, I am investigating."

The fight seemed to go out of Nicky then. "All right. We shall discuss it later. Come with me."

Hank followed Nicky into an apartment, if it could be called that. It seemed to be two crowded rooms. In one of them, a woman sat weeping on the edge of a bed. A young girl lay in the bed.

Nicky said softly, "My niece is quite ill. She's having trouble breathing and her fever is beyond anything I've ever seen before. I told Brigid she should prepare herself for the inevitable, and she screamed."

"Will you allow me to check on your niece?"

"Yes, all right."

Nicky walked toward the woman. This must have been Brigid. Her hair looked reddish in the poor lighting, but her facial features were a softened version of Nicky's. She wore a stained shirtwaist tucked into an unadorned black skirt. There was no pretense here, nothing fanciful, just a family in a bad situation struggling to get by.

"Brigid," Nicky said. "This is Inspector Brandt. He's a police officer who was in the neighborhood. He's offered to see to little Edith."

Brigid sat up straight and looked Hank over. She seemed unconvinced, but nodded once. Hank went to the bed and saw a tiny blond girl laying there. She slept, but there was nothing peaceful here. The girl's breathing was heavy and labored and her skin flush.

"I got ice for them two days ago," Nicky said, "and that seemed to help, but there's no more available anywhere nearby. I fear she's too sick to move now."

"I thought she would get better, but instead, she just pants and wheezes," said Brigid. "I've tried the herbs my mother always gave us, and I tried putting cool cloths on her head, but this heat persists. I thought maybe if it broke, she would improve, but it goes on. The other children have been able to go outside, but Edith cannot."

Hank felt the girl's forehead with the back of his hand. She felt as though she were on fire. Her breath rattled as she exhaled. Hank realized suddenly this girl's breaths were numbered, that she was about to become a victim of the heat like so many before her.

Nicky knelt next to the bed and pressed a hand to Edith's forehead.

"My baby," Brigid said. "My sweet baby girl." Then she started to weep.

Hank looked at Nicky, who was staring at the little girl. Her breaths were coming few and far between. The three adults watched her for several long moments. Hank wanted to do something, though there was nothing to be done. He wanted to take the girl to a hospital, but they'd never make it in time. He wanted to hold Nicky, but of course, that was impossible with his sister there. So instead he sat and waited.

He could tell the moment life left little Edith's body. She went slack and serene quite suddenly. Brigid's weeping became an anguished wail, so she must have noticed it, too. Nicky put a hand on Brigid's back as he silently cried for the little girl who did not deserve death anymore than she deserved to be born into such poverty.

"Let me help you," Hank said to Nicky.

Nicky nodded.

Of all the foolish things to daydream about, the blond man Andrew had seen the night before might have been up there with the most foolish, but somehow this did not prevent an elaborate fantasy in which the man strolled into Police Headquarters to tell Andrew he was forsaking his old life and was in need of rescue. Although Andrew was perhaps on the willowy side and did not cut the dashing figure of a hero—there was a reason he was a secretary and not a police officer—he enjoyed letting this scenario play out, in which he knew just what to do and made life better for everyone. The image presented itself like so many performances of a play in Andrew's mind.

Still, there was a pile of new reports on his desk he needed to sort through and it was Saturday, which meant there was a Police Board meeting. Roosevelt presided over the four-man board, but a consensus was generally needed to move policy forward, and Commissioner Parker, who had no patience for Roosevelt, generally set himself up to be an adversary. Ironically, Roosevelt and Parker had similar ideas for how the city should be run, but lately Parker opposed Roosevelt almost as if for sport. So now Andrew would have to sit in on the meeting while Roosevelt and Parker disagreed on everything and nothing was accomplished.

Most of the reports filed overnight were from officers in nearby precincts who had witnessed people falling from roofs and fire escapes. Most of the victims had gone outside for some relief from the heat and fallen asleep before rolling off a roof or out of a window or falling from a fire escape that had lost its footing. Most of these victims had sustained broken bones and wound up at a hospital, but a few had met their end this way.

"Did you see the paper today?" asked Devery Smith, another police secretary.

"No."

Devery dropped the paper on Andrew's desk. It was a copy of the *World*. "They Fought, They Drank, and a Few Landed in Jail," stated the headline. "Haps and Humors of a Blazing August Day," was printed below it.

"Perhaps these hot days have all been fun and jokes for Mr. Pulitzer," Andrew said, "but he hasn't had to sift through the police reports."

Devery frowned. "Yes, I suspected that would be your reaction. Did you know, Finnegan took a girl to the hospital last night with two broken legs. She had been sleeping on a roof with her father and must have rolled over. A fire escape two floors down broke her fall. Looks like she'll be all right, but the girl is four years old, Andrew."

"It is tragic," Andrew agreed, "though I also have three reports here of violence that broke out on the Lower East Side. For instance"—Andrew held up a report—"a man stabbed another man over a stolen bucket of dirty water. Another savagely beat the owner of a pushcart for selling rotten apples. But, certainly, Mr. Pulitzer, the day was full of haps and humors."

Devery shook his head. "I do not disagree, but sometimes, Andrew, you have no haps or humors yourself. I believe the *World* is merely trying to make light of a difficult situation."

Andrew sighed. "I know. Hard to see the bright side when you have the full picture."

"Ritchley!"

Andrew stood. "If you'll excuse me, Devery, I have a meeting now."

As president of the Police Board, Roosevelt presided over the other commissioners and various others in attendance, including Andrew, five other assistants, and two reporters. Even with the lights out and the windows open, the heat in the room was almost unbearable, which was perhaps why Roosevelt and Parker were even more ornery than usual.

Roosevelt persisted, however, and led the men through his agenda. This policeman was to be commended, this other was to have his suspension lifted. Roosevelt brought up the hotel laws. He had commissioned a report from a Captain Vreedenburg, which he wanted to present to the Board. "Under the old laws," Roosevelt read to a room full of board commissioners, "there were only two hotels in the Fourth Precinct. Now there are *fifty*-two, while others are being opened daily." He went on to say fake hotels were being created for the sole purpose of drinking on Sunday. This, clearly, could not continue.

This went on for some time, and then Roosevelt read a letter from the American Bankers' Association praising the police department. According to the clock in the corner, two hours had gone by and everyone's clothes were soaked through with sweat, despite the fact nearly every man had taken off his hat and stripped to his shirtsleeves. Parker kept looking at his pocket watch. Commissioner Grant wiped his red face with a handkerchief. Commissioner Andrews looked like he might expire right there. The exertion even seemed to be wearing on the indefatigable Roosevelt, who was perspiring profusely as he spoke.

"It might be wise to adjourn for the day," Parker said wearily.

"Might we not take up the promotion of inspectors?" asked Roosevelt. This had been a particular thorn in his side, given that Parker had blocked every one of Roosevelt's recommendations, including that of Hank Brandt, who had taken on the post of Acting Inspector to fill a vacancy while still keeping a pretty full caseload. To Parker, Roosevelt said, "Has anybody seen the eligible list?"

"I don't know," said Parker. "I haven't seen it."

The groan wasn't audible, but Andrew imagined everyone girded themselves for a prolonged argument. Andrew himself fantasized about jumping into the East River if this meeting ever ended.

"I don't know that it would be a wise thing to do," said Grant, warily looking about the room. "Although, if it comes up, I stand ready to vote."

"The reason I want the matter to lie over," said Parker, "is that when I do vote I want to make a statement. That statement I have not prepared, and of course have not got with me."

Someone did audibly groan then. Andrew worried the meeting would never adjourn and he'd die in this very room, baked to death in the summer heat.

Roosevelt tilted his head as if he were contemplating this. "Do you intend to enter your statement on the minutes? For if you do and you have no objections, I may very likely wish to make a statement also, that, I suppose, will be all right?"

"Oh, yes, certainly," said Parker.

The words were conciliatory, but every man in the room knew there would be a dramatic fight at the next board meeting. It didn't much matter to Andrew as long as he got to leave soon. He tugged on the collar of his shirt, hoping it wouldn't choke him where he sat.

"Now, to the matter of Mr. Bryan's visit," Roosevelt said, at last on the final item on his agenda. "The presidential candidate is set to arrive in three days, this heated term shows no sign of abatement, and we have to see to security at Madison Square Garden during his speech."

"If you make it out alive," Andrew told the reporter sitting beside him *sotto voce*, "tell my mother I love her and I died nobly at the side of the great hot bag of air Theodore Roosevelt."

The reporter chuckled, but then made Andrew swear to do the same.

After the meeting, Andrew dutifully followed Roosevelt out of the conference room. Roosevelt paused halfway to his office to wipe his face with a handkerchief. "I grow weary of this nonsense," he said softly.

"Yes, sir," said Andrew.

"As fond as I am of arguing with Commissioner Parker, it would be nice if we could actually accomplish something in our meetings."

It was such an understatement, Andrew nearly laughed. If Mr. Roosevelt was half as frustrated by the deadlock on the Police Board as Andrew was, he was probably ready to burst inside.

"Yes, sir," Andrew said.

"Well. I expect your report later today. Enjoy your afternoon, Mr. Ritchley. Try not to expire in the heat."

"I will do my best, sir," Andrew said as he watched Roosevelt walk away.

Two hours after Edith passed, Nicky sat on the steps of St. Teresa's. He felt drained.

Hank had served the Sharp family quite valiantly. He'd found a priest seeing to patrons on Grand Street and had brought him back to deliver last rites to Edith. He'd gone to fetch Brigid's husband, who had closed his shop for the rest of the day. He'd called in a favor to the coroner's office to expedite removing the body from the house. He'd spoken quietly with Brigid for a very long time, trying to offer her comfort.

Now he walked back up the steps toward Nicky and sat beside him.

"Brigid is speaking with Father Boyce now," said Hank.

"I wanted to get them out of there. I've been trying to save money for them, but Brigid won't take it, and even if she would, I don't have enough to find a house for her whole family."

"You did a lot by going to see her."

"But not enough. Never enough." Nicky shook his head. He'd gotten out of the tenements by earning money on his back, and he'd been thankful for his little apartment, but he'd been selfish because he couldn't rescue Brigid, and now Edith was dead. "She was so little, Hank. No one should die so young."

"This is a tragedy, but it was not one you could have prevented."

Nicky didn't agree. He couldn't.

"I want to offer my most heartfelt apologies," Hank said. "For everything that happened today. I should not have followed you and I immediately regretted it. You have a right to your own affairs. And I feel terribly sorry about your niece and everything you and your family are going through."

Nicky took a deep breath, trying to get his shaky heart to steady. "You have the whole of it now," Nicky said softly. "You're right, you had no business nosing into my affairs, and I did not want to tell you my family was trapped in this way, especially not after I saw your nice house."

"I don't trust easily."

"Nor do I, which is why I was not forthcoming." Nicky tried to keep the edge of anger at bay. He'd been so astonished when Hank had appeared on the landing inside his sister's building that he'd hardly had time to think on what it meant.

Then there'd been a flurry of activity as they took care of little Edith. Brigid had been beside herself, wailing, desperate to try anything to revive Edith, unwilling to leave her side. The Sharp patriarch had woken up from his stupor still drunk and somewhat angry and was noisy and useless as always. Brigid's husband Antonio had broken down as well, and Nicky felt he'd have to hold himself together if anything were to be accomplished.

Nicky stared out onto Henry Street, unable to see now as tears blurred his vision. He blinked them away, hoping Hank wouldn't see them. Maybe with time he'd be able to convince himself this wasn't somehow his fault, but now he kept repeating to himself that he could have done more. He could have insisted Brigid take his money. He could have lived more modestly and helped Brigid and her family move. He wouldn't have moved in with her to help take care of the kids—not when his father was there to try to beat some masculinity into him—but he could have helped her out more. He could have pleaded with their other siblings to help out more. He could have supplemented his income with more men.

He glanced at Hank and knew he couldn't sell himself any longer. Not when he'd had a taste of what it was like to be with a man without the pressure of money changing hands.

"I am angry," Nicky said. "I am angry with you for following me and not trusting me, although I recognize I'd do the same in your shoes. Perhaps you are a good man, but it's not in my nature to trust anyone, the police especially."

"We've known each other, what, four days? I wouldn't expect you to trust me."

Nicky held up his hand. "I am angry you followed me and barged into the building. It's hard to argue you betrayed my trust when neither of us really trusted each other, though. And, well, I needed someone who could keep his head together today."

Hank nodded slowly.

"I accept your apology," Nicky said. "And I thank you for everything you've done for my family today."

"It was nothing."

"Were you supposed to have gone to your precinct today?"

"This afternoon, yes. I found an officer to send word I'd been caught up in something."

Nicky looked down. There was a crack across the step that cut between Nicky's feet like a streak of lightning. "I want to trust you," he said, "but there's some insanity in that, isn't there?"

"Perhaps not." Hank mimicked Nicky's pose, his knees bent and slightly apart. He pulled off his hat and wiped his handkerchief from his hairline down his nose, over his mustache to his chin. "It must be obvious my interest in you goes beyond this case, beyond even a bit of pleasure we might find in each other. It was my pleasure to help you this afternoon. I was happy to be of service, really."

Nicky did want to trust Hank, but wasn't sure he could. "How do I know you won't arrest me when all this is over?"

"You have only my word I wouldn't. As far as I'm concerned, you have done nothing wrong."

"Except wear a gown."

"It's not for me to say. Another cop may arrest you for indecency, but I would not. My intention from the beginning was to make it clear I'm not better than you." Hank shook his head and gazed out at Henry Street. "I don't believe it is in the purview of the police department to regulate morality, but some of my superiors disagree. Certainly if Commissioner Roosevelt discovered some of my past indiscretions, he'd dismiss me immediately. But as long as I have some power over how I do my job, I will stick to solving murders and other crimes. Three men have been killed. What they were doing prior to their deaths is immaterial."

"Is it really up to you to make that determination?"

Hank sighed. "I do not know, but I plan to run my investigation in my own way until someone tells me otherwise."

They were at something of a crossroads. Hank had all of the information he needed for his investigation, so Nicky could walk away now and not feel guilt over his part in this. He could leave Hank to find the killer and go about his life.

Or he could stay.

That Hank had taken control and helped Nicky's family this morning remained something of a miracle to Nicky. In his memory, no one had ever availed himself so selflessly to help Nicky.

"This is what I come from," Nicky said. "My parents came here from Ireland during the famine. They had nothing when they left and even less when they arrived. We lived in a tenement just like Brigid's. I was born after the war, but my father is no war hero. He is a failed farmer who drank to forget his failures. Since he is not at the church now, there's no telling where he is—I imagine he found a saloon to drown in." Nicky took a deep breath, unwilling to look at Hank for fear of what might be on Hank's face. "My mother never quite recovered after she had my younger sister, and she died on a hot day not unlike this one."

"I'm sorry," said Hank.

"This city. When I was a boy, my father would talk about all the opportunities in America. What opportunities? To be crowded into a dark tenement? For a little girl to not get a chance at life because her family has nothing? There are men who come to Bulgaria who have everything. Money, fancy clothes, huge houses. They pay men like Charlie to take care of their needs and then go back uptown to their gold and their wives. They are privileged above all else, but today, my niece died because she could get no relief from the heat."

"Yes. I know."

And Hank *did* know. Hank was a queer police officer, that was plain. His investment in the case was likely due to his own intimate familiarity with the world Nicky occupied.

This was not to mention his years as a police officer as he worked up the ranks, during which time he'd probably witnessed things Nicky could not even imagine.

"New York is a city that will bleed you dry," Hank said. He wiped his face with his handkerchief again. "And yet I would not live anywhere else."

"No. Nor I."

They shared the silence for a few moments. A horse pulled a cab up Henry Street, blowing out breaths like a steam engine did puffs of smoke. The heat bore down on them, wet and oppressive. The street stank of mold and rotting meat. There was a haze over everything, like they had taken up permanent residence in a cloud close to the sun, slowly baking. Nicky had already sweat through his shirt, his waistcoat was damp, and his coat now lay on the step beside him, for all the good taking it off did. Hank was similarly damp, sweat dripping off the ends of his dark hair and pooling at his collar. He put his hat, the dusty brown bowler, on the step beside him, near his own coat, and stared forlornly at the street.

"In all my life," Hank said, "I cannot recall a week like this."

Nicky couldn't either. He wondered even if the one good thing about it, currently sitting beside him, was like an imagined oasis in the desert.

"Is your brother-in-law still talking to the people from the funeral parlor?" Hank asked.

"Yes. He does not have much. He owns a shop, but they only make enough to get by because there are so many mouths to feed. Brigid works a few days a week at a shirt factory near Washington Square. They trade off watching the kids, or my father watches them if he's sober, but sometimes Brigid's oldest daughter Lucy works at the factory in her stead. Lucy is twelve." Nicky's heart squeezed. He could feel his grip on everything slipping away, but if he couldn't keep holding on, he'd fly to pieces.

Hank reached over and briefly rested a hand on Nicky's knee. Then he withdrew his hand again.

The small gesture did more than Nicky could ever express.

"I need to go to my precinct house this afternoon for an hour or two," Hank said softly, his voice low and close to Nicky's ear. "But I will stay for as long as you need me."

It was all Nicky could do not to cry. He pressed his fingers to his eyes as if he could keep the tears at bay and he nodded. "Thank you."

Hank took one of Nicky's hands and held it between both of his. It was too hot to touch, and Nicky's hands were slimy with sweat, but Nicky couldn't pull his hands away. He looked up at Hank and their gazes met. They simply stared at each other for a long time. "You're welcome," Hank said.

Day 5

Sunday, August 9

Temperature: 97°F

Chapter 9

Hank ran his hand up the length of Nicky's spine. They were huddled together in bed, the covers tossed aside, their nude bodies stuck together with sweat, but Hank didn't mind a bit because Nicky lay here with him.

"I had a crazy idea," Hank said.

"Mmm."

"What if we took the train out to Coney Island today? I don't actually have to go to the office and you don't have to be anywhere until tonight, right? Maybe if we went to the beach, we could get some relief from this heat."

Nicky yawned. "It is an interesting idea."

"Just interesting?"

"Well, darling, I imagine every person in the cities of New York and Brooklyn who can afford train fare just had the same idea."

"I think sometimes about what it would be like to leave the city for more than a day or two," said Hank. "To visit somewhere else, I mean. To travel."

"If you could go anywhere in the world, where would you go?"

Hank thought about the question for a few moments. "Italy."

"Italy?"

"Yes. My friend Amelia went to Europe after she and Jonathan were married. She toured everywhere. France, Spain, Italy. I made her tell me about every place. She loved Paris because of the food and the fashion, but the way she described Italy . . . there's so much art there. Just out on the streets. And the Roman ruins. I'd like to see those."

Nicky burrowed into Hank's side and threw an arm over his chest. Nicky's body was like a heavy wool blanket. Hank still didn't care.

"I know there are museums in New York." Hank put his arm around Nicky and held him close. "But it's not quite the same."

"Mmm. Just like you can walk to the piers and look out at the water, but it's not the same as going to the beach."

"Where would you go, if you could go anywhere?"

"As far as possible," Nicky said. "Maybe China or Japan. I have a gown made of fabric imported from China, and it's so beautiful. I'd like to see the place it was made. It must be beautiful, too."

"I'd like to see that gown."

"Maybe I'll wear it for you one day, darling."

Nicky had nearly ceased with the pet names since their talk on the steps of St. Teresa's the day before, but they snuck back in sometimes. Hank was all right with that, as long as he didn't feel like Nicky was hiding something or deflecting him. That wasn't the case here. Instead, Nicky's words were seductive in a way.

Hank was falling for Nicky hard and fast. That could not be denied.

He stroked Nicky's hair.

Nicky sighed, and it sounded happy. Sunshine streamed in through the windows of Hank's bedroom, bouncing off his white sheets and making parts of the room glitter. It was a little like being inside a fluffy cloud, everything white and brightly lit, and he was here alone with Nicky. The world outside his windows didn't matter.

"Can I ask you something?" Nicky said, his lips against Hank's chest near one of his nipples.

The movement of Nicky's mouth against his body sent a shiver up Hank's spine. "Please."

"Do you think there's any hope in the world?"

It was such a broad question. A simple question. And yet it was a hard one for Hank to wrap his head around. "There has to be some hope. Or else why bother?"

"Yes, but . . . everything seems hopeless sometimes."

"In what way?"

Nicky turned his head a little, taking his lips away from Hank's skin, but otherwise he didn't move. "When I was a boy, I would go with my family to the Fish Market or up to Washington Square, and we'd see what life outside our neighborhood was like. I used to hope to be a part of it some day. To get out of the tenements and experience the life the city had to offer me."

"Understandable."

"My siblings felt the same. They each left home. They got jobs that paid better than my father's piddling salary and moved to apartments uptown. My older brother William left the city altogether. He lives out in New Jersey now."

"What kept you here?"

"That same hope, I think." Nicky pulled in a deep breath and let it go, his chest quivering where it met Hank's. "When Brigid married Antonio, we thought she'd leave home, too. Antonio ran this business, after all. He's a good man, but not a great businessman, so he struggled all the time. Then they had their children one after the other. So they stayed. That, and Brigid was the only one willing to take care of my father."

"You stayed for Brigid."

"Partly. I thought if everyone else left but I stayed, I could help her."

"I'm sure you did what you could."

"When I was young, I used to hope to be made differently. These queer feelings I had, they were wrong. I wanted to wear clothes meant for women, and I knew that was wrong, too. I used to pray at night for God to change me. To make me like the other young men I knew."

Hank knew all about that. He hugged Nicky tightly to convey he understood. He'd had his own late nights wrestling with the demon of his inverted sexual appetites and gotten nowhere beyond a reluctant acceptance he could not change himself.

"How did you come to be at Bulgaria?" Hank asked, keeping his tone light to show Nicky he didn't judge.

"I actually got my start at Armory Hall on Hester Street. Did you ever go there?"

The name poked at some long-forgotten memory. Hank didn't think he'd been there, but if he recalled correctly, it was old Billy Mc-Glory's concert saloon, a place where management encouraged men to wear women's clothing or fraternize with other men. "I know of it," Hank said.

"It was just a few doors down from the house my family lived in, you know. I saw a man I thought handsome go in one evening and I followed him. What I saw inside changed me." Nicky shook his head. "When I realized some of the women were painted men, I knew I'd found a home. The first time I dressed as Paulina, I did it by stealing a dress from one of my sisters. I could sew a little, so I altered it to fit me. The first time I went into Armory Hall, I'm sure I was not convincing as a woman, but I learned quickly."

Hank closed his eyes and tried to imagine it. Nicky dressed as a shabbier version of Paulina must have been a sight to behold.

Quietly, Nicky said, "The first few men I . . . well. I was so poor, and they had so much money. I could not refuse."

Hank held Nicky and stroked his back. Hank was not the sort who would or could preach about morality, and he was genuinely unbothered by Nicky's past. He felt a pang in his chest, more because Nicky had been put in such a position to begin with. A poor kid in the tenements didn't have a lot of options.

"When Armory Hall finally closed, I was adrift. I thought I might find more reputable employment, but I had limited skills. I worked for a time in a tailor's shop, but I found the work dull and unfulfilling. Maybe that sounds foolish."

"It doesn't," said Hank.

"It didn't matter, because the tailor shut down his shop and moved uptown, and I was again out of a job. I was walking up the Bowery one evening, after a fruitless day of trying to find something I could do to bring in money. I thought I could get work as a store clerk or something. No one would hire me. My clothes weren't nice enough. I was too effeminate. I was the wrong thing for every job. Then I walked up the Bowery and I saw this woman. She was so strange looking. She wore a black gown that didn't fit her quite right. And she looked troubled, so I asked if she was all right."

"You were on the Bowery. Did she proposition you?"

Nicky let out a little surprised burp of a laugh. "Well, she was a he, darling. And he did proposition me. He lost interest when I said I had no money. But then I asked how he came to be standing on the Bowery in this huge gown, so he told me. Then he brought me to Bulgaria."

Hank played with the ends of Nicky's hair. "And you had a home again."

"I did. It was exactly what I'd been looking for, what I needed at that time in my life. Be assured, I did not get pulled into this life. I chose it. I saw a room full of men just like myself and I wanted to be among them. When I discovered I could make as much money in a single night at Bulgaria as I could in a week at the factory where Brigid worked, I made a decision."

Nicky had curled away from Hank in his righteousness, which Hank recognized as a defensive gesture. Hank reached over and pulled him back. He hated to think of Nicky, *his* Nicky, servicing other men, but he accepted that reality. He'd heard what Nicky said. It was why Hank himself had frequented resorts like the Slide in his youth. The Slide had been the home of some of the worst depravity in the city. Men openly embraced other men, danced with them, kissed them. And Hank had loved every minute of it.

"I understand," Hank said, stroking Nicky's damp hair.

Nicky made a little choking sound in the back of his throat. "I've never met anyone like you."

Not sure whether to take that as a compliment, Hank remained silent.

Nicky said, "I ask about hope because a day like yesterday dashes it. I had hope I could help Brigid and her family, but I couldn't, and now little Edith is dead. I had hope I'd outgrow Bulgaria and be able to pursue a more useful career. As a child, I hoped I'd fall in love someday, but men like us do not have that opportunity."

"There is still hope," Hank said on instinct, though he wasn't sure how true that was.

Nicky picked up his head and leaned on his elbows on Hank's chest. "Do you think there is any hope for us? Once you solve your case, is that the end? Or do we continue to spend time together? I'd like that, but I know how your world works. If your bosses find out you spend time with another man, you'll be fired, yes? I imagine it's only worse if that man is a former prostitute who sings while wearing ladies' clothing."

"It wouldn't matter. If they would fire me for loving a man, then it is not the profession for me."

"It would matter, darling. It would. You derive satisfaction from solving mysteries. I can tell. You have the conviction to find a killer murdering prostitutes in a neighborhood most New Yorkers would just as soon set on fire. You are an asset to the police department. But your involvement with me could cost you everything."

What Nicky said was true. It was all true. Hank loved his job. He valued it, and he was good at it. He'd wanted to become a detective from the moment he'd joined the police department and he'd worked hard to get this far. If anyone discovered their liaison, his career would be over faster than he could sign his name. The pending promotion to inspector made this especially true. This promotion hadn't been something he'd strived toward or asked for, and he didn't care for the politics of it or the way it made him such a public figure in the department. But it gave him power and discretion, meaning he had space to pursue the criminals he thought belonged behind bars, and squirrelly men like Stephens, who thought it more important to lock up prostitutes and drunks instead of helping them, could not prevent him from doing so.

But the promotion brought attention to Hank. The smart thing to do would be to give Nicky up. To go back to his celibate life.

But Hank did not want to.

"No one can find out, then," Hank said.

"Be practical."

"One has to have hope," Hank reiterated, "or else what is the point?"

Nicky shook his head. "What made you become a police officer in the first place?"

What was it? Hank hardly remembered. He hadn't aspired to be a police officer, although in the wake of the economic depression that coincided with his coming of age, there were few options available to a middle-class man who had just reached adulthood. "You're right, I do like a mystery. And I had strong convictions as a young man. I joined the police when I was twenty-three, nearly on a whim. The career suited me well." Of course, corruption was the word of the day when Hank had joined. He wondered if he'd risen so far so quickly because he hadn't indulged in any of the pay-offs some officers received to look the other way. His only vice was his love of men.

"I'm sure it does suit you," Nicky said. "Oh, speaking of police, do you know an Andrew Ritchley?"

The abrupt change in subject surprised Hank. "Yes. He's one of the secretaries at Police Headquarters. Mostly he follows Commissioner Roosevelt around. Why do you ask?"

"Charlie—you remember Charlie—met him last night. Andrew implied he understood Charlie and could be trusted."

Hank nodded. "Andrew is a friend."

Nicky raised an eyebrow. "A 'friend,' darling?"

Hank grunted. "Yes, a friend. We've known each other for years. But not in the way you're implying. Is he trustworthy? Yes, I'd trust him with my life. He happens to be . . . of our kind, as well. But he really is just a friend." And it was nice to have an ally, someone within the department who understood where Hank came from. The two of them had met five or six years before, when Hank was still working his way up the ranks. "Why, are you jealous?"

Nicky scoffed, but Hank suspected the 'darling' thrown in there answered his question well enough.

"I suppose, love, I just wanted to know if Charlie could trust this man should something happen to him."

"Yes, but to be clear, Andrew is not an officer. He has the ear of Commissioner Roosevelt, but he can't actually engage in any law enforcement practices. But Andrew is a good man."

"All right."

"And you're getting agitated because you want to be my only man."

"What? Hardly. Of course not. How could I expect such a thing? As you keep pointing out, we have known each other mere days."

Hank had to suppress a smile. "You're my only man, Nicky."

Nicky visibly relaxed, his shoulders going slack. "Well, all right. The same is true of you for me. But I'm not jealous."

"No," Hank said, letting the smile bloom on his lips. "Of course not."

They lay together silently for a few moments. There was a moment of relief when a breeze came through the open window.

"So what do you say, Hank? Shall we adjourn to Coney Island?"

Even though Hank had suggested it, he now had no interest in leaving his house. He did not want to deal with the world outside. "We could just stay here. Fill my tub with cool water and submerge ourselves."

Nicky laughed. "Just like the ocean."

On his way into Police Headquarters, Andrew passed a dozen men and women who had made beds of the sidewalk the night before or who were resting on carts or in gutters. Baby carriages lined one stretch of

Broadway, most of them occupied by howling, squirming infants in scant clothing with worried mothers occasionally rocking them.

Andrew arrived at Headquarters displeased to find it was still as hot inside the building as ever.

Roosevelt had left for Oyster Bay, which afforded Andrew some peace, at least.

Roosevelt's last order before he left town was to deploy all available vehicles—police wagons, hearses, whatever was available—to transport victims of the heat to hospitals. There were not enough ambulances to escort all of the patients.

Andrew got through one long, sweaty hour of paperwork. Headquarters was nearly silent, as most of the regular staff had the day off, although there was still the occasional bustle of activity as people who needed things came in. The morning was fairly calm, though; most of the city was at church. Except for the heat, it was a typical Sunday.

Then it suddenly became atypical.

The baffled-looking guard on duty escorted Charlie from Roosevelt's Friday night frolic to Andrew's desk.

"This kid keeps asking for you, Mr. Ritchley. He insisted. Shall I see him out or—"

"I'll speak with him," Andrew told the guard, who seemed satisfied to return to his post.

Charlie looked rattled, dressed in a suit but shaking as though he were cold, which seemed impossible in this weather. Andrew grabbed a chair from an empty adjacent desk and put it at his desk. He motioned for Charlie to sit, and then he did the same.

"Y-you said you could help me," Charlie said, his teeth chattering. "D-d'you remember me?"

"Yes. I remember. Charlie, right? What is it? What do you need?"

Charlie shivered. "I'd like to report a crime."

Andrew realized Charlie wasn't cold; he was terrified. "I'm just a secretary, not a police officer. Do you want me to fetch an officer?"

"I-is Inspector B-Brandt here?"

"No, today is his day off. I can get someone else for you to speak with."

Charlie shook his head. "N-no. No. I t-trust you. I w-want to t-talk to you."

"All right." Andrew realized he must have successfully conveyed to Charlie he was friendly. "What happened?"

"L-last night. A man came to . . . I work at a resort. B-Bulgaria. On the B-Bowery."

The name of the club tugged at Andrew's memory. He grabbed Hank's last report, which he'd left off to the side on his desk. "Inspector Brandt is investigating a murder there."

Charlie nodded. "L-last night, I . . . there was a m-man."

"One of your customers?"

Charlie frowned. "No. W-well, he . . . he wanted me to . . . but he made me uncomfortable. I s-said no."

"Then what happened?"

"He l-left. But then when I walked out of the c-club to go h-home, he grabbed me. He p-pulled me onto Third Street. D-dark corner."

Charlie started shaking harder and stopped speaking as he clearly struggled to get his breathing back to normal.

Andrew understood. All at once, he knew what had happened.

"He took liberties," Andrew said, carefully reaching over to touch Charlie's knee.

Charlie looked up and met Andrew's gaze. He nodded. Then he went back to shivering.

Charlie had been raped. There was no better way to frame it.

"This man," Andrew said, trying to think the way Brandt would. "Did you get a good look at him?"

Although his body still shook, Charlie managed to nod. "H-he had d-dark hair. F-fancy clothes."

Andrew looked back at the report. That description could have been of anyone in the city, but it also happened to describe the person Nicholas Sharp last saw with the victim. Coincidence, or was it the same man? "You may be very lucky to be alive. How did you escape?"

"After he . . . f-finished, I got away. I m-mean, I r-ran. I l-lost him."

"That's good. I'm glad you did. Did you go home after?"

Charlie nodded.

"Where is home?" asked Andrew.

"B-boarding house. On G-Great Jones Street. I s-slept there. Th-then I came here."

Andrew pulled a piece of paper from his drawer and wrote down everything Charlie told him. As he finished writing, he said, "I'll share this with Inspector Brandt tomorrow. He will pursue this matter. Will you talk to him if he needs to ask you additional questions?"

Charlie hesitated.

Andrew leaned close to him. "Brandt will not care about your profession. He is a safe man to talk to. He'll want to find the man who did this to you and make sure he is prosecuted to the full extent of the law."

Charlie let out a breath. "Nicky said he trusts this Inspector B-Brandt as much as he trusts anyone. That may be N-Nicky's strongest endorsement."

"Nicky?" Andrew glanced at Hank's case notes again. "Nicholas Sharp?"

Charlie nodded. Then his face fell. "I can't go back. To B-Bulgaria."

"Is there someone you want me to send for? Get word to? Can I be of help to you in some other way?"

Charlie looked up and met Andrew's gaze again. Charlie had really remarkable eyes, the color of honey in the sunlight. He said, "Can I stay here for a little while? I f-feel safe with y-you."

Andrew nodded. "Yes. Stay as long as you need."

Day 6

Monday, August 10
Temperature: 100°F

Chapter 10

Andrew woke up knowing he'd done something wrong. It was not a reassuring feeling.

Nothing had happened, not exactly. Oh, sure, a man who was probably a prostitute was lying in bed next to him, sleeping the sleep of the dead, but no money had changed hands and they'd only slept. It was Andrew who had suggested they strip to their drawers—because of the heat, naturally—before climbing into bed. Maybe that was a mistake, now that he was presented with the tousled hair, long neck, and broad back of a very handsome man who was currently sharing his bed.

But Charlie was truly shaken up and had not wanted to go home alone.

Andrew could do nothing but offer him company.

So Andrew had brought him uptown to the apartment he kept on Thirty-sixth Street. Before they got there, they had dutifully gawked at the temperature recorded on the Herald building's thermometer—101 degrees despite sunset approaching—and wondered aloud how long this could go on. Once inside, Andrew had poured them each a finger of whiskey and they'd talked about nothing. Then Andrew had offered his bed, as there was nowhere else to sleep aside from the old divan that was barely wide enough to sit on.

But Andrew still didn't know what precisely it was that Charlie did at Club Bulgaria. He had guesses. He liked his job and so generally stayed away from the fairy resorts on the Bowery, but he'd been to the Slide once, and then, a few years ago, he'd gone to Paresis with Hank, mostly out of curiosity.

Now Charlie stirred and rolled onto his back. It took him a few long moments to wake up, but eventually, he blinked at the ceiling and then turned toward Andrew. Their gazes met and they stared at each other.

Eventually, Charlie said, "What time is it?"

"Early. The sun has barely risen."

Charlie blinked rapidly a few times.

"If you need me to leave . . ." Charlie said.

"No, it's all right. Stay as long as you need to."

"Dawn and it's already so hot."

Andrew mumbled an agreement, but then took a moment to really look at this man beside him. Andrew felt foolish for so easily trusting him, but then, no ill had come from it. Instead, it was just Charlie, wearing only his drawers, all of his skin on display. Andrew could see now the dark roots of the hair on his scalp and his dark hair everywhere else. His skin was pale, as befit a man who likely slept away his days so he could work all night. He had those honey-colored eyes as well as a face that was a bit heart-shaped, but still masculine and quite striking. Andrew found Charlie unbearably attractive.

Not a single thing could happen between them. Not with what Charlie had been through.

Charlie lay on his back but turned his head toward Andrew, who rolled onto his side. "Thank you for taking me in. I slept better last night than I have in ages."

"I'm glad."

"You didn't have to trust me."

"Then don't make me question if I should have."

Charlie nodded. "I just meant, I . . . that is, you know what I do to make a living. You must."

"I have a notion."

"I did not have a lot of options. My father threw me out of the house when I was sixteen. I washed up on the stoop of Julie—Mr. Juel, he owns Bulgaria—and he put me to work. I've been there for almost ten years. I suppose you can't really call me a working *boy* anymore."

Andrew's heart broke for Charlie. "No, I suppose not."

Charlie turned his head again to face the ceiling. "I don't think I can go back."

"Do not return, then."

"Easy for you to say."

"Perhaps, but ... perhaps we can find you more respectable employment."

"We?"

And there it was. Andrew's true intentions were in the open now. "I just meant, I'm willing to help you if you want my help."

"I do." Charlie turned his head again and met Andrew's gaze. Andrew suspected Charlie understood what he was saying and returned the sentiment.

"Slowly, perhaps," Andrew said. "You'll need some time to recover."

"I'll be forever grateful."

Feeling daring, Andrew reached over and took Charlie's hand. He threaded their fingers together. "No need. I'm happy to do whatever you need of me."

Charlie smiled, a true genuine smile that lit up his whole face. So Andrew smiled back. And for a few minutes that morning, the world felt perfect.

Hank was up early for no good reason. Nicky hadn't come back after his shift singing at Bulgaria, and being alone for the first night all week had made him feel out of sorts. Then he felt foolish for relying so much on Nicky's company, which only served to make him feel more at sea. This was not to mention that being in his house was like living inside a pot of boiling water, so he decided to head to the precinct house early. The mechanical fans might make the precinct house not completely unbearable.

A couple of weary-looking newsboys stood on the corner of Sixth Avenue. Hank gave a nickel to each of them and took the papers. He read as he walked east. "An Epidemic of Sunstrokes," said the *Herald*. The *Tribune*'s headline declared in large capital letters, "DEATHS BY THE SCORE!" It took only a cursory examination to determine both papers had dedicated several pages each to the various tragedies that had resulted from this plague of heat. Hank tucked one paper under his arm and paged through the other as he walked. Apparently the death toll had overtaxed the coroner.

There was also a long explanation of why the heat felt so oppressive—extraordinarily high humidity, according to one expert interviewed in the *Herald*—although a significant portion of the explanation made little sense to Hank. It didn't matter. The heat was terrible and had been unrelenting since August fourth. Humidity reaching 97 percent that Sunday seemed significant and perhaps explained why the temperature felt twice what the thermometers read.

Apparently, the hottest spot in the city was the patch of asphalt in front of City Hall, at which people were just keeling over left and right if the papers were to be believed. Allegedly, the thermometer on the City Hall steps had read 112 degrees.

Other parts of the paper were reporting on William Jennings Bryan's scheduled speech at Madison Square Garden in two days and how the police were being mobilized. Hank, who had only a marginal interest in national politics, wanted no part in a big speech, especially if they intended to pack the Garden in this heat. He hoped to be home Wednesday evening. Perhaps with Nicky.

When Nicky had left the night before, Hank had lodged a protest—"Even on Sunday?"—and he'd been neatly deflected—"My devoted admirers are expecting me, darling."

Hank would see Nicky again in just a few hours, though, when they got ready to go to Amelia's charity ball, and Hank looked forward to that. Well, not so much the charity ball, which sounded dreadfully boring and stuffy and full of Amelia's over-moneyed new friends. But he looked forward to seeing Nicky again.

He dumped the papers in a trash receptacle on the way into the precinct house. His first order of business would be to update Stephens on his plans, although he hoped, as with the follow-up visit to track down Nicky at Bulgaria, Stephens would beg off.

Stephens sat at his desk, frantically scribbling on a pad of paper, oblivious to Hank's presence. Hank stopped and rapped on the desk three times. Stephens head shot up and he stared at Hank.

"Brandt. I hope you're having a pleasant morning."

"It begs for an 'is it hot enough for ya?' sort of joke, but I'm afraid I'm not up to the task."

Stephens grimaced. "Well. I read your notes for the Club Bulgaria case."

Hank couldn't decide if this was good or bad news. "And? Any insights?"

Stephens looked put out, like a child who had just had his favorite toy taken away. "I can't imagine I thought of anything you hadn't already thought of. Your notes are quite . . . thorough."

Hank didn't like Stephens's tone. "What are you implying?"

"I just want to verify your interest in this case isn't prurient."

"Prurient?"

Stephens held up his hands. "I don't know what you do with your spare time."

Hank wanted to punch Stephens, but he refrained. Instead, he said, "I don't like what you're implying."

"Good. As it should be. Now what is your plan?"

So Hank gave Stephens the briefest rundown, bringing Nicky in disguise to a society party to see if he spotted the slumming killer.

"Are you sure the killer was slumming? Could it not have also been another prostitute? A jilted lover? An intoxicated customer?"

"It could be any of those things," Hank said, "but as we have no other leads, I thought this worth trying. If it proves fruitless, I'll have to come up with something else."

"Or we could drop the case. There may be no solution to this one."

Hank figured Stephens disliked the unsavory nature of the parties involved. "Perhaps," Hank said. "If you want to rid yourself of it, that's all right. I'd like to pursue it, at least for a few more days. If I still have nothing on, say, Wednesday, I'll reconsider."

That seemed to satisfy Stephens, who nodded. "All right. Because another homicide came in, this one on the other side of the precinct. Tenth Street, near Tompkins Square. If my hunch is correct, it's a wife killing her lover."

Hank was a little disturbed by the amount of glee Stephens displayed. "All right. Would you like me to accompany you to the scene?"

"Yes, let's do that before the heat becomes too unbearable."

Andrew supposed there was a certain inevitability to the chaos visited upon Police Headquarters Monday morning, given this was an election year and one of the candidates for President of the United States planned to give a speech in a mere two days. The heated term, as Roosevelt called it now, showed no signs of letting up.

Will MacLachlan, a reporter for the *Times,* sat on a bench outside eating an apple and shooting pointed looks at Andrew, so Andrew walked down the steps of the Headquarters building and sat beside him.

"Good morning, Andrew. A fine day isn't it?"

"Oh, yes, perfectly fine."

Will smiled. "Aside from the obvious, I suppose. What can you tell me about arrangements for Mr. Bryan's speech?"

"Not much."

Will sighed. "I stopped by Democratic Campaign Headquarters this morning, and there is so much scrambling, no one had time to speak with me. I suspect even they do not know what will happen when Mr. Bryan arrives."

"All I can tell you is the police department is furnishing security, and we will need it, as they plan to fill Madison Square Garden."

"In this heat?"

Andrew shrugged, trying to look nonchalant. He agreed it was madness to put so many people in one venue when Will's very paper reported daily death tolls from the heat now. But it was out of his hands. "Democrats from all over the country are pouring into town. Bryan himself is scheduled to arrive tomorrow. The date has been set for months."

"The consequences of packing Madison Square Garden in such conditions can only be guessed."

"It promises to be . . . uncomfortable," said Andrew.

"Dangerous."

Disastrous, Andrew thought. "I received word from Commissioner Roosevelt this morning that he intends to spend the day in Oyster Bay. Probably just as well. As ever, the Police Board is deadlocked over every issue, and anyway, Roosevelt wants nothing to do with Mr. Bryan's speech."

"Ah, yes," said Will. "I imagine his plan is to hope McKinley is elected and thus gives Mr. Roosevelt some appointment out of town."

"I believe that is his intention, yes, though you didn't hear it from me. Never let it be said he neglected the police department."

"No, indeed. My wife's family owns a saloon on William Street. I ever tell you that?"

"I had no idea."

"Business is down, Andrew. Sunday is the day most men are most interested in libations because they have no other obligations to speak of. But Commissioner Roosevelt thinks we should honor the Lord's Day by abstaining. That makes so little business sense, it's a wonder no one has run him out of office yet."

"Not for lack of effort. Roosevelt is stubborn."

"Hmm. Well, anyway. I'm working on a story set to run tomorrow on Mr. Bryan's visit, so if you have anything you can share about preparations, I'd greatly appreciate it."

"I'll write something up and have it sent to your office this afternoon."

Will stood and tipped his hat. "Much obliged. I'll be sure to mention how accommodating the New York Police Department is acting, unlike the mayor's office."

Andrew nodded. Mayor Strong had made not so much as a peep about the heat wave or any sort of relief effort for the elderly or the sick, and so Andrew had received piles of reports about the dead from the coroner's office and no way to fix the situation. He stood and shook hands with Will before they parted ways.

On his way back up the steps into Headquarters, Andrew was accosted by O'Hanlon, a city coroner. "Ritchley. You must do something."

"About?"

O'Hanlon tore his hat from his head and wiped his thinning hair off his forehead. "Seventy-seven cases are on my list for review today. One of my clerks collapsed from the heat this morning. I need some more help. Can you get some sort of relief? Another worker? Just a man who can write in English would be sufficient."

"Sir, the staff is already overtaxed—"

"I saw a child who had been cooked to death yesterday. Literally cooked to death. The child resided in one of the Lower East Side tenements. Her mother brought her up onto the roof of the building for some relief from the heat, but the building had a tin roof. It had been heating in the sun all day. The child had severe burns all over her back." O'Hanlon shook his head. "I gave an interview with a reporter to try to get word out not to do that, but of course, the people who need the information can't even read English."

"I'm sorry."

"My colleague Fitzpatrick has written to Mayor Strong to ask for more staff. I thought I'd appeal to your office as well. As it is, yesterday, I had to investigate a great number of cases that required me to walk more than two flights of stairs. I was certain on my last trip I would expire in the stairwell. Surely you can also appeal to the mayor's office. We'll need to suspend the rule that a coroner must investigate before a body can be removed. People will become ill."

"I'll see what I can do," was all Andrew could offer. It seemed reasonable to expect the mayor's office to continue to do nothing.

Lord, what a day this was turning out to be.

"That's all I ask. I realize the stress the police department must be under, between the heat and Bryan's visit and whatever else."

"You have no idea."

Chapter 11

From Hank's vantage point sunk into a threadbare chair in Nicky's living room, he could see Nicky staring at himself in a mirror, shaving with extreme care. Hank had the case notes open in his lap and had intended to work, but there was something completely fascinating about watching Nicky get ready.

Nicky finished shaving and disappeared into his bedroom, so Hank went back to his case notes, even though he was distracted. Nicky moved with such grace, and though he appeared delicate, there was a masculine strength to him. Hank had never met anyone like him.

"Darling, I could use a hand."

Hank rose and walked into the bedroom, where Nicky was now half done-up, a fluffy crinoline covering his legs and a corset loosely wrapped around his waist.

"You don't have to do this, you know," said Hank. "I'm sure you'd be equally as a convincing as a young banker. Or we could pass you off as an apprentice of Jonathan's."

"I want to do this my way." Nicky tugged at his corset and pressed the front against his chest. "I need you to do the strings in the back. Pull me in tight. We want it to be convincing." He paused. "Usually, Charlie helps, but we are not at Bulgaria, so you'll have to do."

Hank took a moment to analyze the pattern of lacing at Nicky's back. It was a bit like solving a puzzle. He took the loosest strings in the middle and pulled, satisfied when the halves at the top and bottom came closer together.

"Really tug, love. Don't worry about hurting me."

That this process might be painful for Nicky hadn't occurred to Hank until just then. Uncomfortable, certainly, but painful Hank hadn't anticipated. "Are you sure?"

"Yes. Really pull. That's the only way it will get tight enough to cinch me."

So Hank pulled, taking a few minutes to solve the puzzle of which strings to pull and which to loosen to best get Nicky laced into the corset. When Hank succeeded, he tied the loose strings into a bow.

Nicky walked away, toward the blue gown hanging from the closet door. He made quick work of sliding into it. He turned around and waved a hand at Hank. "Come, let me abuse your slavish devotion to me. Do up my buttons while I do my makeup."

Hank could have spent hours watching Nicky. Nicky took a length of white cloth from a hook near the mirror and draped it over his manufactured décolletage. Then he went about covering his face with all manner of different things, each in its own little bottle or flat metal container.

"I will likely sweat all this off," Nicky said as he brushed powder across his face. "And then where will I be?"

"The ballroom should be cool, at least." Hank looked down to better concentrate on getting each tiny, satin-covered button through its designated hole.

"They can afford ice uptown," said Nicky.

Hank finished with the buttons as Nicky finished tinting his lips. Hank moved out of the way and then followed Nicky to the closet, where Nicky extracted a round hat box.

"I think I shall be a brunette tonight," Nicky said, pulling the top off the box to reveal a wig. This wig was carefully constructed and styled. Nicky picked it up and walked back to the mirror. He carefully placed it on his head and then pinned it in place. The effect of the brown hair—darker and richer than Nicky's natural color—on Nicky's pale skin was striking.

"Did the man you saw with Edward see you as Paulina?"

"Undoubtedly."

"You're not worried he'll recognize you?"

"Paulina is a blonde, darling. And I quite deliberately used softer makeup. No need to paste it on as if I were a clown if I am not going to be under the stage lights."

"Right. Of course."

Nicky grabbed a wide black ribbon off his dresser and tied it around his neck, effectively covering his Adam's apple. "People see what they want to see, Hank. You show them an outline, they will fill in the rest. Tonight I am Alice McGraw." He raised his voice a half-octave and spoke softly. "My father is part owner of the New York Giants, but oh, I care nothing for baseball." Nicky smiled placidly and then burst into a tizzy of girlish laughter.

Nicky looked like a woman. From the stylishly pinned up brown hair atop his head to his pale collarbone and shoulders to the long lines of his body, he looked every inch a woman. It was uncanny and a little unsettling. If Hank hadn't watched the transformation himself, he never would have believed Nicky stood before him. That would perhaps help with the ruse. "All right, Alice. I suppose you and I have been courting."

Nicky smiled. "If you like." Nicky turned back to the mirror and examined himself once more.

Hank walked closer to Nicky and took his hand. "I would like to court you. If circumstances were different . . ."

"I know, love. But you are a police inspector and I could get arrested for wearing the wrong clothes in public. I do believe we are doomed." He ran his hands over Hank's shoulders and down the lapels on his coat. "You look handsome all polished up. Not that I would complain if you came here half-dressed and unshaven."

Traveling uptown proved to be difficult. They hired a cab, even though the horse pulling it panted and labored up the street with tremendous effort. It was hot inside the cab, the air still and stifling. Hank wanted to strip off his coat and cast aside his top hat, but he knew he had to look presentable at Amelia's party.

They pulled up to the house on Fifth Avenue. Hank caught the astonished look on Nicky's face as Hank helped him out of the cab, but Nicky quickly schooled his features to look as though this were just any other day.

Hank conferred with Graves as they were let into the house, explaining his presence and Alice's as briefly as he could. Graves merely leveled his gaze and said, "I assure you, Mr. Brandt, your presence in this house is far more welcome than some of the other guests."

"Much obliged," said Hank, tipping his hat.

Graves led them to the ballroom. It was nothing like Mrs. Astor's—or so Hank presumed, having only heard stories—but it was nicely decorated. Amelia had worried over each piece of art that hung on the walls, where to place each sculpture, whether there should be plants. The result was lush and lavish but still comfortable, with fine touches like the damask curtains and the carefully chosen striped wallpaper adding a warm touch. Already there were about a hundred guests milling about, all of them dressed extravagantly and expensively. At least, by some miracle, the air was blessedly cool inside.

Hank held out his elbow and Nicky took it. "Please alert me if you see anyone you know," Hank said.

"I will," said Nicky, bringing back the affected voice of Alice.

They began a loop around the periphery of the ballroom, greeting people Hank didn't know. Hank looked for Amelia and did not spot her until she approached.

"Hank, dearest, how nice of you to grace us with your presence at last."

Hank allowed his cheeks to be kissed. Then he said, "Allow me to introduce Alice McGraw. She is my companion for the evening."

Amelia shot Hank a mystified look, but turned the full force of her charm on Nicky. "How delightful to meet you, Miss McGraw."

"Please, my dear, call me Alice," said Nicky.

"Oh, of course. And you must call me Amelia." Amelia turned back to Hank. "This is quite a surprise."

"You were the one who insisted I attend your ball."

"Yes, and there are a number of people I'd like you to meet. I just did not anticipate you would be escorting a young lady to these proceedings. I wish you had given me some warning."

"Pardon my ignorance," Nicky said, "but what charity are you raising money for?"

"The Society for the Prevention of Cruelty to Children," said Amelia. "We're raising money to help some of the children in the poor neighborhoods of New York who are suffering through this blasted heat."

Nicky faltered for a moment, but he pasted on a smile and said, "What a worthy cause. I should like to donate."

Amelia smiled. "Well, we're going to have a bit of an auction later. A number of guests have donated personal possessions that will be for sale. Mrs. Schermerhorn has donated a necklace I think would look quite fetching on you. Perhaps Mr. Brandt would be interested in taking a look."

Nicky managed to blush. He extracted a fan and waved it at his face. "I shall take a look at it when it comes up for auction. No sense in poor Mr. Brandt giving up a substantial chunk of his police salary just to decorate me. Besides, he's useless with jewelry. No appreciation for it."

"I know," said Amelia. "Nor does he care for fashion. What are we to do with him?"

"I seem to be standing right here before you," said Hank.

Amelia laughed. "I neglected to say before, Alice, but this dress is absolutely stunning. I've never seen anything quite like it."

"Why, thank you. I had a hand in designing it myself. I work with a man named Claude, who has a shop in Greenwich Village. He apprenticed at Maison Worth."

"Indeed?"

Nicky raised an eyebrow. "Do not tell me it is not something you always wanted to do. When I was a little girl, I would spend hours looking at the drawings in my mother's books. Of course, when I was young, hoop skirts were still all the rage. I am happy we as a society have moved on from that. My mother's dresses were so heavy."

Nicky and Amelia spent a good minute nattering on about fashion. Hank could only shake his head, bewildered.

Jonathan called for his wife from across the room. Amelia looked at him and smiled. "Duty calls, I'm afraid. Oh, but Alice, I do believe we will be friends. Please feel free to call on me here any time."

"Thank you. You are most kind. I suppose I will have to bring Mr. Brandt along as well."

"If you must. Or we can just speak as ladies without our men present. That is, unless I am misinterpreting this situation?" Amelia looked between them.

Nicky wrapped his hands around Hank's arm and said, "I seem to have consented to court this man."

"After all this time," said Amelia. "I never would have imagined."

"Yes, well," Hank said, trying to come up with some way to either convey to Amelia this was a ruse or to explain nothing had changed. He came up empty, and Jonathan repeated his call.

Amelia smiled. "Well, you lovebirds, the orchestra Jonathan hired is quite good. I hope you'll take advantage and dance for a bit." To Nicky, Amelia added, "Mr. Brandt is a lovely dancer. He was always my favorite partner. Until I met my husband, of course. And, speak of the devil, my spouse is about burst, so I must attend to him. I will speak with you both later." She departed.

"Was any of that true?" Hank asked when Amelia was gone.

"What, the fashionable bits?" Nicky looped his arm more firmly around Hank's as they continued their trip around the periphery of the ballroom. "Quite a bit of it was, in fact. Claude did apprentice at Maison Worth before moving to the States."

"And the women here would have never encountered Claude because he has a . . . different clientele, I imagine."

"Yes. And he indulges me. I do so love fine fabric, and he can get some from Europe at competitive prices. I really did spend hours examining the fashion plates my mother liked. She was a seamstress. Mostly she made simple dresses and crinolines at home and sold them to the dressmakers uptown. She spent what little money she had to spare on pictures of fine gowns. She taught me a bit about how to sew as well. When I was young, I thought it was quite the injustice that men could not wear fine gowns."

"This is a problem you have handily solved."

"Yes. Perhaps not in a way in which my mother would have approved, God rest her soul."

"Yet now you look like you belong in this ballroom. Far more than I do."

"Thank you, darling."

"You are beautiful, you know. I wish I had a way to express how much. I'd love to buy you that necklace, but I fear it is far too expensive for me."

"It's all right. That you don't seem to find me ridiculous means far more to me."

"You aren't ridiculous."

Nicky smiled. "Speaking of things that *are* ridiculous, that statue over there is." He gestured toward a marble statue of a mostly nude woman with a sheet draped around her waist but somehow not her breasts. There was something not quite right about her face.

"Failure of the artist, or did he just have an unattractive model?" Hank asked.

"Maybe it's modern. There's probably a deeper meaning in making Venus ugly or something."

"Could be."

They reached the edge of the dance floor, where finely-dressed couples rotated around the floor in the motions of the waltz. "Can you dance?" asked Hank.

"Can you? I would not have guessed."

"Amelia and I grew up together. Our mothers were great friends. Both hoped we would rise up to another level of society. So we were taught manners and societal graces as children." Hank sighed as he scanned the ballroom. He recognized only a few faces, but mostly it was a blinding spectacle of brightly-colored gowns and sparkling diamonds. "I think our mothers expected us to marry each other. But I could not, and then Amelia met Jonathan Cooper. Her mother was so thrilled."

"The moral of this story is that you learned to dance."

"Yes. Shall I show you? Can you follow?"

"Of course, love. I am a professional dancer."

Hank took Nicky's hand and led him to the floor. He lifted his arms and Nicky stepped into them, completing the circle of the dance frame. So Hank led Nicky and tried not to feel too overwhelmed by the fact that, for the first time in his entire life, he was dancing with someone for whom he had romantic feelings in public view. Not only was it public, but half of New York high society was here.

Of course, this was in part because Nicky subverted his gender.

Hank couldn't help but think that, in a perfect world, none of this would matter. It wouldn't matter if he fell in love with a man or a woman, it wouldn't matter if they were rich or poor, it wouldn't matter if Nicky seemed to love wearing gowns as much as he liked dressing as a man. Of course, in a perfect world, children wouldn't be dying in the heat of the tenements while the upper echelons of society drank wine and danced. There was something perverse about raising money for children with this kind of grand affair. Hank wondered if Amelia even had an inkling about how many children had died just this week.

He tried to push that aside so he could savor the moment dancing with Nicky. Nicky was a good dancer, and some training was evident in the precision of his steps, his grasp of the rhythms of the dance. Hank did enjoy holding him close and guiding him around the dance floor. Perhaps there was even a bit of scandal in holding a woman so close in polite society, though Hank hardly cared because when would he ever get another opportunity like this?

So they danced, and for a few moments, all Hank could see was

Nicky, those blue eyes gazing back at him, the inherent beauty of his face—striking even without makeup, though no less beautiful with the addition of rouge and other paint—and the way the little earbobs on each of Nicky's earlobes caught the light. Hank hadn't noticed those before.

Nicky smelled good. A little sweaty, perhaps, but that was unavoidable. He had a perfumed air about him, something soft and floral, likely intended to mask his otherwise masculine scent. But Hank knew what was really underneath all of it, and it made him want Nicky all the more.

He could easily fall in love with this man.

Of course, that was a complication his life did not need. He had long heeded Amelia's warnings not to get involved, and if anyone knew what was really happening beneath the surface, it would cost Hank his job at best, and it risked Nicky's life.

"What are you thinking about so hard?" Nicky asked.

"You."

"I'm right here, darling, for you to gaze upon. No need to think on the matter further."

"Perhaps I was cursing Fate for bringing you to my life but making us impossible."

"Yes, well." Nicky turned his head and looked off into the distance for a moment, although he never once made a wrong step. "Given the circumstances, I would quit Bulgaria tomorrow if I could afford to. If I had any other means of employment."

"Surely you have other ways to earn a living."

Nicky sighed. "Yes, but none that allow me to look like this. Julie at least lets me be myself. Paulina is an essential part of me. You must understand that."

Hank could not quite grasp the idea. "Are you saying you would rather be Paulina?"

Nicky whispered, "Are you asking if I would rather be a woman? No, darling, I am quite content with the way God made me. But it would be like cutting off an arm if I had to give up Paulina." He adjusted his hand on Hank's shoulder. "I have no other way to explain it."

"If there were a way for you to keep Paulina but get out of that place . . ."

"If I knew of one, I would take that path tomorrow. It took me years to get to where I am now. I don't like working for Julie and I don't like having strange men paw at me. But Julie pays me and I like to sing." Nicky looked up and met Hank's gaze. "You want to protect me, and I appreciate that, but I've been taking care of myself for years now."

"I know. But even if we never see each other again after this is over, I'll worry."

Nicky leaned his forehead against Hank's. In the heeled shoes Nicky wore, they were close to the same height. Hank closed his eyes and leaned in, taking in Nicky's sweet smell and the feel of their bodies close together. He didn't think he'd ever have an opportunity like this again and he wanted it to last.

The song waned and, when those gathered to dance turned to applaud the orchestra, Hank stole a kiss, daring to cause a scandal. Nicky's lips were soft and undoubtedly the press of them against Hank's would turn Hank's red, but Hank didn't care.

If anyone noticed, they didn't react.

When the orchestra struck up again, Hank swept Nicky back into his arms and led him through another waltz. Nicky laughed breathlessly, the sound like music. They glided together for a long moment and Hank sank into the pleasure of the dance.

Then Nicky seized in Hank's arms and gasped aloud.

"He's here," Nicky said.

Hank was instantly a police detective again, keeping his face neutral but alert and aware of his surroundings. He held Nicky close, clasping their hands together, his other hand at Nicky's back. "Where?"

"By the Ugly Venus."

Hank steered Nicky around so that Hank could look. Jonathan was having what looked like an intense conversation with Brigham Knight near the statue. Both had dark hair and were dressed expensively. Could Jonathan have been the man slumming? He hardly seemed the type, but then, Hank didn't know him at all. Or was it Mr. Knight? Knight seemed too preoccupied with his buildings to be the sort. Hank usually trusted his gut, but both men felt wrong for this crime. Still, he was inclined to trust Nicky. "The man on the left or the one on the right?"

"Left. The man with darker hair. With the green waistcoat."

Brigham Knight.

"I know who he is," said Hank. "Are you certain?"

Nicky started to breathe faster and harder. Thinking quick, Hank grabbed him by the shoulders and steered him away from the other dancers. He found an unoccupied chair near the refreshments table and shoved Nicky onto it.

"Is everything all right?"

Hank looked up. Amelia had appeared at his side. "Alice is overcome by the heat," Hank said.

"I will get her some water."

It was clear Nicky's attempts to calm down were for naught, as he kept glancing up toward the Ugly Venus and then inhaling sharply. Amelia returned with a crystal glass full of water, and even though Hank's mouth watered at the sight of it, he let Nicky take it and drink from it slowly.

"I'd like to have a word with Mrs. Cooper, if you will be all right for a moment," Hank said.

"Yes, sorry. The heat, you know. I'll just sit here."

Hank met Nicky's gaze, which somehow confirmed for him that things were all right. Hank took Amelia by the elbow and steered her away from the crowds.

"Is Alice really okay?" she asked.

"I hope so."

"I must say, Hank, I am shocked to see you at a party with a woman. And not only a woman, but one you are clearly quite smitten with. Not that I'm begrudging a change of heart, but—"

"Nothing has changed. Forget about Alice for a moment. What can you tell me about Brigham Knight?"

Amelia balked. "What? Nothing. He's a friend of Jonathan's. Why are you—are you here in another capacity? Are you being romantic with Alice as a cover because you're here to investigate Mr. Knight?"

Hank merely raised his eyebrows.

"You are an astonishingly good actor. I really believed you and Alice—"

Hank held up his hand. "There is more to the story, but I can't tell you now. I need to know about Knight."

"I don't really know him well. He's related to the Vanderbilts by marriage, but I think his wife is a lesser-known cousin. I've only met her once. She's sickly and rarely goes out in public. Poor thing never quite recovered from the last time she gave birth. They have three children, all daughters."

"All right."

"He's been meeting with Jonathan to discuss buying the steel for this project near Madison Square, but Mr. Knight doesn't even have the land in his possession yet, so Jonathan isn't selling."

"That is wise."

"You met him last week. Did he provoke your investigative instincts?"

"No, actually. I thought him innocuous." Hank lowered his voice. "Alice is a witness to the case I'm investigating. She recognized him."

"What should we do?"

Hank glanced back at Nicky, who sat in the chair, rocking slightly, a hand pressed to his forehead. "I want to talk to Knight, but I might need to get Alice out of here."

"I can speak with her while you speak to Mr. Knight."

Hank took a few seconds to weigh his options and then nodded. He watched Amelia pull a chair up next to Nicky and begin a conversation. Hank proceeded back across the ballroom to do the same with Knight.

When Hank approached, Jonathan tossed his head back to laugh at something a grinning Knight must have said.

"Ah, Mr. Brandt," Jonathan said. "I saw you come in earlier. The woman on your arm was quite lovely."

"Yes, thank you." Hank made a show of being bashful. "That's Alice McGraw. My new sweetheart, I guess you could say. I like her a great deal."

Jonathan slapped him on the back. "Capital! Amelia does so worry about your lonely heart, what with all your long hours as a police inspector."

Knight gave him an appraising look, his gaze traveling the whole length of Hank's body. It sent shivers up Hank's spine, but he tamped down a reaction.

"Yes, well, quite fortuitous circumstances. She is over there now, chatting about gowns and ribbons with your wife."

When everyone turned to look, Nicky seemed remarkably better, engaged in what looked like a pleasant conversation with Amelia.

"Yes, women do carry on," Jonathan said.

"A police inspector," said Knight. "Where do you work most often?"

"Downtown. Seventeenth Precinct, though I work in the Tenth and Fourteenth as well sometimes. I work between Fourteenth Street and Canal Street, basically. And I'm only an acting inspector until my promotion is approved. With all the deadlock on the police board, that may never happen. I'm straddling a line in the interim, still working a few cases."

"Are you working on anything interesting?" Jonathan asked. "Amelia mentioned you had a tough case."

Knight leaned closer. Hank wanted to arrest him right then. "Murder on the Bowery, but evidence is scarce. We are likely to give up on the case without solving it. The details are also quite salacious. Unfit for present company."

Knight nodded. "Does that happen a lot? Unsolved cases, I mean."

"More than I'm comfortable admitting." An exaggeration. Hank had an excellent record when it came to solving his cases. That was a big part of why he'd been nominated for the promotion to begin with. "It is difficult with these resorts on the Bowery. Brothels, really. Horrific things. The police department doesn't want to put its resources on another dead prostitute, not when there are more important crimes to solve."

"Not when there are saloons to close on Sunday, you mean," said Jonathan, shaking his head in disgust.

"Yes, well, I do not make these decisions. If you would like an ale on Sunday, take it up with Commissioner Roosevelt."

As Hank fell into conversation with Jonathan about the relative merits of the Sunday laws, he kept an eye on Knight, who silently listened. There was nothing obviously amiss, but something about Knight struck Hank as off. He wasn't sure if it was just that Nicky had alerted him to the possibility that Knight was up to something or if he was acting genuinely suspicious; nothing was obviously out of place. But Hank was now hyperaware of every move Knight made, every gesture, every twitch of an eyelash.

Hank looked back at Nicky and Amelia. Nicky looked distressed again. "I believe I need to return to my Alice. The heat has quite affected her. I hate to dash out of the party, but I believe I must take her home."

"Of course, Hank," said Jonathan. "It was a pleasure to see you."

"Indeed. I thank you for your hospitality, Jonathan. And Mr. Knight, it was nice to see you again."

"Likewise."

Hank nodded and walked back across the bar. He bowed in front of Nicky and offered his arm for him to take. As Nicky stood, Hank whispered to Amelia, "Can you get me Knight's address?"

"Yes, I believe so. Jonathan must have it. His family is on Fifth Avenue, but farther down. I can't recall which block. I will find it for you."

"Bless you, Amelia. Miss McGraw, with your permission, I believe we should bid this party adieu."

"Yes, darling. I find I am quite tired suddenly."

"It is this infernal heat," said Amelia. "Whoever makes women's clothing and all these layers never thought of our well-being on a ninety-degree day."

"Agreed." Nicky reached out and took Amelia's hands in both of his. "Amelia, my dear, it was a delight to meet you."

"And I you! I hope we get to see each other again in the near future. You and Hank can come for dinner, perhaps."

"I'd like that." But Nicky's smile didn't quite reach his eyes.

Graves was deployed to help track down a cab. Once Nicky and Hank were headed downtown, Nicky said, "Mr. Knight. He is our man." It wasn't a question.

"Yes, I believe so. A party was not the correct place to make a confrontation. I intend to call on him at home tomorrow evening."

"Not by yourself."

"I'll bring Stephens. Why, are you concerned for me?"

Nicky tutted. But then he said. "You know I am."

"I'll be careful, I swear to it." Hank took a deep breath. "Seeing him rattled you. Are you all right?"

"I am better now that we are away from the party. That man, seeing him tonight . . . I believe I've seen him about Bulgaria before. Even if he is not our killer, he is a dangerous sort. Please, Hank, I do not know what I would do if—"

"I'll be extremely cautious," Hank said. "I promise."

"Good. Let's go home, my love. I find I am quite exhausted."

Chapter 12

At the request of Commissioner of Public Works Collis and a written memo from Mr. Roosevelt, Andrew accompanied a team to the corner of Canal and Ludlow Streets. He'd protested the whole way, his work regarding the Bryan speech unable to wait, but the powers that be had ordered him to oversee the men who carried out the plan.

The air was pungent, smelling of sweat and dead animals, and the streets were littered with the corpses of dead dogs, great piles of horse excrement, and what might have been blood in one of the gutters. A few curious onlookers had wandered over to see what those assembled were about to do. Their presence reminded Andrew of something Hank had said the day before about the conditions in the tenements. Andrew had read *How the Other Half Lives*, and he knew full well what condition the residents of these old, crumbling buildings had to endure, but seeing this street on such a night was something else entirely.

That they were a week into one of the worst heat waves in Andrew's memory and no one had thought to do this sooner alarmed Andrew. He knew full well how many people—how many children—in this small district had expired since the heat wave began because many of those coroner's reports passed over his desk.

Commissioner Collis stood on the corner and explained his plan to everyone as a team of a dozen workers unfurled great hoses. They were going to flush out the Lower East Side.

"The water," Collis said, "will cool the asphalt and also wash away the accumulated detritus on the streets. By twelve o'clock tonight we shall have thoroughly washed every street in this section between Houston and Division Streets. Let each gang take a street. Hitch on to every fireplug and don't spare the water. It's a terrible night, and many lives may depend on the way you work. Flood the streets and cool the air. Now go ahead."

A glance down the streets where Andrew stood showed there were already perhaps a hundred children outside. As the teams started their hoses, a few came to cautiously splash around in the cool water. Then more joined as their parents looked on. Andrew had been skeptical of this plan, but as he heard the laughter of children, he couldn't help but think this was a smart course of action. Already, the air around them felt cooler. Andrew was tempted to jump into those streams of water himself, but he refrained.

A woman in a tattered dress holding a small child to her bosom walked up to Andrew and said, "I cannot thank you enough for what you are doing."

Andrew watched as more children jumped into the streams of water, many squealing with joy and laughter as they played together. He turned toward the woman. "Do you believe this helps?"

"Oh, yes, sir. Can you not feel how much cooler it has become since they turned the water on? And look at the children at play! It is like a vacation for them." She sighed and adjusted the weight of the child on her hip. "We cannot afford the train fare to the beach, you see, though I know that is how many people cope with this weather. Have you ever been to the beach, sir? I hear it's nice."

"I have been. It is nice."

"I'm sure it's lovely. Well. Thank you, all of you. I must go attend to my sons now."

When she left, Commissioner Collis walked over to stand next to Andrew. "I would call this a success. Already a great deal of the rubbish has been pushed aside. That will help with the smell."

"Yes, sir."

"Tomorrow, we shall repeat this on Mulberry Street and in Chinatown."

"A fine plan, sir."

"You'll write a letter to Roosevelt about this, yes? I'd like to think he approves of such a plan."

"He does."

"Good. I shall write to Mayor Strong. I'd like him to allocate more resources to these efforts."

Andrew thought it unlikely Mayor Strong would allocate resources to anything, given his taciturn response thus far, but he nodded. "I shall report this to Roosevelt first thing in the morning. It seems this has been a successful effort."

Collis smiled. "Yes." Then his face fell. "I can only hope other departments in the city will follow my example. Commissioner McMillen of the Parks Department was also asked to shorten the work day of his employees, but alas, he is too tied up in bureaucratic nonsense." Collins waved his hand. "I want to convince Mayor Strong to issue some sort of order mandating city workers not be forced to spend eight hours laboring until this heated term breaks, but he seems disinterested in doing anything but sitting inertly at his desk."

"Yes. And it is not just laborers who are feeling the ill effects of this weather," Andrew pointed out. "Six police officers have died of heat stroke so far."

Collis shook his head. "It is a shame. We could be doing more to prevent this. I want to do more."

"Yes, I agree."

"I even talked to Commissioner McMillen about lifting the ban on people sleeping in the parks. At least if people are going to leave their houses, they could sleep on the ground instead of on roofs and fire escapes."

Andrew knew as well as anyone the toll those decisions—or failure to make any decisions—took. He'd seen the coroner's report on a five-year-old who had fallen off a fire escape to his death just the night before.

"So much tragedy," Andrew murmured.

"We could be doing more. We should be. But you know how things work in this city. By the time relief efforts are in place, the heat wave will be over, and all this will be for naught."

Andrew opened his mouth to reply, but Collis shook his head and walked back to his men.

Hank helped Nicky out of his garments, and Nicky gasped in a deep breath as the corset stays were finally loosened.

"That can't be comfortable," Hank observed.

"Yes, well, beauty is pain, darling." Nicky peeled off his garments and stretched out his body, hoping to get the blood moving back where it needed to go.

Hank peeled off the corset and rubbed Nicky's back. "This is fascinating to me," Hank said. "Peeling away your disguise. Like unwrapping a present. Or like watching a fantastical transformation."

Nicky laughed softly. "You are easy to impress at times."

"Perhaps." Hank leaned over and kissed the top of Nicky's spine. The gesture struck Nicky as sweet and affectionate. It was one of Hank's best qualities; he could be so giving in his passions and he could be this nice to Nicky when they were having a quiet moment alone.

Nicky and Hank worked together to get the rest of the gown and its accoutrement off of Nicky's body. Hank hung up the gown and undergarments as Nicky wiped the makeup from his face. And that was funny, too, how they could prepare for bed together without saying a word. Hank simply understood what needed to be done.

As Nicky finished with his face, Hank walked up behind him and put his arms around Nicky's chest. Nicky leaned back against him.

"You're perfect," Hank whispered against the space where Nicky's neck met his shoulder. "You were perfect tonight."

"Thank you." Nicky's stomach flopped. He lifted his hands to touch Hank's face, his hair, but he was nervous, too.

"I do not believe anyone suspected your real identity, but how could they? Tonight it seemed like Alice was *you*. The way you acted and moved was so lovely and graceful and *natural*."

"I have had a great deal of practice, darling."

"I've never met a man like you," Hank said. "But I am amazed by everything about you. Your smarts, your beauty, your bravery."

Nicky guffawed. "I'm not brave. Tonight was terrifying."

Hank ran his hands over Nicky's belly, over his chest. "Bravery is not a lack of fear. Fearlessness is stupidity. Bravery is being terrified of something and doing it anyway because it needs doing."

Nicky melted back into Hank. "You really think me smart."

"One of the smartest, dearest men I have ever known."

"You're only saying that because we are both nearly naked and pressed together."

"No, Nicky. There is something special about you. I want to be near it. I want to be with you."

All the emotion in Hank's voice made Nicky nervous, so he said,

"Come to bed with me, love. We'll keep each other hot and sweaty until dawn."

"Mmm. I don't want to sleep. I might miss something."

Nicky was sympathetic. He lifted his hand and ran it down the side of Hank's head, across his face. He closed his eyes and just felt the roughness of Hank's skin, the spikiness of his stubble, the thick brush of his mustache. Nicky thought Hank smart and capable and very handsome but couldn't figure how to say so in a way that did it justice.

And he was acutely aware that their time together was finite.

"So let's stay up all night," Nicky said.

"All right. Who needs sleep?"

Who indeed? Nicky turned in Hank's arms to face him. He gave Hank a brief kiss on the lips and then took both of Hank's hands. He led Hank to the bed and sat. He looked up at Hank and decided to show everything. He felt strongly for Hank, and vulnerable, and attractive. Hank smiled down at Nicky and then climbed onto the bed beside him.

"Let me honor you," Hank said. "Let me make love to you as you should be made love to."

"Yes," Nicky whispered.

When they kissed, any reservations Nicky had melted away.

Day 7

Tuesday, August 11

Temperature: 97°F

Chapter 13

Nicky wanted every morning to begin like this. Well he'd like the heat to be less overbearing, but he was so comfortable he almost didn't mind it. He lay in bed with Hank, propped up on his elbows and meeting Hank's lazy, sleepy gaze, and the two of them just stared stupidly at each other. Hank reached up and ran his hand over Nicky's cheek before cupping it and lifting his head until their lips met. The kiss was soft but passionate, Hank's lips moving sensually over Nicky's, Nicky's heart melting as he sank into Hank's embrace.

Hank had pulled the curtains closed the night before to keep some of the hot sunlight out, and it helped a little, although the room was dim as a result. Nicky's building bordered three others, and the view out his bedroom window was partly obscured by a rusty metal fire escape, so the room never got great lighting, but it seemed particularly dark this morning. It had the effect of making Nicky feel like he and Hank were alone in a cave.

"Let's never leave here," said Nicky.

"Mmm. Make love to me."

"I'd be happy to."

And Nicky wanted to. He wanted to love Hank. Wouldn't the world be a better place if the two of them could just be together, if there weren't something inherently backward, inverted, or wrong about them? Nicky had met enough other men like himself over the years that he'd come to understand this inclination was just a facet of humanity, but this did not mean he could not be arrested for it. He'd been arrested for indecency early in his days playing Paulina, and it hadn't gone anywhere, but the officer who had put him in jail had told him he wouldn't be so lucky next time. He'd been extremely careful about how he comported himself outside the club ever since.

Nothing was ever easy, and maybe a life of ill deeds meant Nicky was unworthy of love, but that didn't stop him from wanting it. Hovering now above Hank made him crave it more than anything else. He could love Hank. Hank could love him. In a different time, in a different place, they could be happy together.

But alas, this was New York City in 1896 and it was appallingly hot outside. Nicky knew his time with Hank would be short, and he should make the most of it.

He dropped his head and kissed Hank, really kissed him, mouths open, tongues tangling. Hank groaned beneath him and thrust his hands up into Nicky's hair.

"I want more," Hank murmured.

Nicky moved on top of Hank and pressed their hips together. Hank was hard and Nicky got there when the immediacy of Hank beneath him subsumed any thoughts in his head. Hank ran his big hands up and down Nicky's back and Nicky bucked and writhed and moved against him. Hank's hands were rough and hot and made Nicky's skin tingle. All of it made Nicky tingle from his forehead to his toes. Nicky threw his head up, and Hank moved in to plant kisses against Nicky's Adam's apple. Nicky moaned and pressed his hands against Hank's chest, feeling Hank's nipples harden under his palms.

"More," Hank said.

Nicky wasn't sure what more he could give. He sensed Hank was asking for something specific. "Hank, I can't—"

"You're so beautiful." Hank looked up and met Nicky's gaze. "Your eyes, your skin, all of it. I've thought about you whenever we've been apart nearly constantly for the last week."

"Hank . . ."

Hank kissed Nicky, stifling any abashed protest Nicky could make.

"What if I allowed you inside me?" Hank asked when they parted.

Nicky balked. The morning had taken a strange turn. How could a man like Hank even want that?

Hank stroked the side of Nicky's face and gazed at him with a kind of soulful longing Nicky didn't understand. Hank said, "I know. I know a hundred men came before me and used you. They used your body for their own pleasure. I know why there are acts you won't do, intimacies you won't allow. I can't pretend to know what that's like, to put yourself in their hands the way you did. I don't know first-hand about the risks or the pain or the scars they left behind. But I know a thing or two about men and the world you have lived in. So I understand why you have limits, why there are things you won't let me do."

Hank's gaze flitted over Nicky's face. He gently ran his thumb over a scar on Nicky's chin, a reminder of the time a man had cut open Nicky's face with the ring on his fist.

Nicky said nothing. Hank likely did understand.

"I know, too," Hank said, "that while this act can be selfish on one person's part, it can also be an act of trust and affection. It shows a tremendous amount of trust to take someone into your body, does it not?"

Nicky's heart fluttered and started to pound. There was so much kindness in Hank's voice, and Nicky knew not why he deserved it. Then something occurred to him. "How do you know?"

Hank took Nicky's hand and held it to his bare chest. "I had a lover once. A real lover, a man I spent time with regularly." Hank looked up toward the ceiling, his gaze unfocused now, perhaps lost in the memory. "We were not together long, but I cared for him a great deal. We met at the Slide, of all places, during one particularly wretched night when I drank too much whiskey. He took to me, I suppose, helped guide me home, and then he just never left." Hank shook his head, a small smile touching his lips. Emotions played out over Hank's face, and even though Nicky couldn't read them all, he could fill in the fondness and the sadness regarding this.

"What happened to him?" Nicky asked.

"He died." Hank sniffed. "Some disease, the doctor couldn't say what for sure. He fell ill one day, and then quite suddenly he declined and then he simply . . . never woke up again." Hank's whole face went slack for a moment and then he closed his eyes tightly.

"My deepest sympathies," Nicky murmured. "I apologize, I did not wish to bring up bad memories."

"No, it was my fault for mentioning him." Hank turned on his side and moved Nicky so they both lay facing each other. Hank put a hand on Nicky's hip. "What I intended to say here was that there can be trust and intimacy between two men. I know because I've experienced it and I've tasted it. I've come to care about you a great deal as well, and I want to show you that. I want you to be inside me because I like how it feels and I trust you. And perhaps it is foolish of me to trust you, but how can one ever know what is possible if one doesn't risk something?"

"You trust me."

"Yes. And us together, we can use our bodies to care for each other. That is what I want."

Nicky was overwhelmed. Hank doing this showed a remarkable amount of trust, and the gesture and the obvious affection in Hank's gaze touched Nicky. Tears stung his eyes.

"To be clear," Hank added as he ran his palm over Nicky's hair. "I'm not commanding you to do this. Merely offering myself to you."

And there was nothing to do but for Nicky to bury his face in the space where Hank's neck met his shoulder and weep with relief and joy and shame and everything boiling inside him. He clutched at Hank and pulled him close as Hank's arms came around him. For Hank to make this offer seemed crazy and perfect.

"I want to," Nicky said.

Nicky thought quickly. He hadn't done this in so long he stalled while he thought about what he should do. They needed help to make this happen. Nicky remembered at once the little bottle of scented oil he had on his dresser. He kissed Hank again and whispered, "Stay here. I will return."

He hopped out of bed. His heart raced as he anticipated the act. His thoughts were everywhere. Hank moved him, aroused him; Nicky wanted everything with Hank. He picked up the bottle and took several deep breaths, trying to get his heartbeat back to a normal pace. Then he approached the bed, where Hank lay splayed out, naked and breathtaking, his body scarred and muscular and hairy, his muscles rippling beneath his skin, his gaze bright and intense.

Nicky climbed atop him. "Are you certain of this, Hank?"

"Yes."

That was unequivocal. Nicky poured some of the scented oil on his fingers, dribbling a bit on Hank's stomach. Hank reached down and ran his fingers through the little puddle and then reached between his legs and ran those fingers over the entrance to his body. Nicky backed up a little to watch him. Hank was so gorgeous and arousing, touching himself in that way, rubbing oil against his balls and cock as well. Nicky groaned because how could he not? He reached between Hank's legs and moved his fingers to mingle with Hank's. There was a dance they did together, their fingers moving against each other and inside Hank. Hank groaned and thrust his hips against Nicky's hand.

So Nicky prepared Hank the way he'd want to be prepared himself if any of his past lovers had taken the time. Hank threw his head back and arched his back off the bed, and his body was all tight muscle and ecstasy. As Nicky thrust his fingers inside Hank, Hank took his own cock in his hand and stroked, keeping it hard, continuing to writhe with pleasure.

"More, Nicky."

Nicky poured more oil on his hands and stroked his own cock, looking up at Hank as he did so. His gaze met Hank's and it held. He did the rest by instinct. He guided himself toward Hank's entrance, positioned himself without breaking his gaze away from Hank's. And began to press forward without losing the connection to Hank. He went slow, because Hank winced as Nicky pushed through the barrier to his body, but soon enough Hank thrust against him again.

"Yes," Hank whispered. "Oh, that's good."

And it was good. Hank's body squeezed around Nicky's cock, making him feel crazy with lust and arousal, the pleasure an acute thing. Hank reached over and pressed his big hands against Nicky's buttocks and pulled him in farther.

And then Nicky was completely inside Hank and something in him shifted. There was a warmth spreading through Nicky's chest, a tingly affection for Hank. Hank's heart was in his eyes as he gazed up at Nicky. When Nicky began to worry he'd hurt Hank, Hank leaned up and kissed Nicky hard. So Nicky began to thrust slowly, experimentally moving in and out of Hank. It was beautiful and amazing and felt so great Nicky never wanted this to end. Hank moved against him, encouraging more movements.

Hank whispered Nicky's name, and Nicky heeded the call and kissed him and thrust his hips and made love to Hank. Hank was handsome and trusting and important and Nicky needed that in his life. Being inside Hank was a revelation, something that brought all new pleasure to Nicky, something he'd never quite experienced before even though he'd been with plenty of other men. No, being with Hank was unique. This moment was special. But Nicky was slowly losing his grip on it.

Nicky picked up the pace of his thrusting as his insides churned. His heart raced, sweat poured off him, and he could feel the telltale sparks and knew he was going to spend soon. Hank stroked his own cock, his hand a blur as he shifted his hips up against his hand and against Nicky. Then Hank let out a long groan, loud enough to wake the neighbors, and shot hard against his belly. His body squeezed Nicky and Nicky lost his grip. He kissed the side of Hank's mouth, felt the sweat glue their skin together, and pumped a few more times until everything was just pleasure and white light. He went blind as he climaxed, pulsing deep into Hank's body, grasping at Hank's shoulders for something to hold onto lest he fly apart.

When Nicky came back to himself, Hank was frantically kissing his face everywhere.

"Astonishing," Hank said. "That was beautiful and just . . . astonishing. You really are remarkable, Nicky."

Nicky could barely speak. He pressed his forehead against Hank's chest and then slowly picked up his head again. "Thank you, Hank. Thank you."

"Together, Nicky. You and I should be together. Like this. Forever."

"I want that."

"I know it's hard. I know there's no earthly way for this to work. But I couldn't live with myself if I did not fight for it, because what we have between us is so good. It's so good. Do you not agree?"

"I agree. I do. I just don't see—"

"Shh. Just pretend for a little while. Let's stay here and not worry about the outside world for a little while longer."

"All right." Nicky settled against Hank's side and laid his head on Hank's chest. "We'll pretend. Us together. Like this."

"Mmm, yes. Forever."

"Anything for you, Hank."

Chapter 14

When Hank arrived at the precinct Tuesday morning, Andrew was already sitting at his desk, waiting for him. Hank felt a little guilty for lingering in bed with Nicky and being this late for work, but not that guilty.

"I have a name," Hank said.

"He struck again," said Andrew.

Hank cursed. "When?"

"Sunday night."

Hank's face fell. "He killed someone Sunday night and you didn't think to tell me until now?"

Andrew crossed his arms over his chest. "All right, to begin with, the victim is not dead. Second of all, neither of us has been at our respective desks much since before Sunday. And I didn't think you wanted me to simply leave you a note in plain sight."

Hank let out a breath and tried to relax his stance, but he didn't like having a victim he didn't know about. "How do you know the crimes are related?"

"I don't, but as you would say, I have a hunch." Andrew stood and brandished a sheaf of paper. "A prostitute named Charlie came to see me Monday. I had seen him when I was out the other night and gave him my card."

"I know."

Andrew's eyes went wide. "Do you now?"

Hank hesitated. He did not want to make his relationship with

Nicky apparent, so he said, "I did a bit of espionage yesterday, accompanied by Nicholas Sharp."

"Your witness."

"Yes. He accompanied me to one of Amelia Cooper's parties. He identified the man he saw with Edward. Brigham Knight. An architect."

Andrew's face did not display any recognition. "All right. And Charlie knows Mr. Sharp from Bulgaria, so Sharp mentioned Charlie had my card."

"He did, yes."

"You think this architect is the killer?"

"I don't know for sure, but this is the first solid lead I've had."

Andrew grimaced. "Mr. Sharp identified him."

"Knight is friendly with high society and has some familial claim to his place there, but he doesn't strike me as being completely embraced. That doesn't mean anything, but this does. Nicholas Sharp told me when I first interrogated him he saw Edward with a well-dressed man and figured the man to be an uptown aristocrat. So, acting on a hunch, I brought Mr. Sharp to a society party uptown, and Sharp identified Brigham Knight as the man he saw with Edward. Which means nothing, I suppose."

"But your instinct tells you this is the man."

Hank considered the problem before him. "I need to go interrogate Mr. Knight, and I had intended to bring Stephens, but Stephens has proved to be quite hostile toward the case. In the event he decides to be unavailable to accompany me to question Mr. Knight, would you like to accompany me?"

"Me?"

"You know as much about this case as anyone. I trust you."

Andrew shook his head. "This is highly unusual. I don't do these sorts of things. I file reports and take notes for Commissioner Roosevelt. I don't accompany officers to question suspects."

It was a crazy idea. Hank wasn't sure why he'd landed on Andrew as the ideal person to help in this matter. He only knew it was even more foolish to go to see Knight on his own, and he needed a companion he could trust. Then he remembered something. "If Sunday's victim wasn't murdered, what happened? And how did you know? Was it reported to another officer?"

"No." Andrew took a deep breath. "No, the victim came to me directly."

Andrew's reluctance annoyed Hank. He couldn't figure why Andrew was being so coy. "Just tell me what happened."

Andrew let out a breath. "The victim was Charlie."

Hank uttered an oath. "What happened?"

"I think the killer found him, Hank. A man pulled him into a dark spot near the resort and buggered him there. Against his will, I should add."

That horrified Hank. No one should have been defiled in such a way. "Lord almighty," he whispered.

"Yes, I thought so as well. He was shaky when he came to see me. Completely out of sorts. I believe what he says is true. He says he was able to get away, but he believed his life was in danger."

"He may be the key to this case, Andrew. Do you realize that? Charlie has direct knowledge of the killer."

"Assuming his assailant is the killer."

That was true. There could have been more than one aggressive man. "I think if we interview Brigham Knight and find a way to get Charlie to look at him again, that might be the thing to pull the case together. If Knight is the same man Nicky saw and the man who assaulted Charlie, we can hang the whole lot of the charges on him."

"Nicky?"

Hank froze. He'd slipped. He never slipped. What was Nicky doing to him? "Nicholas Sharp. He goes by Nicky."

Andrew raised an eyebrow. Perhaps he was onto Hank.

"You must not breathe a word of this . . . familiarity," Hank said.

"You know I wouldn't." Andrew looked at the papers in his hand. "Though tell me. This familiarity. How deep does it go?"

Hank said nothing.

"Right," said Andrew, handing his notes to Hank. "Well, I just came down here to pass this along. Someone attacked Charlie, and he's not doing well in the aftermath. When he came to speak to me, he shook the whole time. I mean violently shook to the point where it affected his speech. The man who did this, whoever he is, is a menace and needs to be taken off the streets."

"And I will do everything in my power to see it happens."

"I know you will." Andrew stood. "I must be getting back to Headquarters."

"All right. I'll be in touch. Particularly if I need you to accompany me to talk to Knight."

Andrew grimaced. "Hank . . ."

"Think on it."

Andrew nodded. Then he walked away.

Andrew daringly took the elevated train back uptown during his lunch break to check on Charlie.

Hank wanted him to go question his suspect, and Andrew couldn't think of a worse idea. It was against procedure. It was far outside the scope of Andrew's job. He had enough work to do with the Bryan speech the next day and, well, all the people expiring in the streets from the unbearable, unending heat.

And yet Andrew wanted to be involved with this case. It felt important to be involved, and he had a personal stake in it now. Sort of. If Hank wanted back up, Stephens refused, and Andrew was the only one Hank trusted, then Andrew would do it. Even if it was a terrible idea.

The thermometer on the *Herald* building read 103 degrees, and Andrew felt every one of those degrees as he crossed the street to his building. The dog a police officer had shot the day before was still there, and the smell was astounding, one of the most horrific things Andrew had ever encountered. Flies buzzed around the corpse. Andrew put a hand over his nose and hurried into the building.

Andrew's apartment was small. He'd been renting it from a family friend for a few years, and it suited him, but having someone else stay there made him self-conscious. There wasn't much in the way of decoration. Most of the furniture was second-hand and out of style. His salary as a secretary was not going to be buying him a Fifth Avenue mansion anytime soon, though, so it would have to do.

When he went into the apartment, he found Charlie napping on the bed. Andrew sat on the edge of it and nudged Charlie awake. Charlie woke with a start, and then blinked a few times and stared at Andrew. He smiled.

"I snuck away from the office to pay you a quick visit. I can't stay long."

Charlie frowned. "To make sure I'm not stealing your things, in other words."

"No, actually." Andrew reached over and lightly ran his fingers down Charlie's naked arm. "I wanted to be sure you were all right. And, well, I just wanted to see you."

Charlie furrowed his brow as if this confused him. "Truly?"

"You trusted me. I'd like to return the favor."

Charlie closed his eyes and slumped into the mattress. "I do not deserve your support."

"I want to offer it."

Charlie sat up. He met Andrew's gaze. "You came all the way uptown just to see me?"

"Yes."

Before Andrew knew what was happening, Charlie had cupped a hand behind his head, pulled him close, and then they were kissing. The kiss was a hot shock. Andrew closed his eyes and leaned into it, happy to be kissing Charlie, loving the press and texture of his lips, the taste of him. He opened his mouth and licked into Charlie's, and the taste was a little sour, but Andrew didn't mind because this was so delightful.

Unless Charlie thought he owed Andrew.

Doubt crept in. Andrew wondered if Charlie was doing this out of obligation, if he was accustomed to using his sexuality to pay for things, if he thought he had to do this for room and board. Andrew didn't want that. He lost momentum, pressed his lips together, and pulled away.

"Did I do something wrong?" Charlie asked.

"No. No, nothing wrong, but . . . I hope you don't feel like you have to kiss me. Or do anything with me. Especially not after what you've been through."

Charlie's face fell.

Andrew felt the need to backpedal. "Not that I don't want you to kiss me. I want to kiss you! Very much. But I want you to . . . want to kiss me. Not for you to do it because you feel you owe me something."

Charlie appeared to consider this. "Nicky told me a couple of nights ago he had a new man in his life to whom he gave his love freely. Because he wanted to. It made me jealous."

Andrew spared a thought for Hank. Hank had been coy, but Andrew could read between the lines. Hank was cavorting with a witness on a case, not something Andrew really approved of, but given his own situation, he supposed he couldn't throw stones. "You want to be able to do that."

Charlie shrugged and looked down at the mattress. "I was never interested in women romantically. When I landed on Julie's stoop, he told me there were other men like me, men who liked other men. But I started, well . . . right away. Julie put me to work. So I've never . . ."

"You've never been with a man who wasn't paying for it." Or perhaps there were other men who forced Charlie, but Andrew was too horrified by that idea to voice it out loud.

Charlie nodded. "Some of them I liked well enough. I had a couple of regular customers at Bulgaria. They were kind to me. Sweet. Bought me gifts. Some were handsome. One man was astoundingly beautiful. I've always wondered what happened to him."

Andrew felt his own pang of jealousy. "He left?"

"He stopped coming to Bulgaria sometime this past winter."

Andrew must have been making a face, because Charlie added, "I just mean, it hasn't been all bad, my profession. I did it because for a while it was the only option I had, but I honestly didn't hate it."

It didn't escape Andrew's notice that Charlie was speaking of his profession in the past tense. "All I want you to know is I genuinely like you and care for you, so if you want to be with me, I want you to choose to be freely," Andrew said.

Charlie looked up. "I do."

Charlie kissed Andrew again, but this time Andrew felt no guilt. He pressed his lips against Charlie's and tried to convey with pressure and movement how overwhelmed he felt suddenly.

Andrew was hot and aroused, not just because of the weather, and he wanted to stay, to linger in that bed with Charlie for the rest of the afternoon, but he had to get back to the office before anyone missed him. More to the point, Charlie was still fresh from his recent encounter, and Andrew didn't want to risk traumatizing him further.

So he pulled away. "I have to leave."

"Will you be back soon?"

"Tonight, yes. I may have an errand to run with Hank—Inspector Brandt—this evening, but I will come home as soon as I can."

"I will be here. I won't steal anything."

Andrew could only guess at what Charlie's life had been like to this point. He didn't want to linger on it, not in this moment. Thinking on it broke his heart. "I shall look forward to seeing you, then."

Charlie gave Andrew a bright smile. This situation was unorthodox, but it might work out. It was enough to give a man hope. Maybe the heat would never cease beating down on the city, but Andrew had this.

Reluctantly, he made himself leave to go back downtown. He turned back to get one last look at Charlie before he left his apartment. Charlie smiled again. So yes. Andrew had this.

Chapter 15

Stephens wanted no part of the trip to see Brigham Knight, which surprised Hank not in the least, and as he was pushing things with his deadline, it made sense. Stephens seemed preoccupied with the Tompkins Square murder, anyway. It was the sort of crime more up Stephens's alley, anyway; no moral ambiguity, a pretty clear villain, enough sordid details to keep it interesting. In the meantime, Hank asked Andrew to come with him to Knight's.

"I still think this is highly inappropriate," said Andrew, although he, at least, was done up in his best suit, a dark brown affair he had to be boiling within.

They were walking from the elevated train to the Fifth Avenue home of Brigham Knight, so Hank figured Andrew had decided it was too late to back down.

"You don't have to do anything. You can take notes if you really want to, but I mostly just need someone else's take on the matter. So just stand there and say nothing. Listen if you care to." And he needed someone to support him and back him up if Knight became difficult, but articulating that to Andrew seemed like a fool's errand, given how riled up he already was. Hank was confident if the situation did get hairy, he could count on Andrew's instincts to back him up.

Or this had been a terrible idea.

Andrew harrumphed. He held his hat firmly on his head as a carriage sped by them, kicking up the rare gust of wind that, alas, smelled of rotting food and horse manure. Hank pulled his handkerchief out of his pocket and covered his mouth.

Andrew was agitated, more than was reasonable in proportion to the situation, and Hank wondered if there wasn't something else on Andrew's mind. Hank bided his time. If Andrew wanted to say something, he would. If he didn't, it was none of Hank's affair. They walked silently for a block.

"You should know," Andrew said as they crossed Park Avenue. "Charlie Evans has been camping out at my house since Monday."

Hank nearly choked. He did stumble, although he managed to keep his feet beneath him. "He what?"

"I realize the difficulty of this situation. Please do not lecture me. And please do not force me to point out my suspicions about you and Nicholas Sharp. Which, given how much time you must have spent with him . . ."

"No, I—"

"It's fine, Hank. I don't judge you."

"I know. But others might. And it's inappropriate. He's a witness."

"And yet."

Hank sighed. "Yes."

"Anyway, Charlie is only sleeping. He's spent the days sleeping away his troubles in my bed." Andrew kicked a stray rock down the street. "This weighs on me, which is why I'm being so forward. Nothing has really happened between us, but not because I do not want it to. Normally, you know me, I am the soul of discretion, but I just . . ."

"Trust me, I understand."

Andrew smiled ruefully. "You always do."

Hank pulled the piece of paper out of his pocket on which he'd recorded Knight's address, which he'd gotten in a note from Amelia earlier in the day. The address had, naturally, been accompanied by a quick missive explaining that Amelia just adored Alice and that she was quite delighted Hank had changed his mind about a few things. He would have to set her straight soon, but he'd worry about it after he'd resolved his murder investigation. If, that was, Nicky even stayed with him. He wasn't at all sure that would be the case.

He wasn't sure he'd survive the week, either. Heat aside, it might be only a matter of days before someone found out about Nicky. Hank knew he risked his job the longer he stayed with Nicky. He was at a point now where he wasn't sure how much he cared.

Well, actually he did care a great deal, and he knew he was being cavalier and foolish, but his brain was cloudy, and he wanted Nicky in his life. He blamed the heat for his foolishness.

"I believe the Knight house is on the next corner," Hank said.

"Yes. Lead the way."

They walked up Fifth to what was likely the most modest house in the neighborhood. Hank said, "Be careful what you say. Ask questions if they occur to you, but mostly leave the talking to me."

"I understand, Hank."

They walked up the steps in front of the narrow brownstone. Hank rapped on the door. He wasn't sure what to expect—a butler? Knight himself? Silence?—so he put his hands behind his back and waited. Andrew shot him a wary glance.

A gaunt man with graying hair answered the door.

"I'm Inspector Henry Brandt with the New York City Police Department," Hank said. "I'd like to speak to Mr. Brigham Knight. Is he at home to callers?"

"May I ask what this is about?"

Andrew's concern about the situation was written all over his face. Hank regretted asking him to come along. He would certainly betray any cover they had. "I met Mr. Knight at the Coopers' charity ball last night. Quite a grand affair. We had a conversation about architecture I was anxious to continue." He looked at Andrew, fidgeting beside him, and tried to convey he should stop moving. "This is my colleague, Mr. Ritchley. He also has an interest in architecture."

The butler nodded. "Very good, sir. I do believe Mr. Knight is available. Please follow me and I will escort you to the parlor."

The butler brought them to a sparsely decorated sitting room on the first floor. The only thing remarkable about it was the shelving lining the walls. Brigham Knight owned a great number of books, which crowded the shelves, wedged into any spare space.

"Try not to look like you're about to have a coronary incident," Hank said to Andrew once the butler had left.

"Apologies." Andrew huffed out a breath. "I'm sorry, I shouldn't have come. I am not well suited to this sort of work."

"Can you think on your feet and fire a gun?"

"Yes."

"Then you're all the help I need."

This didn't seem to placate Andrew much.

Brigham Knight arrived a few moments later. Hank stood and shook hands with him.

"Mr. Brandt! A pleasure to see you again."

"Likewise. This is my colleague, Mr. Ritchley."

The two men sized each other up and shook hands.

Hank said, "Do you have a few minutes to talk? I have a few questions."

"Of course. Any friend of Jonathan Cooper's is a friend of mine. Please have a seat."

Hank took his time settling into his chair so he could think on how best to approach this situation. "Did you enjoy the ball?" he started.

"Quite a bit, yes. And I am always happy to support Mrs. Cooper's causes. Ethical treatment of children last night, yes?"

In light of what Hank had witnessed with Nicky's family, the charity took on even more import. "Specifically aid to children in the Lower East Side tenements. Aid that is greatly needed. I've been there quite a bit the last few days, in my professional capacity. It is terrifyingly hot in those buildings. A child died on my watch a few days ago. That is not an experience I care to repeat."

"No, I can't imagine you would."

From Amelia, Hank knew Knight was from out of town—Illinois or one of the other Midwestern states, she couldn't remember which—and so he probably didn't have a lot of experience with that level of poverty, unless he visited it voyeuristically. "Have you ever been there?" Hank asked.

Knight waved his hand. "I rarely go below Fourteenth Street, honestly, unless I go all the way downtown. Another architect I work with frequently has offices on Broadway near Trinity Church."

"Right, of course." Hank reconsidered his strategy. Perhaps some honesty would be in order. "Well, I'm afraid my visit here is not altogether a happy one. You see, I'm investigating an incident that occurred last Wednesday, so I've been checking in on anyone who may have seen anything."

"I can't imagine how I can be of help. Last Wednesday?"

"Where were you that evening?"

Andrew pulled a notepad and a pencil out of his pocket and posed as if he were about to write down something important.

"I do not recall exactly. It has been so hot, the days run together. I believe I went to a dinner party that evening."

"Where was this dinner party?"

"Delmonico's. The William Street location."

"So you were downtown?"

"Yes. Unless that was Tuesday." Knight raised his shoulders and shook his head. "I'm afraid I can't recall. Whichever night I did not go downtown, I spent the evening here at home reading."

He was lying. Hank knew it in his gut. Perhaps there had been a party at Delmonico's, perhaps it was even with this architecture colleague with the office on Broadway, but that would not prevent Knight from heading back up to the Bowery resorts after dinner. The walk would have been a little arduous in the heat, but not unmanageable. "Well, whichever night this was, did you go straight home after dinner?"

Knight made a show of considering his answer. Hank knew Knight meant for him to infer that he had trouble recalling, but he suspected Knight was cooking up a strategy. Nicky had identified him as the man at Bulgaria, so even if he wasn't the killer, he had been seen there. That he'd lied didn't do much to convince Hank he was honest about anything.

"We may have adjourned for a stroll afterward. One of my dinner companions is somewhat obsessed with the work of Jacob Riis. He wanted to see 'how the other half lives' or some such. I thought it a bad idea, but I did accompany him on a walk through some of the lower parts of town."

"Does this companion of yours have a name?"

"Joseph Rooney. He lives on Little West Twelfth." Knight grinned. The expression sickened Hank—he knew it was meant to be a, "See how accommodating I can be?" gesture.

Andrew scribbled on his pad.

Hank didn't want to play his hand just yet. He doubted he could convince Knight to confess, and he didn't want to spook the man, either, lest he get a sudden urge to flee the city.

"Well. Just curious. Which is to say, all I really have to go on is a vague description of a man who could be one of hundreds in this city. So I've been asking about for anyone who might have been in the area, and as you've mentioned your architectural projects and I know there is some construction happening near Cooper Union, I thought

I'd check if you'd seen anything. Very likely, I'll have to abandon this case."

"This is the same case you mentioned at the Coopers' soiree?"

"Yes. Just some trouble with a prostitute." Hank waved his hand. "I do know sometimes the uptown folk like to check out what is happening in the resorts in that area, so I've been asking around. I'll leave you to your work now. Though if you do find yourself downtown again, be wary. There has been quite a bit of violent crime."

"Of course."

"If you can think of anything strange, send a note to Police Headquarters addressed to me or Mr. Ritchley. I'd be happy for any leads."

For show's sake, they made small talk for another few minutes before Hank pulled out his pocket watch and declared he was running late for an appointment. Knight escorted Hank and Andrew to the front door and said, "I am not certain I can help you with your investigation. I really don't know anything. I hope you find what you're looking for."

"Yes, as do I, but many of these cases do not have satisfactory resolutions," Hank said. "Stay away from some of the seedier neighborhoods for a while. Especially Greenwich Village. The crowds at the resorts and clubs on Bleecker have been bustling, but the heat is bringing out everyone's worst behavior."

"Of course. I have no business downtown."

Hank wondered if Knight was aware of how much he gave away, the way his body tensed or he grimaced before he remembered to act and correct the behavior. Hank nodded and bid him to have a good day. Once Hank and Andrew were down the block, Andrew said, "I do not know what you hoped to accomplish there, but I am not sure we determined anything beyond that Mr. Knight is a liar."

"Yes. But now we've established that, at least."

They walked another block while Hank considered his next move. Andrew must have found that frustrating, because he let out a disgusted grunt and said, "What the devil was the point of all that?"

"I'm planting seeds. I suppose next we must speak with this Mr. Rooney about Knight's alibi."

"Knight will get to Rooney before we do."

"Only if he has a telephone. We should go visit Mr. Rooney at once."

Andrew frowned. "I am having trouble seeing how we tie all these strings together. You have nothing but some vague hunches."

"I don't know what else to do. I want to catch this man. I need to think on it more."

"I want you to catch him." Andrew shook his head. "Unfortunately, I have a speech at Madison Square Garden tomorrow to deal with, so I'll be unable to help you much more, but I'm deeply uncomfortable with all of this besides. I'm your friend and I'll help you as much as I can, but before you go pushing headlong into a difficult situation, consider the real consequences of your actions. If you push too hard, especially against a member of the city's elite, it could cost you your job."

It seemed everything about this case could cost Hank his job. He sighed. "I'm going to keep an eye on the Greenwich Village fairy resorts for the next few nights either way. Perhaps he'll turn up there again."

"Be careful, Hank."

"I'm always careful."

Andrew looked unconvinced.

Hank and Andrew returned to Headquarters, where Hank found a directory and looked up Mr. Rooney's address. After wishing Andrew luck with Mr. Bryan, Hank walked to Little West Twelfth, not far from his own house.

Rooney was a short, balding man with glasses, who smiled kindly as he let Hank in. "I don't wish to take up too much of your time," Hank said. "I'm merely looking to verify the whereabouts of a man last Wednesday night."

"Brandt, eh? Any relation to the Brandts who lived on West Tenth Street?"

That brought Hank up short. "Er, yes, actually. I still live in the house on West Tenth Street."

Rooney laughed. "Henry! Of course. Our fathers fought together, you know. The old Eighty-second Regiment. Antietam, Fredericksburg, Gettysburg, yes?"

"Yes, sir." Hank's father had been a part of the Eighty-second Regiment, but Hank had no idea there were other veterans living in the neighborhood.

"I was about twelve years old when the war began," said Rooney. "You must have been a wee babe."

Hank was in awe of this strange situation he'd walked into. "Yes, sir. Born 1860. I was not quite a year old when my father left for war."

Rooney nodded. "I left for West Point shortly after my father returned home. I had this idea I'd be a soldier and go South to help with the Reconstruction. Turns out I am not quite suited for military life." He shrugged. "Our families seem to have lost track of each other after your father passed. I am very sorry for it. And now you are a police inspector!"

"Well, acting inspector. The promotion is pending police board approval."

"Yes, of course. I read about the police board troubles in the paper." Rooney gestured toward a worn armchair, so Hank sat. Rooney sat on the settee across from him. "Now, what can I help you with, young Henry Brandt?"

Hank nearly laughed. No one really called him Henry except in very formal settings. "Well, sir, I am actually just verifying a dinner party took place last Wednesday."

Rooney thought on it. "Yes. I had dinner at Delmonico's with a few of the fellows from an architecture firm. I'm investing in a property uptown, you see."

Hank hoped it wasn't the foolish proposition of a sliver of a building on Madison Square. "Are you acquainted with an architect named Brigham Knight?"

Rooney nodded. "Yes, and he was at that very same dinner. Very bright young man. He has a lot of incredible ideas. I think he might just be the next Stanford White."

Hank doubted that, particularly if he got his way and put Knight behind bars. "Do you happen to know if he went straight home after dinner?"

"Yes, I believe so." Rooney looked at the ceiling. "Well, I saw him get in a cab, at any rate. Why do you ask?"

"A witness spotted a man fitting his description at the scene of a crime I'm investigating. It's probably of no consequence, but I thought he might be a witness."

"All you've to do is ask him yourself," Rooney said. "I've known him a few years and have never known him to be anything but honest."

Hank nodded. This was getting him nowhere. Knight must have known Rooney would back up his alibi; Hank wondered if Knight made sure to be seen by prominent people before he went to the Bowery resorts so he'd have plausible alibis lined up.

"What sort of crime are you investigating?" Rooney asked.

"Oh, nothing too significant. There was a scuffle involving a man and a prostitute."

Rooney chuckled. "Ah, what has this city become?"

Hank stood and looked around. The house was nice, but utterly masculine. "Are you married, Mr. Rooney?" he asked.

"Confirmed bachelor, I'm afraid."

Hank nodded and wondered if perhaps the relationship between Knight and Rooney was more than a business acquaintance. He shook Rooney's hand and smiled. "Given we are neighbors, we should have dinner sometimes, perhaps. If you have any recollections of my father, I would be happy to hear them."

Rooney winked. "Oh, I recall a few war stories. I imagine you've heard a lot of them."

"Probably. But it's not every day I meet someone who knew my father. I . . . I miss him a great deal, still."

"He was a fine man, as I recall. I can make tea, if you'd like?"

Hank glanced at his pocket watch. "Unfortunately, I need to get back to my precinct house. I do thank you for your help. I apologize for taking up your time."

"It was no bother at all, Mr. Brandt. Please call on me anytime."

Hank left Joseph Rooney's house feeling like he hadn't accomplished much beyond perhaps gaining a new acquaintance. He knew in his gut Knight was his man, but proving it felt impossible.

Day 8

Wednesday, August 12

Temperature: 103°F

Chapter 16

The knock on the door came as Hank finished breakfast. He didn't feel especially enthusiastic about going back out in the heat. Making sweaty love to Nicky in the wee hours of the morning had not precisely cooled him off.

Nicky stood at Hank's hallway mirror, fiddling with a plaid scarf before scoffing at his reflection and tossing it aside. "I cannot live with this weather," he said. "It is so difficult to adorn myself properly."

And then the knock at the door.

Hank went to answer it and was surprised to find Amelia there.

"What are you doing here?"

"Shopping with Isabelle Cartwright, so I was in the neighborhood. I told her I wanted to stop by to see you, but the hats in a shop on Seventh Avenue distracted her. I told her I'd meet her back there after I said hello to you."

"Oh."

"I apologize for arriving unannounced."

"It's all right. It's just I have company—"

Amelia pushed past him and into the house. She clearly spotted Nicky immediately, and he stood there looking just as shocked to see her. He was dressed relatively plainly, at least, in a white shirt and crisp brown trousers. His dark blond hair was elegantly combed atop his head into a wave and he'd rouged his cheeks as was his wont. He was Nicky, in other words. And not, alas, Alice McGraw.

Nicky and Amelia stared at each other for a long moment.

"Er, well. I had not expected this," Amelia said.

Hank stammered, but managed to say, "Amelia, this is—"

But Nicky pushed passed him and held out his hand to her. "Perhaps we should dispense with illusions here, love," he said to Hank.

Hank's heart beat so fast he worried it would burst. If he hadn't already been sweating, sweat likely would have bloomed on his forehead. He went cold everywhere, though, shocked and unable to verbally reconcile this man before him and the person Amelia had met two days before.

"I don't—" Hank started. There could have been a logical explanation. Nicky had dropped by to say hello. It wasn't obvious he'd spent the night. It was rather early for callers, but Amelia was here, so . . .

"Nonsense. This is all nonsense." Nicky crossed his arms over his chest. "We could just admit we've been caught, darling."

Hank stopped breathing. "Yes, but—"

"I can't believe you would betray Alice in this way," Amelia said, venom in her voice.

Nicky turned to her, alarm on his face. "That is not precisely what is occurring—"

"I thought you'd changed, Hank." Amelia swished past him into the foyer. "I thought things were different this time. That girl was lovely and she suited you well. I don't understand why you couldn't have just . . . that is, I don't know why you . . ." She grumbled and turned to face Nicky again. She gave him a good long look. Then she gasped. Something in Nicky's expression or the way he moved his hands must have tipped her off, because she said, "Alice. You're Alice."

Nicky balked, but then dropped his shoulders. "Yes. In the flesh, darling."

Hank was surprised into silence, shocked Nicky wouldn't even bother to deny it.

Amelia said, "This does explain a great deal."

"Amelia," Hank said, finding his voice. He could not tell if she was disturbed by this situation, upset with him, or if she just thought this another strange day in the life of Hank Brandt. He took a step forward and gestured toward Nicky. "This is Nicholas Sharp." He put a hand on Nicky's shoulder and then took it away. "I wanted to tell you, but there was no good opportunity to—"

Amelia slapped Hank across the face.

It smarted. "What did you do that for?"

"My god, Hank, do you have any idea what could have happened to you?"

Hank held his hand to his face.

Amelia started pacing and shook her head. She wore a dress made of what looked like heavy red fabric, and under all the layers, she must have been boiling, but Hank knew he had to focus on the matter at hand and not her clothes.

She said, "I cannot believe you, Hank. Did you really bring a man dressed as a woman to my charity ball, at which a number of New York's most prominent people were in attendance, and expect no one to notice?"

"No one did notice," said Hank.

Amelia screamed low in her throat and threw her hands up. "You are so reckless sometimes. If anyone had caught you—"

"They did not."

"—you could have been arrested or worse. Both of you."

Hank, feeling defensive, took a step backward. "Allow me to point out, first of all, I am an officer of the law. I knew what I was doing. Nicky dressed the way he did of his own volition. He is . . . something of a professional."

Amelia gawped at Nicky. "A . . . professional?"

Nicky stood with his hips cocked and his arms up with his wrists twisted out, a pose perhaps best suited for a female nude statue. His voice lilting, he said, "Yes, darling, a professional. I work as a female impersonator. I sing on a stage at a fairy resort. Are you irredeemably scandalized yet?"

Hank tried to shoot Nicky a look—this had just gone too far—but Nicky turned away from him.

Amelia blustered for a moment, looking for all the world like she was about to throw a tantrum as she'd done dozens of times when they were young, but she managed to calm down somewhat. She let out a breath that blew the front fringe of her hair away from her face. Then she stood there with her fists clenched at her sides.

"This is all completely absurd," she said with remarkable calm.

"Amelia, I'm sorry," Hank said. "I am so very sorry. I wanted to tell you honestly what the situation was about, but I never had the opportunity. And I needed to get Nicky in the same room as some of what you call the most prominent people of New York so he could identify a potential suspect. Which he did, by the way. Your husband's friend Mr. Knight? He spends his evenings slumming at fairy resorts."

Amelia's eyes went wide. "He what?"

Hank held up his hands. "I apologize for manipulating the situation the way I did, but I could find no better alternative plan. Nicky spotted Knight and identified him as the man who was last seen with my murder victim. You should tell Jonathan he'd do well to stay away from Mr. Knight."

"And you trust this Nicky."

Hank hadn't realized he'd been referring to Nicky by his familiar name. He looked back at Nicky, who stood ramrod straight now. All of his defenses were up. Hank half expected him to mince his way out the door in an effeminate flourish.

So Hank risked telling the truth. "Yes, I trust him. The affection you witnessed between me and 'Alice' was not all show."

If he hadn't been so worried two of the people he cared for most in the world were about to walk out the door and out of his life for good, Hank would have laughed at the comically exaggerated shocked expressions both were making. They froze in a strange limbo where no one moved or spoke for several long moments.

Amelia broke the silence when she said, "You lied to me."

And Hank had to admit, yes, he had, but he said, "Perhaps by omission, but we needed our cover. I did plan to tell you when I solved the case. Had Knight discovered Nicky was not the woman he appeared to be, he might have recognized him from the club. Who knows what harm might have befallen him then?"

Amelia resumed her pacing. Nicky backed away and leaned against the stairwell, as far as he could be from the fuming Amelia without leaving the foyer. The only sound was the rhythmic clack of Amelia's heeled shoes against the wood floor.

"You think I would have betrayed your trust?"

"No. Not on purpose."

"You jeopardized everything. You jeopardized my ball, my reputation. You put your own life and Mr. Sharp's at risk. And you came to my ball not to support my cause but because of your own agenda. Is that about the sum of it?"

"I do support your cause. I was happy to give money for the children in the tenements."

Nicky jerked slightly. He was in Hank's peripheral vision now as Hank tried to concentrate on Amelia.

"Would you have come to the ball had you not wanted to identify a suspect?"

Hank hesitated just a moment too long before opening his mouth to respond. Amelia made a frustrated noise that was more than a grunt but less than a scream.

"Amelia," Hank said. "I love you and you are my greatest friend and I feel tremendously guilty for having used your ball in this way, but I thought it was the right thing to do at the time. I still believe it was the right thing to do, because it has connected Mr. Knight to this crime."

"What if he is not your killer?"

"Then he's innocent, I suppose, though he lied to me about his whereabouts the night of the murder I'm investigating, and he's lying to you all about his after-hours activities."

"Says Mr. Sharp."

"Yes, and I believe him."

"Perhaps I should leave," said Nicky.

"No. Please stay," said Hank. He turned back to Amelia. "And you, please accept my sincerest apology. I would have told you about Nicky when the time was right."

"Am I correct in assuming his presence here in the morning means he is your lover?"

Hank bristled at how intimate the question felt, but he nodded.

Amelia sighed. "And here I had thought you had seen the light and changed your nature. That it was possible for you to fall in love with a woman and make a family and be happy finally."

"I do not think that possible."

Amelia nodded. "You know it does not bother me that you are . . . an invert. I love you no matter what. But I want you to be happy."

"I know. But happiness the way you mean it may not be possible, either."

Amelia frowned and glanced out the window.

Nicky stepped forward. "Far be it from me to intervene in a dispute between friends. But I worry we've lost sight of what is important here." He cleared his throat. "Mrs. Cooper, I am deeply sorry for my deception. It was never my intention to cause trouble at your ball. I am, actually, deeply grateful I was able to attend such a soiree. Never in my life have I seen a ballroom as nicely appointed as yours."

This seemed to mollify Amelia somewhat; she blushed and smiled faintly.

"This particular deception was entirely my idea," Nicky went on. "Hank initially suggested I dress as one of his police colleagues or as a young banker. I'd be a pal who came with him to pay homage to your cause. But as you can see, I am hardly the rough police officer type. I thought I might be more convincing as Hank's young lady friend. So the fault for that particular crime lies entirely at my feet."

Amelia glanced at Nicky and then looked back at Hank.

"I worry for you, you know," Amelia said. "I worry about you a great deal. One of these days you will get caught, and you will lose your job or worse. If anyone at Police Headquarters has even a suspicion, your promotion will never be approved."

"That outcome is a strong possibility," Hank conceded. "But until such a time as that occurs, I intend to be the best inspector I can be, which means solving this murder within reasonable means. A man is assaulting and killing young men in my precinct. I cannot just let it go."

"No. I realize that."

Amelia looked up and met Hank's gaze. He understood her frustration with him was borne of concern. He knew she wanted him to be happy, but something about the way she expressed that, framing his happiness as depending on changing himself, struck Hank in the gut.

He might never find happiness. But he thought he could get some semblance of it with Nicky at his side.

He did not know how to convey that to Amelia.

"Your anger is justified," he said. "I should have explained the situation to you before my arrival. But it is too late to change what happened now."

Amelia nodded.

Although he regretted angering Amelia, the rest of it could never be regretted or forgotten. He'd danced with Nicky in the ballroom as if it were a perfectly normal thing to do. He'd hold that memory close for a long time to come.

"I should be returning to Isabelle," Amelia said, gesturing toward the door. She picked up the parasol she must have dropped when she came in. "Mr. Sharp, it was a pleasure to meet you again, this time as yourself."

"Yes." Nicky bit his lip. "I meant what I said, darling. I do sincerely wish you and I could be friends. I think we'd get on brilliantly. But I understand if you want nothing to do with me."

"It's not that precisely. I just need some time with this, I suppose. It's not every day I meet Hank's . . . friends. I've never met one such as you before."

"I am one in a million," Nicky said with a hollow smile.

"I suppose I can find it in my heart to forgive you both if your actions were in the service of solving a crime. Do not do this ever again, though." She held up her hand and pointed at Hank. "We've been friends for too long for you to lie to me."

"I know. I won't do it again," said Hank.

Amelia took her leave, which kept Nicky and Hank in the foyer for a long silent moment.

"She really cares for you," Nicky said.

"Yes."

"I've never had a friend like that. One who just accepted me as I am. But she accepts you."

"Yes. And I treasure her for it. I do not know what I would have done if she had not accepted my apology."

Nicky touched Hank's arm, ran his fingers down the length of it. "Once we have put ourselves to rights for the day, would you please escort me home?"

"Of course. I can walk with you on the way to the precinct house."

"Thank you, love."

Nicky smiled. It didn't quite go to his eyes. Hank could only imagine what he was thinking, but didn't dare ask.

And so an hour later they walked together along West Fourth Street. The morning was not exactly serene. There was a large mound near the corner of Seventh Avenue that might have been a dead horse but could have been anything. People were sitting along the edge of one building atop quilts and towels, as if they'd slept there. It smelled horrifically, like urine and decaying flesh. And it was still so hot and humid merely walking was like pushing through a pool of boiling water.

And still, a calm fell over Hank as they walked, a contentment, daresay a bit of happiness. It was so at odds with how he woke up most mornings, heat or no, he wanted more time to savor it.

Hank was reluctant to go to work, in fact, because he didn't especially want to part from Nicky. He had the sense all of this was about to come crashing down around him. The dread sat like a stone in his belly.

Nicky fiddled with his scarf as they walked east. The scarf seemed like an eccentricity in this heat, though Hank also knew the color was meant as a way for Nicky to identify himself. A red ascot or scarf was often a signifier to other inverts that they were in good company. Hank had known a lot of men who had particular eccentricities—bleached hair, for example, or a predisposition toward tight trousers—that were also signals only men in the know would be able to interpret.

A bright red scarf on a hot day, no matter how flimsy the material, seemed like a beacon now.

Hank wasn't sure how much he really cared, though. The concern for others spotting him walking with Nicky felt borne more of habit than anything tangible he felt.

"Can I see you tonight?" Hank asked.

Nicky finished fussing and dropped his arms to his sides. "Well, darling, you are in luck. Tonight is my night off. Perhaps we need a few hours in which we put all the nonsense aside. Shall we have a little night on the town?"

"I'd love to." Hank genuinely would love to spend a night out with Nicky. He wanted an opportunity to talk with him, have a drink, bask in the energy of a saloon with like-minded men. "It has been a while since I spent nights doing anything but reading at home or police work, so I'm not sure where to go anymore."

"I know a few places."

They made arrangements to meet at a spot near where Nicky wanted to go once Hank got off work. Hank said, "I look forward to it."

"I as well, love."

Andrew read through various reports, both from police captains and in the newspapers, about the event at Madison Square Garden. According to one of the papers, some thirty thousand people had applied for tickets, most of whom were turned down. Madison Square

Garden had a capacity of ten thousand five hundred seats but room for about seven thousand more to stand. Filling the space to capacity in the deathly persistent heat seemed like a colossally idiotic idea.

There was some concern at Police Headquarters that this would be a repeat of President Cleveland's speech in 1892, in which a woman had fainted and caused a panic. That day had been hot, too, though nothing like the last week had been. Police Chief Conlin had made it clear he wished to avoid such a calamity and had requested a police surgeon be on hand to treat anyone with illness from the heat.

Somehow the burden had fallen on Andrew to relay the various requests and reports to the correct people. Thus Wednesday morning was utter chaos.

All so William Jennings Bryan could accept his nomination as the Democratic candidate for President of the United States in style. What happened to the candidates quietly accepting at home by writing a letter? Candidates for president were not supposed to be so flashy.

Worse, it wasn't at all clear from the news media that this was a ticketed event, not a public rally. For whatever reason, Bryan's talk was a major draw for city residents. Well, Andrew thought, it wasn't every day a presidential candidate came to New York to formally accept the nomination. Grover Cleveland had done it four years before, but he was a hometown man. Why Bryan had chosen New York as the scene of his triumph, no one knew, but maybe Andrew was being too cynical. The papers had been raving about the event for two weeks, so the police department expected a large turnout. It was possible thousands of people would show up. Andrew could easily picture a riot of people who were turned away.

It was creating a mess for Andrew.

"The police are providing cots and we've got pillows and blankets on loan from several hospitals," a captain whose name Andrew couldn't recall said as he stood beside Andrew's desk. "We're also bringing in ice and several large tubs. Dr. Nammack claims the best way to cure heat stroke is to submerge the patient in an ice bath." Dr. Nammack was the police surgeon.

"All right," Andrew said. "You've already got most of this in place, I hope."

"Yes, or it will be within the hour. We want to be ready for Mr.

Bryan and the crowds we anticipate. It seems very likely we will have to turn people away."

Andrew nodded. What a mess.

George Stephens arrived at police headquarters then, which was just what Andrew needed. He didn't trust Stephens; he understood why Hank thought he was a weasel.

"Mr. Ritchley," Stephens said. He ran a hand down the front of his perfectly crisp uniform. Stephens never had a thread out of place, even in the heat, which was enough to draw suspicion.

"I am quite busy this morning, Inspector Stephens. Preparations for the Bryan speech at Madison Square Garden. Was there something you needed?"

"I have some concerns about my acting inspector. I'd like to know who best to bring them up with. He outranks my precinct captain, so I thought coming to you to file a report would be the best course of action. Since you have the ears of the superior members of the police department, that is."

"Concerns about Hank Brandt?" Andrew's pulse accelerated.

"I think he's behaving in a wrongheaded manner where our current cases are concerned. Spending undue time on this matter involving the fairy prostitutes on the Bowery and not on more important cases."

"Right. He's made headway on the Bulgaria case, though. I've read his reports."

"See, the particular issue I have is I suspect . . . no, I shouldn't say."

Andrew rubbed his forehead. "What? What do you suspect?"

Stephens leaned close and lowered his voice. "Brandt may very well be a fairy himself."

Andrew had to fight to suppress his reaction, though he knew he utterly failed. Stephens smiled briefly before schooling his features again. Probably he'd misinterpreted the horror on Andrew's face.

"Let us not breathe a word of this just yet," Andrew said, trying to seem conspiratorial. "Wait for Brandt to incriminate himself. If you're right, he will. No one can keep a secret from this police commission, as you may have noticed."

Stephens nodded. "All right. I will look into the matter a little, if you don't mind."

"Not at all." Andrew's panic was mounting. Stephens meddling could very well blow up the whole investigation, but Andrew couldn't figure out how to make him back off without giving too much away. "Let me know if you uncover anything."

"I will." Then Stephens left.

Andrew watched him go. He knew he needed to talk to Hank immediately. If a lunkhead like Stephens had figured out Hank's secret, Hank wasn't safe anymore.

Chapter 17

Hank met Nicky near the corner of Bleecker and Mulberry Streets. Nicky wore a gray suit, the jacket open to reveal a matching waistcoat and a crisp white shirt. He'd tucked a red ascot into his collar. His blond hair was a little disheveled, likely due to sweat or whatever pomade he used melting in the heat.

They greeted each other as old friends, which Hank supposed said something about their relationship now.

"How was your day?" Hank asked.

"All right. I went to see Brigid. She is not faring too well." Nicky sighed. "I tried once more to persuade her to move to another neighborhood. I offered my apartment again. She won't move her whole family there while I still live there, and there is also the nagging issue of my father, who disappeared for a few days but finally turned up again." Nicky shook his head. "Father has lofty ideas of better accommodations for the lot of them, but unless he can conjure up the money to pay for it out of thin air, there's not much that can be done. And Brigid is not thinking straight and is digging in her heels because the tenements are closer to her husband's shop."

"That is a difficult situation. I wish there was something I could do to help."

Nicky shook his head. "Until Brigid decides to be less stubborn, there's nothing for it." He paused at Bleecker and took a moment to decide which way to walk. "Let's go this way. I trust your day was better than mine?"

"Not really. Andrew told me today my part-time partner suspects I am up to no good."

"The properly suited Inspector Stephens, yes?"

"Yes."

"Suspects you are a Prancing Nancy?"

Hank laughed despite himself. "Yes."

"Well, darling, I'm afraid I have bad news."

Hank laughed harder. The situation really was absurd. "It's not funny," Hank said between gasps as he tried to calm down. "And yet."

"I know."

Hank wheezed and then managed to pull himself together enough to keep walking. "I do not know what the future holds. It seems to me if Stephens has suspicions about me, he plans to speak to my superiors. We've had enough differences of opinion, and he is just ambitious enough, he likely went to Andrew thinking he had a sympathetic ear who would pass those suspicions up the chain of command. Even though I know Andrew will keep my secrets, if Stephens is starting to make noise, my days as a police inspector are probably numbered." Hank took a deep breath. "I love my job, I do, and I want to keep it, but my priorities have shifted this week. I decided this afternoon my main objective right now is to catch Brigham Knight and get him off the street. Once that is accomplished, who knows?"

"You would really sacrifice your career to catch this man?"

"If it means keeping you safe, yes."

Nicky tilted his head. "Do you mean 'you' as in the citizens of New York or 'you' as in the boys who work on the Bowery or 'you' as in me specifically?"

Staying on his current course was a risk. The smart thing for Hank to do would be to drop the case. But would that only postpone the inevitable if Stephens was already meddling? And what was the real answer to Nicky's question?

"All of those," Hank said.

Nicky grimaced. "It may be foolish, what you are doing. Have you always acted this brashly?"

"Really just since meeting you."

Hank wasn't sure if that was a problem.

The first stop on their Roosevelt-esque walkabout of Greenwich Village was the Pit, a saloon with something of a reputation for being the place the inverted men of New York descended into hell. It wasn't as bad as its reputation, which Hank knew firsthand, unless it had changed in the two years or so since he'd had to modify his habits for the sake of his job. Being here now was still a risk, though; even if everyone inside was sipping milk and knitting shawls, rumor about this place would be enough to get Hank fired for being there.

Why was he sabotaging himself in this way?

"Perhaps I should give some thought to moving on from the police force when all this is over," Hank said.

"Is that what you want?" asked Nicky.

"What I want is to be with you."

Nicky blushed and ducked his head. "I appreciate your hell-bent romanticism, dearest, but think about what you are saying. Carrying on like this could be a terrible idea. I want to be with you, too, but not if it means giving up your life."

They descended the stairs to the Pit's main room. Hank paused after he stepped away from the foot of the stairs. "Make a promise to me," he said.

"What?" asked Nicky.

"We worry about it all tomorrow. Tonight is for us. We will enjoy each other's company. We'll have a few drinks and maybe we'll dance and we'll cavort around the dark places of this city as if we were young again. Yes? The rest can wait until morning. My job, yours, the police, the city, the heat, all of it can be dealt with tomorrow. Tonight we put it all aside. All right?"

Nicky tilted his head and considered. "All right. I can make that promise."

"Good." Hank offered his arm. "Come with me. Let us explore what this particular road to Hell is like, yes? Have you ever been here before?"

"Once last year." Nicky hooked his hand into the crook of Hank's elbow. "I was dressed as Paulina at the time."

"A bold choice."

"A Tuesday night."

Hank guffawed. "Come. I'll buy you a drink."

Nicky scanned the room. It didn't seem remarkable at first. It was dimly lit with a bar off to one side. A bartender poured drinks while a half-dozen men leaned on the bar. There were tables peppered about where groups of men were socializing or, more likely, making transactions.

Perhaps that was what made this not just any saloon. It was not the sort of place men came after a long day of work to have a few drinks before going home to their families. Nor was it the sort of place one went for a dinner party or celebration of any sort. No, it was the sort of place men went to meet similarly inclined men. Nicky therefore regarded each table with a certain amount of skepticism. How many of those flirtatious glances or soft laughs or sweet touches were genuine and how many were feigned?

Because that was how *this* world worked. The men with money and power paid the men without for their love and affection.

And yet that was not the case with Hank, who even now kept a hand on Nicky at all times. The movement was warm and possessive. Hank wanted the men gathered here to know Nicky was his. Hank's protection was a powerful thing. No money had been exchanged between them. Instead, their relationship seemed built on genuine attraction and affection.

But how long could that last?

"Would you like something to drink?" Hank asked.

"I would like a gin fizz."

Hank's look of skepticism was so exaggerated, it made Nicky laugh.

"You want a what now?" Hank asked.

"The bartender will know. It's basically gin and fizzy water with a splash of lemon juice. I can't handle ale, you see. It's too bitter."

Hank furrowed his brow. "All right. Wait here. I will return shortly."

Nicky took a step back to lean on the wall behind him. It was an excellent vantage point. He felt invisible, like he blended into the shadows, which allowed him a view of some of the men in the room.

Few were expensively dressed. The men seated at the table nearest him—there were three—seemed young but weren't working boys. They were, perhaps, men out on the town for the night, friends from nearby New York University. Perhaps they had wealthy parents and this was their one bit of rebellion before they found women to marry and made proper families for themselves.

Within Nicky's earshot, two men were engaged in a clear transaction; one man, who looked barely out of short pants, caressed the chest of a much older gentleman who leaned toward him. Perhaps this was a man stepping out on his wife or one of the older inverts who sometimes frequented Paresis or Bulgaria looking to recapture his youth with a young man in his bed.

By the time Hank returned with two glasses, Nicky had made up stories about four or five of the clusters of people around the room.

"See anything interesting?" Hank asked.

Nicky took the proffered glass and took a long sip before he said, "Nothing too out of the ordinary, darling. Though it has brought to mind . . . were you ever one of the youths who got lost in places like this?"

"Perhaps."

"Perhaps you left home and attended college or the police academy and your fit of rebellion involved getting lost in a haze of sex and liquor at the Slide or some other even more disreputable place."

Hank shot him a cocky half-smile. "I won't deny it."

Nicky laughed. "Oh, you delight me, darling. You have a look about you like you just walked off the site of some monolithic new building under construction, as if you lift great metal beams or some such for a living. If I saw you on the street, I would assume you had a wife and children at home on whom you doted. And yet."

"I continued to be a great disappointment to my mother until her death because I did not marry Amelia."

"I imagine so. I quite like Amelia. I do believe she got the better end of the bargain, though, and not just because her husband has more money than the Queen."

"Perhaps."

"Which is not to say you would not make a good husband, just given what I know about your sexual predilections, I imagine you would not make a good husband to a woman."

"Is there any other kind of husband?"

Nicky smiled. "There were these two old men who used to come to Bulgaria to hear me sing. John and James. War vets, the both of them. Quite a romantic story, actually. Met in the army. James was wounded at Gettysburg. When John realized James hadn't returned from the battle, he realized he loved his fallen friend and went back to look for him. James survived his injuries. Bullet to the hip. Spent weeks in the hospital, endured several surgeries. You could tell when you spoke to him he ached from his wound still. But the two of them loved each other deeply. They lived together in an apartment uptown. Like husbands, they said." Nicky sighed, sounding perhaps a little dreamy, as he'd always liked that story. "So you could be that sort of husband."

"I suppose."

Nicky laughed softly. "The romantic and the practical man in you are often at war with each other, aren't they? Do you think you could be that kind of soft-hearted fool for another man?"

Hank shrugged. "I could be. That is, it was a sweet story. But do you really see me as the sort who would settle down in such a way?"

"You already have a house. You could move a man in there with you, call him a boarder, live together for the rest of your lives."

Hank guffawed. "I am surprised to find you of all people so idealistic." He shook his head. "I have given some thought to what life could be like, but let's face it, as soon as it became clear to someone at Police Headquarters who lived in my house, my job would be at an end."

"And yet you risk your career by getting caught here with me."

Nicky couldn't quite understand what was going through Hank's head now that they were here in the Pit. He watched Hank sip from his ale and stare out at the crowd. There might have been an ulterior motive here, or Hank had given up trying to maintain his discretion.

"Darling," Nicky said, "*are* you indeed sabotaging your career?"

"What about you?" Hank asked, turning his head quickly and staring at Nicky. "Would you take up with another man in a house and live domestically? Give up Paulina and stop performing at Bulgaria? Find a more respectable means of employment?"

"What do you mean by respectable?" Nicky bristled. He knew full well what Hank meant but resented the word. Perhaps Nicky's chosen profession was not respectable in the eyes of most of the citizens of New York, but Hank, at least, had seemed to have some respect for it.

"Apologies. I merely meant I wondered if you might find some other means of paying your rent. Perhaps you could find work at a restaurant or a shop. Hang up your gowns and start a new phase of your life. Move in with a man and live as husbands, as you put it. Have the little romance you seem to desire."

Nicky was offended by the whole idea that he would—or that he should have to—quit being this part of himself. He paused to give the question due thought, however. His first instinct was to blurt out that he could not give up Paulina, which was true. He loved those gowns, he loved to sing, he loved *being* Paulina, even if it was in a seedy resort for fairies. Bulgaria itself he could have done without, and Julie was an abrasive and oppressive employer, but working there gave him the opportunity to embody this part of his personality in a real way a few nights a week, and he'd always be grateful to Julie for giving him that opportunity.

"I couldn't give up Paulina, no," Nicky said, "but I could take her elsewhere. I wouldn't necessarily be confined to Bulgaria."

Hank tilted his head and sipped his ale for a long moment, so Nicky did the same, letting the burn of the alcohol tingle his throat.

"You want the romance, in other words," Hank said.

"Eh, perhaps. If someone like me *could* have a romance, I'd want it. I realize no decent woman would ever have me, nor do I want to get married, but I could live with a man in some sort of companionate relationship. Spend our mornings in bed together, go out at night together, make sure we each have someone in our lives to take care of us and care for us." Nicky paused and made a risky choice. "Kind of like we have been doing for the last week."

Hank let out a breath. "Well, you do bring up an interesting point. That is, I have an idea that may seem a little crazy, but I think it might make us both happy."

"Well, then, I'm all ears, darling."

A makeshift hospital had been set up in the basement of Madison Square Garden. Why cancel an event in which illness and injury seemed a foregone conclusion, Andrew thought, when a city needed the prestige and the income? Better to pretend you cared about public health and make a show of it than to actually act in the best interest of the people.

The auditorium had already reached a nearly unbearable temperature, without anyone inside yet.

Charlie stood at Andrew's side in borrowed clothes. Andrew had gotten him a job as a runner for the evening. That was, Charlie would run information to anyone who needed it, and the police department would pay him a flat fee for his trouble. Andrew and Charlie stood now to the left of the dais that had been erected at one end of the arena. They were both looking out at the permanent seats and rows of chairs on the floor. Four policemen were set up at the corners of the auditorium, each holding a white flag with a red cross on it. The object was to hold up the flag near the ailing audience member until help could arrive, although Andrew suspected there would be more than a few of those tonight. Four flags hardly seemed adequate.

Madison Square Garden was the largest such venue in the world, and it was a mere six years old, sitting in triumph aside Madison Square Park. The nude Diana statue atop its tower scandalously aimed her arrow into the skyline. Andrew hated the whole structure; he thought it too big, too ostentatious. But here he was, overseeing his own handiwork as one of the architects of this particular event, no matter how against his will his involvement had been.

"This will be a disaster," Andrew said.

Charlie rubbed his back, and then seemed to realize himself and jolted and withdrew his hand. "Are you always such a pessimist?"

"Probably."

"We're ready to open the doors!" bellowed Finnegan, who was part of the security detail for the night.

The sense of foreboding that had plagued Andrew all day hit him with the force of a punch to the face.

Two of the officers stationed at the auditorium doors pulled them open, and there was an immediate rush to get inside. The riot Andrew had anticipated would pop up outside the auditorium doors was happening right here before his eyes as people pushed each other aside to get the best seats.

The officers with flags were in motion at once. It took a while to get the crowds to calm down and take their seats. Andrew knew there were nearly three hundred officers on hand, and still their combined power couldn't keep people from pushing each other at walls and climbing over each other to seats. Andrew watched with horror as one woman fainted and had to be carried out by one of the officers with a flag.

Andrew wondered if the people had brought more heat in with them.

"This is intolerable," whispered Charlie. "It's like the inside of a furnace in here."

Andrew nodded. He looked away from the chaos and back toward Charlie. "Are you all right?"

"Yes, I'm fine. Hot, but I'll survive." Charlie paused. "Am I really going to see Mr. Bryan speak?"

"I believe so. Provided there is no other crisis that requires either of our attentions, you should be able to watch him speak from right here."

"I've never been to an event like this."

Charlie's excitement was a palpable thing. Andrew supposed it must have been a novel experience to be this close to someone as famous as William Jennings Bryan, even if they were all slowly baking inside the Garden. Andrew smiled at Charlie, trying to get caught up in his enthusiasm, before turning back to the audience.

The commotion had settled and now the audience sat murmuring. Most of the men had taken their coats off and a number of people in the audience had palm-frond fans they were waving frantically at their faces. The Garden was now a sea of moving fans and white shirtsleeves.

The band started up a few minutes later, but not even the blat of a horn could grab the attention of the chattering, fan-waving crowd. Members of the Democratic National Committee filed in and took their places on the dais, just as had been preordained, but the vice presidential nominee, Arthur Sewall, did not rouse much of an interest from the crowd. But up in the stands, far from what Andrew could see, someone shouted, "Three Cheers for Bryan!" The band struck up "My Girl's a Corker," a song Andrew did not particularly like.

Charlie started giggling. "This is a lewd song choice for a political event."

"Indeed."

During the part of the song when the lyric was, "She's got a pair of hips, just like two battleships," Mrs. Bryan appeared on the dais. That sent Charlie into peels of laughter. A wave of laughter and murmurs moved throughout the audience, which Mrs. Bryan seemed to take as enthusiasm. She grinned and waved at the crowd.

There was a little more fanfare, and finally Bryan arrived on stage. There was a gaffe involving one of the other runners trying to hand Bryan a little flag, which Bryan refused to take. Andrew had never seen the man in person, although he'd seen renderings in the papers. He was strikingly handsome, a bull of a man, better looking in person than he had been in the papers. Maybe that was part of his appeal to the American public. Bryan had been traveling across the country as part of his campaign tour, and he'd been greeting the American people all over, unlike his opponent McKinley, who had mostly been waging his campaign from his home in Ohio.

Bryan walked to the podium with a large sheaf of paper in his hands. He began to speak, and as he did so, he swayed a little and kept the papers close to his face. The first ten or so minutes of the speech lacked any kind of rhetorical flourish, which was a surprise because Andrew had been hearing for weeks Bryan was a gifted orator. And yet, Andrew had trouble paying attention to the speech. So did the audience, who slowly began to leave the auditorium.

The longer the speech went on, the more people left. They left in droves, the clatter of their shoes against the floor making so much noise it drowned out some of the speech. Charlie shot Andrew an alarmed look.

"What is happening?" Charlie whispered.

"I think they're all bored."

Andrew escorted Charlie over to a pair of abandoned seats, and they sat, prepared to weather the storm, such as it was. Bryan went on for another hot, interminable hour. Andrew had trouble following the speech; he spoke for a bit in the middle about gold and silver but his themes were so anathema to the economics of the city Andrew thought that section only served to make Bryan look more out of touch. By the time Bryan finally sat, it looked to Andrew as if two-thirds of the auditorium had emptied.

And here Andrew had been anticipating a riot of heat stroke and spectators who couldn't hear or see.

Arthur Sewall then stood to give a short speech. He kept it brief, perhaps aware he'd lost all but the most faithful of Bryan supporters.

Andrew wondered if Bryan hadn't just lost a whole nation. All those days of planning, the terrible heat, the crowds, and . . . that was it? Andrew supposed he should have been glad the riot he'd been anticipating had never materialized, but he couldn't help but feel disappointed.

Charlie seemed utterly mystified by all of this, too. "I couldn't make sense of Bryan's speech," he said quietly as they stood after the rally ended.

"Nor I. What a disappointment. I'd heard he's a wonderful speaker, but that was dull and . . . long."

"Yes."

A harried Finnegan approached and said in his lilting Irish accent, "The clean-up crew is about to take over. There's no need for you to stay here and continue to cook in your suit. Go home, Mr. Ritchley. You as well, Mr. Evans." Finnegan paused. "You're sure you've never worked in the police department before, Mr. Evans?"

Charlie laughed softly. "I believe I would have remembered."

"You were a great help to us tonight. If you want a more permanent job, I may have one for you. That is, if Ritchley doesn't hire you first."

Charlie's eyes went wide. "I . . . yes. I would be interested."

Finnegan nodded. "When the heat clears, if you still aren't permanently employed, please come by my precinct. Ask for me there. Ritchley can give you directions."

Charlie nodded. "Thank you. Sincerely."

Andrew and Charlie watched Finnegan walk away.

"How is it I have turned from breaking the law to helping enforce it in just a few days?" Charlie asked.

"It has been a strange week," said Andrew. He turned to Charlie. "Let's adjourn."

Charlie nodded, still looking a little dazed. "Yes, please. I thought you'd never ask."

Nicky took another sip of his drink while he waited for Hank to speak. Then a movement on the other side of the room caught his eye. He wasn't sure what had brought the man walking along the opposite wall to his attention, if it was just the brief movement of his arms or his shoulders, a familiar gesture that pulled at something in Nicky's memory, but suddenly the dip of those shoulders arrested him and could not look away. It took him a long moment to determine why. Then it hit him all at once.

Brigham Knight.

He gasped.

Hank apparently was not paying attention and, as he faced Nicky, he would not have seen the movement behind him. Instead, he said, "I have been giving some thought to our respective situations, and I can't help but think perhaps there is something to this idea we could be together, that is, you could—"

"Hank," said Nicky.

"No, let me finish. I want to say this—"

"Hank, not now. This is not the place to have the conversation." In his head, Nicky was practically screaming. He knew he was the sort who could attract attention, but he didn't want to attract Knight's. He knew all about how his blond hair reflected the light—something he'd discovered after playing around with the stage lights at Bulgaria while wearing a series of blond wigs—and he knew the scarf at his throat was bright enough to penetrate even the dim light, and he knew he tended to gesticulate wildly when he talked, which would catch the eye of a passerby the same way the sudden flurry of a flock of pigeons on the sidewalk could call to anyone who happened to be walking by. Maybe Knight wouldn't recognize Nicky, but he would definitely recognize Hank.

Hank's face fell. "Oh. Well, I suppose it does not matter. It was a foolish idea."

Oh, god. Hank was about to say or do something romantic and Nicky had crushed it, hadn't he? Nicky brought his hands to Hank's cheeks and cupped his face. "Oh, no, my love, no. That is not at all the issue. I want to hear every word of what you have to say. It's just that Brigham Knight is on the other side of the room, and frankly that is my greater concern right at this moment."

Hank's eyes went wide. "He's here?"

"Yes, I believe so. Behind you."

Hank let out a burst of swear words.

Nicky's horror at having spotted Knight had delayed the realization that Knight seeing Hank here could create a whole new batch of trouble.

"Should we leave?" Nicky asked. That seemed the best solution. They'd need to abandon the drinks Hank had probably paid a premium for, but they were also much closer to the doorway out than Knight was. All they had to do was go back up the stairs and then quickly move to another block. Knight would never even know they were there.

But Hank hesitated. He seemed to have frozen in place.

"What are you waiting for?" Nicky asked.

"We could catch him in the act."

"Hank."

Hank seemed to be more in tune with what was happening on the other side of the room than with Nicky, suddenly.

"Where is he?" Hank asked.

"Almost directly behind you."

Nicky, scandalously, was not wearing a hat, but Hank was. Nicky pulled the brim of the old dusty bowler over Hank's eyes and then hooked his hand around Hank's neck. He moved in as if he were going to kiss Hank, but instead turned slightly so Hank could see the back of the room by moving his head. Nicky watched Hank's gaze follow the man across the room.

"It's definitely Knight," Hank whispered.

"I know." Nicky didn't want to lose sight of the objective here, but being this close to Hank was distracting. Even as sweaty as he was, Hank smelled good, salty and musky, a bit like sex. The stubble on his chin and the hair at the edge of his mustache brushed against Nicky's bare cheeks.

"I should follow him," Hank whispered.

"He'll see you."

Hank put his hand on the small of Nicky's back. They swayed slightly in a strange approximation of dancing. "When will I have an opportunity like this again?" Hank clutched at Nicky pulling him close. "I could catch him in the act. Suppose he is here tonight to find another victim. If I catch him before he kills again, I could be saving that young man and any others who come after."

"Or you could make it clear who you are and why you're here and he marches into Police Headquarters tomorrow morning and tells everyone. Then you are no longer a police inspector and can do nothing to save any of Knight's intended victims." Nicky leaned close again and pressed his hand more firmly against Hank's neck. He hoped he portrayed the illusion they were having a quiet, intimate moment. "You said yourself, your partner is no longer interested in helping you solve these crimes. Certainly no other member of the police department has the time to bother with saving the so-called morally corrupt men of Greenwich Village. You're our great hope, Hank. Don't throw it away by getting caught."

Hank dipped his head. He briefly rested it on Nicky's shoulder before he picked it back up. "You're right. I do not know why I feel so reckless. It feels like a wasted opportunity, but perhaps we *should* leave."

Nicky imagined he could see the calculations happening behind Hank's eyes. Perhaps this was a chance to catch Knight doing something illegal, but it could just as easily incriminate Hank. It was a difficult decision to navigate.

And, indeed, they waited too long to decide.

"He's headed this way," Hank whispered.

Before Nicky could figure out what was going on, Hank had taken both of their glasses, put them on a table, and then grabbed Nicky's hand to yank him out of the room.

As they ascended the stairs, Nicky asked, "What are we going to do?"

At the top of the stairs, Hank pulled Nicky up and then shoved him out the door. "You're leaving."

"What?"

Hank looked around and then walked out onto the street. Nicky followed. Hank said, "You have to leave."

"What? Without you? Why?"

"It's one thing for me to get caught here. I can take care of myself. I will figure out what to say to my superiors. I'll tell them I followed the suspect here. But you can't be seen with me. If Knight decides to retaliate, he may come after you. It's for your own safety that I ask you to leave."

Nicky understood what Hank said and even saw some wisdom in it, but it felt wrong to leave Hank there to fend for himself. "Are you certain that is the best course of action?"

"Yes. Let me pursue Knight. Let me catch him at his game. That is my profession. It is what I have been trained to do. You must leave and get to safety. All right?"

A flurry of emotion swelled up in Nicky. He was terrified, exhilarated, worried for Hank, worried for himself, and so touched Hank wanted him to stay safe. He wanted to tell Hank this last week had been amazing, and though he now sensed it was coming to a close, he would not soon forget it.

But instead, all he said was, "All right. I'll go. I'll be home later if you care to call on me when it's all over. Be careful, Hank."

"I will be."

Nicky reached over and briefly squeezed Hank's hand. Hank smiled faintly before he turned and went back into the saloon.

Nicky decided to walk home, so he turned and walked back toward his apartment. But before he'd gone more than half a block, a hand clamped down over his mouth. His back met with a wall of muscular chest. In his ear, his abductor hissed, "So you're Brandt's little plaything, are you? Do you suppose he'll miss you?"

Then pain blossomed on the side of Nicky's head and everything went black.

Knight wasn't in the Pit when Hank returned. Hank walked the perimeter, cut through the center, spoke with a few patrons, and became increasingly convinced Knight had either found his victim for the night while Hank was upstairs or he'd left. But how could he have left? Hank had never taken his eyes off the entrance. He would have seen Knight leave.

To the bartender, Hank asked, "Is there a way out of here besides the front?"

"There's an exit out the back. It's only really used by employees, but—"

Hank ran out the back before the bartender finished speaking.

There was a short hallway with slimy walls that led to a staircase up to street level. The sour sweetness of discarded liquor bottles and stale beer stung Hank's nostrils as he rose to the street. He saw a trash bin had been kicked over and its contents spilled on the flat stone that paved the area behind the saloon.

Hank stumbled through the trash area and emerged onto Mercer Street, a little surprised to be there at first. It took him a moment to get his bearings. That may have proved a moment too long, because there was no sign of Knight or anyone here, aside from a few people clearly intent on making the street their bed for the night, and a couple of children on a fire escape up above.

Although there in the gutter was a bit of red fabric.

Nicky.

It wasn't Nicky's red scarf. The material was wrong, as Hank saw when he picked it up. But it might have been used by Knight as a kind of decoy or a way to lure potential victims. Or it belonged to another man frequenting this part of Greenwich Village and it had been discarded either because of the heat or during a tryst in this crowded not-quite alleyway. Or it was entirely a coincidence. Hank tossed it aside and stood, not sure what to do now.

To the children up on the fire escape, who probably had the best view, Hank shouted, "Hey, did you see a man blow through here a few minutes ago?"

A little girl nodded.

"Did he have dark hair? Was he wearing nice clothes?"

"He had on a hat," said a boy. "It was a nice hat."

It wasn't much to go on, but it must have been Knight. How else would he have gotten out of the building. "Thanks. Be safe up there. Try to stay cool. Drink water if you can."

"Sure, mister," said the boy, his voice laced with sarcasm.

Hank sighed. This neighborhood was no place for kids, let alone kids that young hanging out on a fire escape to get away from the heat inside. Lord knew what all they saw at night. Hank wanted to tell them to go back inside, but knew better. Instead he gave them a little wave and moved on.

He looped back toward Bleecker, worried he was too late. There wasn't much to see there, either. A few men lingered near the front entrance to the Pit. Hank approached.

"Crazy night, eh?" Hank said, trying to sound casual.

"I'll say!" said one of the men.

Another man with curly hair that grew longer than his ears and what looked like makeup on his face in the waning light elbowed the first man in the ribs. "We were just nattering on about the heat. 'Hot enough for ya?' You know. And then this man in a dark coat comes sneaking about."

Hank leaned close. "A sneaky man, you say. Someone I should keep my eye out for?" He added what he hoped would be interpreted as a flirtatious expression at the curly-haired man, who was effeminate in much the way Nicky was, though not nearly as attractive.

The curly-haired man laughed. "If you're going to go leering at men like that, then I imagine so. We watched him abscond with a gentleman just up the block."

Hank's heart seized. "Abscond?"

"I assumed they were together," a third man said. He was wearing a bowler with a red ribbon tied around it and sported a handlebar mustache that curled on the ends. "Not the first time I've seen a bit of rough play in this neighborhood."

"The man he absconded with, what did he look like?"

Hank must have sounded too eager, because all three men gave him an odd look. "Oh, uh, a bit of a fairy. Blond hair, red scarf. Quite lovely, actually." The first man looked back up the street as if he might still find the man standing there. "I might have tried my luck, you know, had our darkly-dressed friend not taken him away."

"Which direction did they go?" Hank asked.

Now everyone looked concerned. "Er, why?" asked the curly-haired man.

Hank stepped forward and lowered his voice. "I tell you this not to alarm you but because I want you to be careful with whom you go home tonight. I am a police officer investigating a series of murders committed on the Bowery."

Everyone gasped and balked and tittered. It almost looked as though they might run off.

But Hank pushed on, hoping his friendliness would buy him time enough to explain himself. "I am a man of, I would guess, inclinations similar to yours, so you will come to no harm at my hand if you help me right now. I happened to spot my suspect in the Pit just a few moments ago and I believe he escaped through the Mercer Street exit of the building. He may have come back up here. You say he absconded with a man who fits the description of my . . ." Here Hank stalled, not sure how to quantify Nicky. He sighed. "My lover. He's about this tall." Hank held up his hand to approximate Nicky's height. "Blond, thin, and he wore a gray suit and a red scarf."

"That could be him," said the man in the bowler. "Oh, dear. It looked like they knew each other or were just playing around. That's been known to happen around here at night, especially one such as this when everything feels so hot and crazy."

"They went toward the Bowery," said the first man.

"Thank you kindly, fellas. And like I said, be careful tonight."

Hank ran down Bleecker toward the Bowery, though he knew he was likely too late. When he got to the corner, he looked both ways and . . . nothing.

He cursed.

If Knight had really taken Nicky, which Hank still wasn't completely certain of, he could still be nearby. But where would they go? A dark alley? Hank jogged down the street and looked between the crevasses between buildings and saw nothing. Panic was making it hard to think, but Hank looked around him as he ran through possibilities. Would Knight have known Nicky was with Hank, or was his abduction a coincidence? Could Knight be trying to get to Hank by taking Nicky? Could they have gone uptown to Knight's house? That was a good distance from where Hank now currently stood. He supposed Knight could have pulled Nicky into a cab. Hank watched one labor up the Bowery, the horse panting as it went. So Hank jogged up the street, hopping to peek into the open cabs for anyone who looked like Knight or Nicky.

Then all of a sudden a wave of dizziness hit him, so powerful he doubled over. Cold sweat broke out all over his skin as he leaned on his knees and tried to collect his breath. It was still unbearably hot, too hot to run after cabs, too hot to be wearing the coat he had on, too hot to do much of anything but stand there panting. As the dizziness waned, Hank stood back upright but knew an opportunity had been missed. Even if the horse driving the cab were just plodding along, a cab headed uptown would already be well ahead of Hank.

And that still assumed Hank's guess was right.

Hoping against hope Nicky had merely gone home, Hank walked to Nicky's apartment. He spent most of the trip there turning over worst-case scenarios in his head.

He questioned why he was so invested. Nicky was a witness and a good lover, but Hank had been preparing himself to move on when the case wrapped.

Except he didn't want to. He wanted to keep Nicky in his life.

He reached Nicky's building in what felt like record time. The door was propped open and a man wearing only trousers and a scuffed pair of shoes leaned against it. As Hank approached, he could smell sour liquor and vomit, and the man's eyes had the tell-tale glassiness of a drunk. Hank pushed past him and ran up the stairs. He pounded on the door to Nicky's apartment. Then he leaned his head on the door, hoping to hear, "Just a moment, darling, I'll be right there."

But there was nothing.

"If you're in there, Nicky, please come to the door," Hank yelled. "It's Hank. I just need to know you're all right."

But he knew it was futile.

Hank's next stop was Club Bulgaria. Not even Charlie seemed to be there tonight. Hank pulled aside one of the working boys and said, "I'm looking for Paulina."

"It's her night off, mate," the boy—and he really looked young enough to be barely on the brink of manhood—said. "But try back tomorrow." He had a bit of a cockney accent, but whether it was real or a put-on was hard to say.

"There's a boy who works here named Charlie."

"Not here either. Hasn't been to work all week, in fact. If he's your favorite, you're out of luck, as I think he might be out of a job." Then the boy ran his hands up Hank's chest. "I'm sure I'd do all right by you, though. You're right handsome, you are."

"Look, if Charlie or . . . Paulina come by, I need to speak to them right away. My name is Hank. Will you tell them to call on me either at home or the Seventeenth Precinct house?"

The boy's eyes went wide. "Are you a copper?"

"Yes," Hank whispered. "I will not arrest you. I just need to find Paulina."

"Is she in trouble?"

"No. Not how you mean. I fear she may be in danger. That goes for you, too. Be extremely careful with the gentlemen you entertain tonight. There is a killer among them."

The boy nodded solemnly.

Hank walked back out onto the Bowery, fretting he'd never catch up with Nicky. He hailed a cab and went west to his house, hoping Nicky had gone there to surprise him. But there was no sign of Nicky there, either.

With some reluctance, Hank faced the fact Knight had taken Nicky. Hank didn't know where to look and he was losing time. The best idea he had was to search Knight's home. He watched a cab lurch up the street with some effort and decided he might get uptown faster if he took the elevated train. That meant walking back east, though, and every bit of time he spent traveling was time Nicky might be suffering at the hands of Knight. If Andrew's assumption that Knight had also assaulted poor Charlie was true, and if Knight was indeed capable of the worst kind of violence, then who knew what kind of danger Nicky might be in.

It took nearly a half hour to get uptown, according to Hank's pocket watch. He started to run toward Fifth Avenue when, again, the heat thwarted him. He had to pause and lean against a building to catch his breath and keep from fainting. He had trouble breathing, too, although that was as much from worry over Nicky as it was from the heat.

When Hank arrived at Knight's house, it was empty and dark. The house was sandwiched between two other narrow houses, so there was no way to see into or get around the house.

He walked up and gazed into the dark window at street level. It was obscured slightly from the street by the staircase that went up to the first-floor stoop. But when Hank got close, his heart rate sped up. He tried to formulate a plan beyond "grab Nicky and run."

But the more he examined the window, the harder his heart sank. No one was here.

He backed up and walked up to the front door. No signs of life. From what Hank could see the windows were all dark. Of course, it would make sense for Knight to conceal the fact he was home.

Then a voice off to Hank's left shouted, "You there!"

Hank turned and saw an old man poking his head out of the front door of the house next door. "Yes?"

"Are you skulking about Mr. Knight's house?"

"I am looking for Mr. Knight. He doesn't seem to be answering his door. Do you know if he's home?"

The man stepped out onto his stoop and crossed his arms over his chest. "My wife makes something of a habit of watching the comings and goings of Mr. Knight. A dreadful occupation, if you ask me. Mr. Knight leaves at all hours of the day and night on lord knows what sorts of missions. He's an architect, not a police officer."

"Well, I am a police officer," Hank said. He pulled his badge from his pocket and flashed it at the man.

The man seemed delighted. He clapped his hands once and leaned forward. "Has he finally gotten caught at something for which you will arrest him?"

"I'm afraid so," said Hank.

"Well, I'm sorry to say he is not in. My wife told me right before we sat down to a late dinner that he had gone outside. The front door has a rusty hinge, you know, and it squeals like a cat caught under a carriage wheel when he comes and goes, so we always hear it. Even the door downstairs makes this dreadful clanging sound because the mailbox bangs against the iron gate."

Hank peered over the side of the staircase to the downstairs entrance, which was built into the stairs. There was indeed a large metal mailbox hanging onto the outside gate there, and it looked like one of the screws was loose, such that the mailbox was hanging slightly ajar.

"I see," said Hank.

"He has not been home, or we would have heard. That, and the missus is always curious about him."

"Are there any other entrances to the house?"

"I daresay no. Well, you can get in from the back yard. But we can see it from the terrace out back on which we were having dinner. Too dreadfully hot to eat inside, you know."

"In other words, Mr. Knight is not here."

"We would know if he were, certainly."

Hank felt defeated. He'd just about run out of places to look. "It is quite late for dinner," Hank pointed out.

"Yes, well, it is also quite late not to be in bed, but Essie has trouble sleeping these days, you see. So we were sitting out on the terrace, hoping to cool off, just chatting, you know. I came to the front of the house to grab a cigar from the case I keep by the window when I saw you hovering near the door. Thought you might be Knight himself. I have a spare key, you see."

A bit of hope fluttered in Hank's chest again. "May I borrow the key? I need to make sure Knight is not home."

"Ah, yes, of course. Anything for the New York City Police Department. Just one moment, if you please."

The man went back inside. He emerged a minute later with the key. Hank bounded down the stairs of Knight's house and up the stairs of his neighbor.

"I take it you do not like Knight much," Hank said as he accepted the key.

"Dreadful man. How his family abides him, I've no idea."

"And where are they?"

"Off on Long Island at their vacation home. Near Oyster Bay, I hear. Trying to get friendly with the Roosevelts to hear Mr. Knight tell of it. They left a week ago. Mr. Knight told me he had to stay behind on some sort of company business."

"I see," said Hank. "What of his butler?"

The man scoffed. "Bane is his name. I believe this is his night off."

"So the house is truly empty." Hank looked around, wondering what to do.

"He is a strange man," the man whispered conspiratorially. "Out at all hours of the night, keeps dubious company when his wife is not home."

Hank took a deep breath. "All right."

"Why are you arresting him?"

Hank had to tamp down a reaction to the man's giddy enthusiasm. "He may be a suspect in a violent incident downtown."

The man nodded gravely. "I knew I couldn't trust him. Well, I hope you find him. Just slip the key into the mail slot when you've finished."

"I will. Thank you, sir."

Hank shook hands with the man and then went back next door. He let himself into a house he was now quite convinced contained no living people. Nor would there be any evidence here. Even if there were a whole passel of servants willing to keep Knight's secrets, Mrs. Knight likely took some responsibility for the upkeep in the main rooms on the first and second floor, or at least periodically entertained company there. Knight wouldn't leave anything incriminating where she could find it.

Hank toured what was clearly Knight's study on the second floor but found nothing of interest there beyond some ledgers. Knight was in the red, so there was that. Hank wondered if his wife knew. More to the point, though, Hank was convinced, other than bringing the occasional boy home for a romp in bed, this was not the scene of his crimes.

So what was?

The hour was late and the heat was still unrelenting when Hank slipped back outside. He'd spent a good hour looking over the house from attic to basement and had found nothing.

Where the devil had Knight taken Nicky?

After dropping the key in the neighbors' mail slot as told, Hank walked back to the elevated train, at a loss for ideas. He figured he'd go back home again, wash up and take stock of the situation, and then head back out to see what he could find.

It took nearly an hour to get back home as the elevated train squealed and struggled on the track with some sort of mechanical difficulty. By the time Hank returned to his house, it was well into the wee hours of the morning.

And there was a note taped to his door.

Day 9

Thursday, August 13

Temperature: 90°F

Chapter 18

The headlines that day boasted of Bryan's spectacular failure, but Andrew thought the real news was that it felt like the heat might finally be waning.

He sat at his desk, picking apart the *Journal*, which had a special section with the headline, "Heat More Deadly than a Great Disaster." The article went on to argue this plague of heat had lasted longer and killed more people than any in the city's history. Apparently it had killed more people than the Great Chicago Fire. Andrew wondered if this could be true, not that it mattered. This whole week had been horrific. One death was too many.

Andrew tossed the special section aside—he didn't need a newspaper to tell him how hot it was—and turned instead to other news. The heat seemed to have expedited the end of the tailor's strike that had begun nearly two weeks ago. Violence had broken out in the Lower East Side tenements the day before.

And the body of a man presumed to be a working boy had been found on Eighth Street near Cooper Union.

Andrew cursed.

Roosevelt himself burst into Headquarters with a trail of reporters behind him. He stopped by Andrew's desk. "Ritchley. I've just come from the mayor's office. I've devised a plan that will offer some relief to the masses, but I need your help."

"All right." Andrew stood and followed Roosevelt into his office. Roosevelt left the door open, probably for the reporters to overhear whatever bit of brilliance he now intended to impart.

"We will be distributing ice to certain neighborhoods via the precinct houses. It will take some effort to coordinate this distribution, so I'll need you to get in touch with the captains. I will be overseeing the distribution myself."

"Ice, sir?"

"Indeed, some of the very poorest citizens have had no relief from this heat. And, as you may be aware, Mr. Morse controls the ice interests in the city. I have finally got Mayor Strong to agree to some measures that would allow the police department to distribute ice for free. Ice is on its way downtown as we speak, so we need to get moving. I would be dee-lighted if you would help me with this matter, Mr. Ritchley."

"Of course, sir."

"Other measures are to be made as well. The public floating baths will be open all night instead of closing at dusk."

Andrew nodded, although that struck him as an odd decision. The floating baths were merely areas of the rivers opened to the poorest New Yorkers for bathing. They were meant to be used primarily for hygiene, not recreation. So few of the tenement buildings had adequate running water, even after the law changed to require it. He supposed there was some wisdom to keeping the baths open around the clock so some of the tenement residents could find some relief.

"We will also," Roosevelt went on, "be suspending the ordinance against sleeping in the parks. If people are going to sleep outside, it might as well be in the parks and not on the streets."

Andrew pulled out his notepad and jotted it all down. He then spent the next hour alternately using the telephone to contact the captains of each precinct—particularly those below Fourteenth Street—and sending Charlie and the other runners out with clear written instructions. At one point late in the morning, Roosevelt stripped to his shirtsleeves and helped haul great blocks of ice off the trucks with his own arms. He set up a station on Mulberry Street and then dispatched a group of officers to bring ice to the homes of every family in a five-block radius. The written instructions Andrew dispatched commanded the captains of each precinct to do much the same.

Once Roosevelt was satisfied the ice distribution at Headquarters was going according to his wishes, he took one of the other secretaries and announced he was going to walk around to investigate whether everything was happening at the other precincts according to his plan. He put Andrew in charge in his absence.

That flurry of activity done, Andrew returned to his work. He'd left the story about the dead man on Eighth Street page-up on his desk, so that was the first thing to snare his attention. He was about to track down the arresting officer when Hank came barreling into the precinct office. He was out of breath and frantic.

"Nicky," Hank said, panting. "He's been taken."

"Taken?"

"Brigham Knight."

Panic lanced through Andrew like a spike of ice to the heart. Could the dead man reported in the paper be Nicky?

"How do you know?" Andrew asked.

"He means to blackmail me. Sent a note to my house this morning telling me if I came after Nicky, he'd expose us both."

Andrew couldn't tell if this was good or bad news. "Another body was discovered last night."

Hank clamped a hand over his mouth. "Not Nicky. Knight wouldn't have power over me any longer if he killed Nicky."

"Correct, it would be a foolish move. Presumably this man expired before Nicky was taken. But I would not underestimate him. He's killed before and likely plans to again." Andrew scanned the paper. "The body was found around nine o'clock last night."

"That was before Nicky and I parted ways." Hank grunted. "Knight. Knight has Nicky. He took Nicky last night from right under my nose. I was out all night looking for him. Then this was at my house when I returned home." Hank thrust a piece of paper at Andrew.

Andrew took it and read it.

I have your precious plaything. He's alive, though perhaps not for long. Try to come after him and I'll tell Mr. Roosevelt what you do when you're off duty.

"Christ," Andrew whispered.

Charlie walked over with a stack of newspapers. "Here were those papers you asked for, Mr. Ritchley."

"Yes, thank you."

"Charlie," whispered Hank.

Charlie turned and saw Hank. His eyes went wide and he gasped. "You're the fellow from that night at Bulgaria. The one who wanted to meet Paulina."

Hank nodded. "Yes, and I apologize for our meeting again under somewhat trying circumstances, though I am also curious as to what you are doing here."

"I got him a job," said Andrew. "Basically a department errand boy. We had to fudge his employment history a bit, but luckily he was charming enough no one questioned my desire to hire him."

"Oh," said Hank. "Well, I am glad, then, you've managed to get out of what must have been a difficult situation."

"Er, yes." Charlie looked at Andrew, a question in his eyes.

"Charlie, allow me to introduce Inspector Hank Brandt."

It took a moment for Charlie to put the pieces together, but Andrew could see the moment he did. He relaxed, the tension leaving his body. "All right. Nice to see you again. Trying circumstances?"

"Something has happened to Nicky," said Hank.

Charlie clapped a hand over his mouth. "Oh, dear. What is it?"

Hank handed Charlie the note. He looked a bit choked up.

Charlie took a long time to read a note. Andrew had seen over the last few days his reading skills were not quite up to the task of doing more than some light filing, but he could read if given enough time to work out how all the letters fit together. When he finished, he pointed to a word on the page. "This? This is referring to Nicky?"

Hank said sotto voce, "Yes. He and I have been . . . spending time together." He took a deep breath. "I don't know who to go to with this, but I fear it's out of my depth. I trust you, both of you. Nicky and I were at a saloon in Greenwich Village last night when we spotted Brigham Knight. I wanted Nicky to get out so he could get home to safety, but I was too late. I thought we'd left the saloon without Knight seeing us, but I must have been mistaken, because he snagged Nicky when I turned away." Hank looked so worried and shaken up Andrew wondered how clearly he was thinking, but the danger to Nicky must have been significant.

"What have you—" Andrew started to ask.

"I've run all over the city. Didn't sleep last night. At first I was just looking for Nicky. Then I got the note. He's not at Knight's house uptown, by the way, so Knight must have another residence or something, or at least a place he can go. I thought maybe we could check the housing records or any media to see if he mentions another house."

"I'm ahead of you there," Andrew said. He reached over to the stack of papers Charlie had just left on the desk. "I had Jacobs down in the records office pull any newspapers that mention Brigham Knight. I really only wanted a picture to be used to verify some witness accounts." He thumbed through the pile until he found what he was looking for. It was a front-page story about a real-estate development deal near Madison Square. Accompanying the article was an image of the lead architect: Brigham Knight.

When Andrew picked up the paper and held it up, Charlie immediately started shaking.

"This is the man, isn't it?" Andrew said.

Charlie nodded.

Hank frowned. He looked grim. He must have understood what Andrew's vague question meant. "We must find Nicky," Hank said.

Hank paced in front of Andrew's desk. Andrew watched him for a moment before offering, "You could go to the clerk's office and check the property records. See if Knight owns property beyond his house uptown. Charlie can go with you to help."

"Yes," said Charlie. "I want to."

Hank looked back and forth between Andrew and Charlie. He looked like he'd aged ten years since the last time Andrew had seen him; his brow was furrowed, his eyes were watery, his hair was disheveled, he frowned. "All right," Hank said.

"Then we'll storm the gates. Don't go in there alone. Find an address, scope it out, yes, but come to me when you're ready to go in there. I'll assemble a team for you."

Hank shook his head. "That will take too much time."

"Storming in there on your own will get you killed."

Hank groaned. "God, I need to get to him. Standing around talking about it is accomplishing nothing."

Andrew reached over and put a hand on Hank's shoulder. "Take Charlie to the records office or talk to the clerk. Find Knight's other possible residences. Talk to his friends. Do whatever you have to do to make a list of possible locations. I will put a team together of friendly officers in the meantime." Andrew met Hank's gaze, hoping to portray he knew which officers would not object to the cause. Because there was something of a fraternity among queer officers Hank had never quite been a party to—he seemed to prefer his outsider status—but Andrew knew who he might be able to get on board, provided they were on duty today. "We'll reconvene here in an hour. Please do not act rashly. We'll get him, Hank, but if you act in haste, you'll get yourself killed."

Hank grimaced but said, "All right." He signaled to Charlie and then left the room.

So Andrew went to his desk to assemble the team.

When Nicky came to, the walls were crying.

It took him a moment to realize he sat in a dimly-lit room underground and the tears were just condensation. The room was so hot and humid even the walls were sweating.

He had a doozy of a headache but otherwise seemed to be in one piece. His hands were tied behind his back with what felt like very rough rope, and it rubbed against and tore into his skin as he pulled at it. He was on the floor of this sweating room and there was an eerie echo as water dripped off the ceiling and onto the hard floor.

A wild, unfocused moment passed while Nicky tried to recall exactly what had happened and where he was. The last thing he remembered was saying good-bye to Hank in front of the Pit and then turning to walk home. Everything after that was just . . . gone.

So how had he ended up in a sweaty basement?

A creak above his head alerted him to the fact he was not alone in the house, or whatever sort of building he was in.

Nicky came all the way awake in a rush as he realized his last conscious thought was of concern for Hank as he left, and he panicked as he tried to recall how he ended up in this room but couldn't. His memory was just blank blackness.

Where was Hank?

Footsteps on a nearby staircase didn't do much to calm Nicky down. In fact, he struggled to take in a breath as he wondered who had put him in this room and tied his hands. And, with his hands tied, he couldn't figure out how to get enough balance to stand.

Brigham Knight turned a corner and stared at Nicky.

Nicky leaned away, his back colliding with the wet wall.

"So you're awake," Knight said.

Nicky frantically tried pulling at the ropes binding his wrists, but that only served to scratch his skin.

Knight said, "I had my suspicions about Brandt the first time I met him. It was nice of you to confirm them last night. I saw you with him and I knew. Foolish of him to let you go."

"What do you intend to do?"

"At first, I merely intended to make trouble for Brandt. Take something valuable away from him. Perhaps even get a taste for myself." Knight leered at Nicky, which made Nicky feel ill. "Brandt surely knows who I am by now. He has identified me as the killer of those boys on the Bowery."

Nicky didn't say anything.

"I cannot be implicated in such a crime. Not that it was me, of course." Knight walked closer to Nicky. "So I shall keep you for now. If Brandt comes looking for you, I will immediately alert his superiors that he has a male lover and frequents places like the Pit."

Knight reached for something in his pocket and came back with a black object that Nicky didn't recognize at first. With a quick flick of his wrist, Knight revealed the object to be a folding knife. He ran a finger along the blunt edge.

"Tell me, sir," Knight said, "are you a prostitute?"

"No." At least Nicky could say so without hesitation.

"Mr. Brandt does not pay you for your services?"

"He has never given me a cent."

"So depraved, the two of you. Certainly my wife would not approve of such things. It's why the men who service me must die afterward. The dead cannot speak. One got away, but he'll likely meet his maker within the week if this heat keeps up."

Nicky's stomach rumbled and he worried he was about to revisit his last meal. He swallowed and his throat stung.

"Just how precious are you to Brandt?" Knight let out a sigh. "He can't be foolish enough to come after you. I've already informed him I plan to ruin him if he does. His career as a police inspector would be over and he'd likely end up in jail for his trouble. A career officer such as himself could not have that." Knight waved the knife and it caught the dim light of the bare electric bulb dangling precariously from the ceiling. "But suppose he is foolish enough to come for you? I cannot be caught. So I will ruin him either way. If not by reputation, then perhaps by slitting your pretty throat."

Nicky gasped. He really was going to be sick. He could feel his stomach burbling. "Please, no. Leave Hank out of this. If you want me, take me, but leave Hank be."

"Hank? You call your Mr. Brandt Hank? Of course you do." Knight chuckled. "Well, dearest, I shall take your pleas into consideration. You really are quite pretty. I like my prey to struggle a bit before I partake, however."

Nicky was sick then. His body felt like it was turning itself inside out. He leaned over and vomited on the hard, scuffed floor.

"Why did you have to do that?" Knight asked. "Perhaps I have terrified you? I am not so completely hideous. I might make a fine lover for all you know."

Nicky missed Hank. It was a tangible need. He didn't know how to face this situation, couldn't fathom how to get out of it, didn't know what to do. But Hank would know. With Hank at his side, Nicky could do anything.

Because Hank cared about Nicky as more than just a plaything. Hank cared about Nicky's well-being. Hank could very well have been scouring the city for Nicky right then.

Or Hank could have decided not to risk his job.

Not knowing how Hank would react to this situation didn't do much for Nicky's nausea. The room now smelled horrifically, but there was nothing to be done for it. Nicky just sat on the floor and stared up at Knight.

"I'll let you think about this for a bit. Stew in your mess. Then I'll be back because I intend to have you to determine what this Hank of yours finds so appealing. Or perhaps I'll pop uptown and let his friends the Coopers know what Hank does in his off hours. Or"— Knight brandished the knife, then ran his fingers over it again— "We'll just have to see what I'm possessed to do."

Nicky's stomach flopped as Knight left the room again. He was overcome with worry: worry for himself, worry for Hank, worry he'd never see the outside of this room again. The smell was barely tolerable, the heat oppressive, and he felt grimy all over. He listened to Knight's retreating footsteps with a sense of foreboding.

How much time had passed? Hank hadn't found him yet, which he didn't think boded well for his prospects. Unless it had only been a matter of minutes. The basement had no windows to the outside and no clock, so Nicky had no sense for the time of day.

There was no way to win. If Hank rescued Nicky, his career was over. If he didn't, Lord knew what Nicky's fate might be at the hands of Brigham Knight. But if Hank didn't find Nicky, perhaps life was not worth living.

With a pang in his chest, Nicky realized that in just a matter of days—and it had only been just over a week, hadn't it?—he had fallen hopelessly in love with one Henry Brandt.

He was doomed.

Chapter 19

The line of people waiting for ice outside Police Headquarters was already around the block before the ice had even been delivered. Women stood holding children on their hips and men in tattered suits stood behind them, with children playing alongside old people teetering on canes. Many people had boxes, baskets, towels, aprons, and all manner of receptacle ready to take the ice away. Once the ice had arrived, the officers started handing it out on the sidewalk, but it soon began to melt and the distribution had to be moved to the cellar inside the building. Andrew, meanwhile, stayed perfectly, unpleasantly hot inside, and thus was at his desk when George Stephens stormed the gates.

Andrew was writing out a note to the Seventeenth Precinct captain when he caught sight of Stephens. He finished the note and handed it off as Stephens arrived.

"A word, Mr. Ritchley?"

"I am quite busy."

"I understand. I just need a moment."

Andrew looked him over. His patience was thin. "Would you like to help me solve the issue of the city-wide *coffin* shortage? So many people have expired in the heat the city has run out of coffins. Can you believe that?"

"I am sympathetic, but I have an issue of some urgency."

"All right." Andrew stood up straight and looked right at Stephens. "What is it?"

"I believe Inspector Brandt is acting contrary to the central tenets of good police work. I wish to file a complaint."

Andrew nodded slowly. "You wish to file a complaint." Not that Stephens's request was a surprise, but Andrew couldn't see the urgency.

"Er, Mr. Ritchley?" asked one of the other runners.

"Yes?" said Andrew.

"Chief Conlin needs a word."

Andrew turned to Stephens. "Excuse me, Detective Stephens. I have to see to something for a moment. Please wait here and we'll see about your complaint."

Probably leaving Stephens to his own devices was a poor choice, but Andrew didn't see the alternative. He spent the whole of his meeting with Chief Conlin imagining Stephens measuring Roosevelt's office to plan his own decorating scheme.

Indeed, Andrew ran into Stephens standing outside Roosevelt's office. Andrew's arms were weighted down with a stack of reports, but he said, "Do you have any proof of impropriety on Hank Brandt's part?" He cocked his head toward his desk and started walking.

Stephens followed. "Not proof exactly, but I do believe he's been fraternizing with a witness. Is that not grounds for dismissal?"

Andrew couldn't hide his grimace. "What has led you to this belief?"

"He's been acting strangely, so I followed him last night on my way home. I happened to see him with our witness. They greeted each other as old friends."

Andrew sighed and eased the stack of reports onto his desk. "Could he have been questioning the witness?"

"I do not believe so. It was a male witness as well. As we discussed yesterday, I do not believe Inspector Brandt is entirely well suited for his position."

Andrew knew he was bearing the brunt of this complaint because everyone knew he had the ear of Commissioner Roosevelt. If Roosevelt knew one of his inspectors was fraternizing with other men, let alone male witnesses, he'd be sure to dismiss that inspector without prejudice. Andrew guessed Stephens's real motives leaned toward gaining Hank's position once Hank was out of the way.

"I'd like to investigate further," Andrew said, handing Stephens a form. "Record your complaint here and I'll look into it."

Stephens squinted at the form. "I will do this right now."

As Andrew started processing reports, Stephens sat at an unoccupied desk and filled out the form. He spent a lot of time looking up at the whirring fan overhead, probably thinking out his responses carefully.

Andrew tried not to let the fact Stephens was making a formal complaint concern him. It would be easy enough to circumvent the form. Stephens was likely unaware how close Andrew and Hank were as friends.

Stephens completed the form and handed it to Andrew with a flourish. Andrew pretended to look it over. "All right," he said. "I'll file this with the internal affairs bureau. Be aware that because of recent events, it may be a while before anyone gets to it. We've got our hands full with the aftereffects of the heated term."

"All the more reason to file it now, so it's in the queue. I merely want to be sure we have only the most upright men as officers in the Police Department."

"Of course. The police commission would have it no other way."

That seemed to satisfy Stephens, who shook Andrew's hand, nodded, and left.

The clerk at the records office managed to uncover a previous address for Brigham Knight, a little house on Pine Street, not far from Trinity Church if Hank's recollection of Manhattan geography was correct. The housing records further indicated the house had never actually been sold.

"This must be where he is," Hank said to Charlie. Then he headed for the door.

Charlie snagged his arm. "You heard what Andrew said. If you go there on your own, you could be killed. That will not be of much help to Nicky."

Hank knew Charlie was right, but that did not keep him from wanting to run straight for this house. Police Headquarters was back uptown, away from Pine Street.

"Perhaps I could go to the scene and look around. Verify Nicky is there. I won't go in until you arrive with the team Andrew is putting together."

Charlie shook his head. "What if Knight catches you? You can't go alone."

Hank groaned. This was an impossible situation. He worried every moment he wasted investigating or waiting was a moment that put Nicky into further danger.

"All right. We'll do it your way and speak with Andrew first."

"Thank you." Charlie touched Hank's upper arm. "He's my friend. I want to rescue him, too. I want for Nicky to be all right. But I want to be smart about it."

So they left the records office with a list of every one of Brigham Knight's previous home addresses, dating back to 1885, just in case. Hank hailed a cab back uptown. Andrew was in conference with a pair of officers at his desk when Hank and Charlie returned to Police Headquarters.

"Ah, Inspector Brandt," Andrew said as Hank approached. "May I introduce you to Officers Sherwood and Polk. They are with the eighth precinct."

Sherwood was vaguely familiar, but Hank couldn't remember ever having met Polk. He extended his hand to each man and said, "I'd tell you it's a pleasure to meet you, but I trust Andrew has given you the brief version of the circumstances."

Sherwood, who had dark hair and a neatly trimmed beard, said, "A young man has been kidnapped by the suspect in a series of murders you've been investigating."

"Ritchley says you can tie four murders and an assault to this same man," said Polk, who had light brown hair and a surprisingly light voice.

"I believe so, yes," said Hank. "And I believe our kidnapping victim is in grave danger."

Sherwood leaned close and said, "This victim has some sort of personal connection to you."

Hank's breath caught in his throat and a long moment passed before he could breathe again.

"I can vouch for these men," Andrew said. "Your secrets are safe."

Hank still struggled to get his breathing back to normal. He rubbed his chest where it hurt. The stakes were so hard to fathom. They were wasting time on pleasantries now, and who knew what fate had in store for Nicky, but Hank still worried he was about to be exposed. "You should be aware, then," Hank said, "my suspect, an architect named Brigham Knight, sent me a letter threatening to tell my superiors about my . . . about the role the kidnapping victim Nicholas Sharp plays in my life should I decide to try to rescue him."

"I suppose it comes down to who makes a more credible accuser," said Polk. "A seasoned police inspector combined with us as witnesses or a man accused of five counts of murder or assault?"

Andrew shot Hank a look that seemed to say, *See? I'm saving you.* Witnesses of good standing with the police department would likely prove invaluable should Knight decide to expose Hank's personal life. It was something Hank was too rattled to think of to do on his own, and he was deeply grateful to Andrew for being so level-headed.

"Yes," said Hank. "Which is why I'd like to go to this location with all possible haste." Hank showed everyone the paper on which he'd copied the Pine Street address.

As a group, they went outside. Andrew tried to talk Charlie into staying behind, which caused a brief delay and an awkward explanation as Andrew told Sherwood and Polk that Charlie was his new assistant. "Assistant. Of course," said Polk.

When they got to the yard in which the police vehicles were usually stored, they found it empty.

"I'm sorry, sir," said an officer posted near the entrance. "All available vehicles had to be deployed as ambulances. None are available."

"There are actual crimes being committed beyond those perpetrated by the weather," Andrew said, hopping mad now.

"How are we to get downtown if all police vehicles are engaged?" Sherwood asked.

"Cab," said Hank. "Come along."

Hailing a cab proved difficult. Most that drove by Police Headquarters were already occupied. Hank was about to yank people out of the next one that came along when Polk finally got one to stop. There wasn't really room for all five of them, but they made do, with Charlie half-sitting on Andrew's lap.

"Is there a plan?" asked Sherwood.

"Since I have you all with me," Hank said, "I have an idea."

There must have been a clock upstairs, because Nicky heard chiming. He held very still to count the chimes. It stopped after three. Was it three in the morning or the afternoon? Nicky bemoaned the fact he couldn't tell if it was day or night in this dark basement.

He supposed he should be glad Brigham Knight had mostly left him alone. Knight came down the stairs periodically, but he was more menacing talk than action. At one point he had come over and whispered in Nicky's ear, "You are a treat too sweet to leave alone for long," and then reached down and grabbed between Nicky's legs. That was the worst thing that had happened so far. Nicky was still whole, he still had his clothes on, and Knight had been pacing upstairs for what felt like an hour. There was a spot that must have been near a vent because Nicky could hear Knight mumbling to himself whenever he got to that spot.

The clock started to chime again, which seemed odd until Nicky realized this chime was different. Could it be the door?

There was a metallic squeal—Knight opening the front door perhaps—and then by some miracle, Knight and his visitor both stumbled into the spot where Nicky could hear them, because their voices rang through quite clearly.

"Terribly sorry to barge in on your afternoon," said a male voice Nicky didn't recognize. "But I work for the city and I've been going door-to-door to check on how people are faring in this heat. How are you today, Mr . . . ?"

"Knight. I seem to be all right," Knight said.

"I'm glad to hear it! Well, if you need any further assistance, you can of course go to your local police precinct. They will be giving away ice near City Hall later this afternoon, as well as at every police station, if that does not prove too difficult a walk for you."

An outsider, even a stranger, might be an opportunity. Nicky tried standing again, but couldn't quite get his feet under himself. Even when he crashed back to the floor, it hardly made a sound. He kicked his feet and he banged his bound hands against the wall, but there wasn't a sound much louder than a slap. It certainly wasn't loud enough for the strange man upstairs to hear.

Nicky let out a breath and fell back against the wall.

Then he heard a third voice upstairs. "Ah, Mr. Polk, sir, could I get a hand with something outside. And you, sir, you look like you've a strong back. Would you mind helping us out?"

Nicky listened to the patter of feet across the floor above him. The voices were mere murmurs now they'd moved out of the magic spot on the floor. If Nicky's guess was correct, they were headed toward the front door. There was a loud slam, but no steps back into the house. Had Knight gone outside?

Nicky resumed his attempt to stand up. He scrambled against the hard floor, his feet slipping. He fell back down with each attempt. He cried out in frustration.

If he could just get his weight forward enough to stand, if he could just wriggle out of the ropes around his wrists, if he could just . . .

He threw his shoulders forward as he attempted to stand. He succeeded in getting over his toes, but then he fell forward, his chest slamming onto the hard floor just before his chin hit. His teeth rattled together as he hit the ground.

That hurt, but he began to cry more out of resignation than anything else. He'd never see the outside of this basement. He'd never see Hank again.

So when he heard someone above say, "Nicky?" and that person sounded like Hank, Nicky thought he was hallucinating.

Then it came again. "Nicky? Are you down there?"

"Hank?" Nicky croaked out, not believing it.

There were footsteps in the far corner of the room, and they sounded like they were descending a staircase. Nicky's heart faltered. Knight could be headed down those stairs to exact his revenge, cutting off whatever magical place Hank's voice was coming from. Or Nicky really had imagined it and it was an omen of the end.

He thought of everyone just then: Hank, Brigid, Charlie, little Edith, his other brothers and sisters, Julie, everyone at Bulgaria, Hank. This could very well be the end, with Knight bounding down the stairs to kill him or whatever he was going to do.

But then Hank called out, "Nicky!" again.

"Hank!" Nicky's voice sounded more like a wheeze than a shout.

But then the voice echoed through the basement. From his vantage point, face-down on the floor, Nicky couldn't really lift his head to see, but feet were slipping over the hard floor and running toward him. "Nicky, my God. Nicky. Are you all right?"

"I can't get up," Nicky said.

"We don't have much time," Hank said. "I need to get you out of here."

Then Hank's arms encircled Nicky. It wasn't quite in the way he would have wanted, but it didn't matter. Hank scooped him up and carried him back toward the staircase. He cursed and murmured Nicky's name the whole way. Then he bounded up the stairs, jostling Nicky and making him realize how sore he was from sitting so long and then from falling on his chest. Nicky groaned, aching everywhere, but relieved Hank had come to rescue him after all.

Except they weren't out of danger.

"Knight is still in the house, isn't he?" Nicky asked.

"Not precisely."

Nicky wanted to ask what was happening, but he didn't dare. Not yet. He could only hope they'd have time to discuss it later.

Hank paused at the top of the stairs. He looked around. "Front or back?"

"Just get me out of the house," said Nicky.

Hank looked down at Nicky and met his gaze. He frowned. "Are you hurt? Did he hurt you?"

"I fell, but it was my own fault. Knight didn't do anything but threaten me."

"Thank God. You're in pain, though?"

"It's really not so bad."

"Out the front."

Before Nicky knew what happened, Hank jogged through the house. It seemed like a nice house, though it was sparsely furnished. And worn around the edges, actually.

Why was he thinking this?

"Can you walk?" Hank asked.

"I think so."

"Good. I have to put you down to get the front door open."

Hank lowered Nicky to his feet. Nicky's knees were wobbly and it took him a moment to find his balance, especially since his hands were still bound. He swayed, but Hank grabbed him and pulled him close. Then he pulled the front door open. As they stepped through the door, Hank wrapped his arm around one of Nicky's.

There were two men in suits standing with Knight on the sidewalk, looking at a horse. "No, the shoe looks fine. The horse didn't throw it," Knight was saying, "but I don't see what—"

"I got him," Hank announced.

Knight turned around and looked back at Hank, his jaw dropping.

His face shifted from surprised to angry in an instant, his eyebrows coming together and his mouth forming a scowl. He took a step back toward his stoop and raised his fist. "Brandt! I should—"

But then one of the suited men grabbed Knight's arm. "Brigham Knight, you are under arrest."

Nicky had no idea how to react. He stood there stupidly, watching as the two men wrestled Knight into a cab. One of them poked his head out of the cab window. "Can you get back to headquarters on your own?"

"I'll figure it out," Hank shouted back.

"Round up Ritchley and the kid, too. We'll meet you back at Ritchley's desk after we process this fella. Driver! To the Tombs. Hop to!"

It all happened so fast, Nicky's head spun.

Hank moved behind him and started to work on the bindings around Nicky's wrists. Nicky winced and grunted as the ropes rubbed against the raw areas of skin, but when the bindings finally loosened it was the sweetest relief.

Then, suddenly, Hank's arms surrounded him again, wrapped him up tightly and pressed his body against Hank's chest.

"Oh," Nicky said. "Hank, I missed you too, but we're in plain view of everyone on this street."

"I have been looking for you nonstop since last night. I am going to hold you. Bully to what anyone thinks."

Nicky melted against Hank. It felt nearly as good to be held as it did to finally have his arms free. So he wrapped those arms around Hank and that felt even better. "Since last night?"

"Knight proved difficult to track down. But thank God I found you before any further harm came to you."

"My wrists are likely bleeding into your shirt."

"I have other shirts."

So Nicky closed his eyes and let himself be held. Even in the heat, even in full view of whoever might be walking down the street, it felt good to be held. Nicky was dizzy as his anxiety began to seep away.

Hank stroked Nicky's back. "Are you sure you're all right? Knight didn't try anything with you?"

"He wanted to. He never got the chance, I suppose. I'm a little sore from being tied up, but I'll be all right. Honestly." Nicky took a deep breath. Their sweaty bodies were . . . fragrant together. Nicky didn't much mind. "You really searched for me since last night?"

"From the moment I realized Knight had left the Pit. I knew in my gut he had taken you. I spent the whole night searching all over town for you."

Nicky grasped onto Hank's back. "Why?"

"Why did I try to find you?" Hank squeezed Nicky harder. "Because somehow, in a mere nine days, you have become the most important person in my life. I don't know what I would have done if Knight had hurt you, or worse. I kept imagining you violated or dead and I raced to get to you before that happened. I am so relieved I made it."

Nicky's chest fluttered. "Oh, Hank. You made it. I'm glad you did. I worried you wouldn't." Nicky leaned away. "Where am I, anyway?"

"Downtown. A couple of blocks from Trinity Church. Knight kept a house here. I suppose it's his little, ah, pied-à-terre."

"The place he took his male lovers, in other words." Nicky turned out of Hank's arms and looked at the front door. "How did you get into the house?"

"Through the neighbor's house. They allowed us to get access through the backyard. I had to climb a fence."

Nicky laughed, more out of relief than mirth. "I'm impressed."

"I snuck through a back door and down to the basement while my colleagues distracted Knight. I left Andrew and Charlie next door, so I should go retrieve them. Then, alas, we must adjourn to Police Headquarters or the nearest precinct so I can record your version of what happened, or most of it anyway. We'll have to be careful about what you say. But I believe with the help of you and Charlie, we have enough to keep Knight behind bars for a very long time."

"That's good."

Hank nodded quickly and then turned to go down the stairs.

"Hank?"

Hank turned back.

"Before everything gets crazy, I just want to say something."

"All right."

Nicky took a deep breath. What he had to say was difficult, and it made his chest hurt. "Since we were separated yesterday, I don't think a moment has passed in which I have not thought of you. I don't know how we will manage what is to come, but I do know I do not want us to be separated again."

"Nor I," said Hank.

That reassured Nicky. "You're the most important person in my life, as well. It should not be possible, but I have fallen in love with you."

Hank's face went through an odd transformation, where his eyebrows rose and fell and his lips pursed and Nicky feared for a moment he'd taken it too far and Hank was disappointed. *Too much too soon.* Or Nicky was wrong, because who could fall in love in nine days?

But then Hank said, "I love you, too, Nicky. We'll find a way, all right? I don't know how, but we will."

Reassured, Nicky nodded. Then his knees went out.

Before he fell, Hank rushed up the steps and caught him.

"Perhaps I still need help."

"Let's go get Andrew and Charlie so we can take care of everything. Perhaps I can have the police surgeon look at you."

"I think I'm all right."

"Still. You've had a rough time."

"Yes."

Hank helped Nicky down the stairs. "It is nearly over."

"Yes. Let us put it all behind us."

Nicky and Charlie were deep in conversation on the other side of the room. Hank glanced up at them periodically, still worried about Nicky, although he had to finish filing his report before he could take Nicky home.

Andrew sat beside him, ostensibly to help him with the report.

"I solved this," Hank said. "There is not a doubt in my mind Brigham Knight is responsible for the murders on the Bowery. However, I am not altogether sure I can prove it, nor am I certain the city will even want to prosecute."

"It is difficult to predict," Andrew said. "They may decide they don't want the bother of prosecuting one of Mrs. Astor's Four Hundred. They may decide the murder of a few male prostitutes was a boon to the city. Or they may decide to make an example of a wealthy sodomite and others like him who enjoy slumming as if the neighborhoods of Lower Manhattan were a tourist attraction."

"Yes," said Hank.

"As a well-regarded police inspector, even an acting one, you have some clout, though I am sad to say Stephens is convinced he has some evidence of impropriety against you. At minimum, he thinks you were overzealous in your pursuit of this particular killer. I think he intends to publicly allege you took improprieties with a witness."

Stephens meddling in his affairs was the last thing Hank needed. He wondered how much traction Stephens could get. Certainly a goody two-shoes like Stephens would get the attention of Theodore Roosevelt and other members of the police leadership, certainly more so than Hank, who they tolerated because he got results rather than respected, or so it seemed to Hank.

"In other words," Hank said, "It may be for naught."

Andrew shook his head. "I am honestly not sure."

Sherwood and Polk walked in then. Polk sat on the edge of the desk Hank occupied and said, "You may feel gratified to learn one Brigham Knight is currently enjoying life as an inmate at the Tombs."

That did make Hank feel somewhat better. "I cannot thank you gentlemen enough for your help in this matter."

"Well, as he seems guilty of what he's been accused of," said Sherwood, "I must say I am pleased to be of service."

"It is a difficult case to prove," said Hank. "First of all, it is difficult to explain how I even knew to look for Nicky without implicating myself. But more to the point, Nicky was tied up in the basement when I found him and he has a few bruises but nothing serious. All we really succeeded in gathering evidence-wise is that Knight is guilty of kidnapping a man. Charlie can testify to one of his other crimes." Hank glanced back to where Charlie and Nicky were talking. He decided it would be inappropriate to disclose the nature of Knight's crime against Charlie. "But as for the murders themselves, I have no evidence to prove Knight was the killer beyond Nicky's assertion that Knight was the last person seen with one of the victims. I believe him, but that's hardly incontrovertible evidence. Any defense lawyer worth his salary will poke holes in my case at trial."

Sherwood frowned. "I suppose most lawyers may rely on the, er, unsavory nature of the victims and the circumstances under which they were killed. If he were charming enough, he might convince the jury Mr. Knight is a hero."

Hank let out a breath. It was frustrating to be in this position. A flimsy case, a personal involvement with said case, and a partner who had no interest in seeing him succeed was not a strong position to be in.

Unfortunately, there was not much Hank could do now but wait to see how everything played out.

The only other thing for certain was Hank's life had changed irrevocably since taking on this case.

Day 10

Thursday, August 14

The Heat Wave Breaks

Chapter 20

Clearly some calamity had befallen the front door to Hank's house, given all the pounding. Somewhat terrified the whole of the New York Police Department would bang their way into the foyer, he ran down the stairs. It wasn't the police. It was Nicky, who had left Hank's bed a few hours before with a key to the house, now pushing through the front door with several trunks. Charlie and Andrew brought up the rear with more trunks.

"What is going on?" Hank asked, not sure if he wanted an answer.

"Well, darling, if it is not obvious, I'm moving here."

"You're doing what?"

Andrew and Charlie lay down the last trunks in the foyer. Andrew glanced at Hank, and then back at the front door. "Hey, I need to be back at Police Headquarters, so . . ."

"Oh, I'll go with you," said Charlie.

"Subtle," said Hank.

Andrew gave Hank a salute and then took Charlie's arm and left the house. When the front door closed, Hank looked at Nicky.

"This was the best solution," Nicky said. "We found a boarding house on Twenty-first Street willing to take in my father for very little rent if he agreed to chip in with the household chores. So now Brigid and Antonio and their kids are moving into my apartment because I'm moving out. She swears they will pay the rent on it, even though they can't afford it. We'll split it, maybe, I don't know. But they're moving in this afternoon, so I had to get all my gowns out of the apartment."

Hank looked around at the four trunks now piled in the foyer. "All right. So you came here?"

"I'm your new boarder."

"Nicky."

"I know it is a great imposition. I acted rashly and I should have talked about it with you first. But after yesterday, I thought perhaps . . . well, that is to say . . ."

"You want to live with me?" Hank asked.

"Yes, my love. I do. I know the arrangement is perhaps a bit unorthodox. But I love you and I want us to be together, and I want Brigid to be all right, so this was the best solution I could come up with."

Hank was startled but not altogether opposed to the plan. "I must say this is a surprise. Then again, this is a lot of house for a bachelor. I suppose another person living here might fill it up better."

Nicky let out a little squeal and then launched himself into Hank's arms. Hank laughed as he caught Nicky, and then he hugged him tight. Honestly, he loved Nicky and welcomed the opportunity to see him more often.

"Oh, Hank," Nicky said. "You will not regret this, I promise. I will be the best houseguest you ever had."

"I thought you were my boarder."

"Whatever you wish, darling."

Hank held Nicky as he looked around at the trunks. He ran through the rooms of his house mentally, trying to determine how best to accommodate this new situation. "There's a second bedroom upstairs where you could store your things. That will be your room for appearance's sake. Not that I get many visitors."

"I appreciate that." Nicky leaned back and grinned. "Thank you for not getting angry about this."

Hank couldn't keep the smile off his face. He stepped forward and pulled Nicky closer into his arms. "I'm not angry. Like I said, I'm happy to have you."

"You didn't say that."

"Well, I mean it." Hank sighed, not wanting to pull away. "I have to be at Police Headquarters very soon for a meeting, but you may arrange your things upstairs in the room across the hall from the master bedroom. I am sure you will find a way to organize it to your liking. And you have a key now, so if you need to leave, you may at your whim."

Nicky sighed heavily against Hank. "Thank you."

"Are you working tonight?"

Nicky hesitated before speaking. "Well, normally yes, but I haven't been to sing in a few days, obviously, so I am not even certain I'd be welcome there anymore." He took a deep breath. "Do you want me to work there? Assuming I still have a job, that is."

"I want you to do whatever you want. If you want to work there, if you still need to be Paulina, then do it. If you want to get another job, that is all right, too. Do what is best for you."

"Really?"

"You said you needed Paulina. I would never force you to quit."

Nicky leaned against Hank. "I love you, darling."

Hank stroked his back. "You have freedom, Nicky. I don't need rent because I own the house. I'd just need a bit for upkeep and food. So if you need to pay rent on your apartment still, that is all right. If you don't want to work at Bulgaria, then find something else."

"Or I could be your kept man."

Hank laughed. "You may do anything you like as long as you stay in my life."

"I will."

"Good. Now I really need to get going or I am going to be late for my meeting."

"Is the meeting regarding Mr. Knight?"

"No, but that is something else I shall have to manage today." Hank wasn't looking forward to the scheduled meeting or to figuring out how to keep Brigham Knight behind bars. He knew his case was thin and he'd be hard-pressed to keep a man of such wealth incarcerated for more than a few days before Knight hired some fancy lawyer to spring him. If he hadn't already. Hank had Knight on kidnapping, but the murders would be difficult to make stick with such flimsy evidence. Hank trusted Nicky with his life, but at the end of the day, Nicky was a former prostitute and current female impersonator and would hardly stand up as a compelling witness in a court of law. Nor would Hank be able to explain how he came to pursue the case without fudging the truth, which he didn't want to do, either.

Which meant the kidnapping charges might be difficult to make stick as well.

And that didn't even compare to what revealing all of Nicky's dirty laundry to a courtroom would entail. Hank could hardly imagine it. Any lawyer worth his salt would impeach the characters of Nicky and Charlie—and Hank, most likely—before flashily declaring an upstanding gentleman such as Mr. Knight could not possibly be guilty of the crimes of which he was accused, and any jury in this city would vote for acquittal before lunchtime.

So the case was impossible.

But Hank said none of this to Nicky. "I'll see you tonight, all right? Perhaps we can have dinner together before you head off into the night."

Nicky pulled away and smiled. "That sounds quite pleasant. We may just domesticate each other."

"That is fine with me," said Hank.

When they left Hank's place, Andrew suggested to Charlie they walk uptown to police headquarters.

Andrew had a lot he wanted to say and no real way to articulate his feelings because he'd never quite been in this position before. Luckily, Charlie spoke first.

"I just wanted to thank you for all you've done for me this week," Charlie said. "You didn't have to help me, but you did, and I will be grateful forever."

"It was no trouble."

"Andrew. You gave me a place to sleep when I needed it. You found me a job at the police department which, trust me, is the last thing I expected. I've walked into Police Headquarters every morning for the last few days wondering how this became my life. That is, just a few days ago, I was still servicing men in the backroom at Bulgaria, but everything is different now."

Andrew preferred not to recall that time. He knew he shouldn't be jealous, but he felt a pang just the same whenever he thought of all those men who'd had Charlie before. Andrew swallowed and said, "I wanted to help you. It was my pleasure, honestly."

"About that," Charlie said. "You never even asked me for anything in exchange for your help. You are . . . you are an angel."

Andrew barked out a laugh. "Hardly." He sighed. "I mean, if I'm honest, part of my motivation for helping you is I think you quite handsome. That first night I met you, I found you striking."

"Yes, but many other men would have taken me in and then used me. You never did."

Andrew couldn't keep the blush off his face at the memory of some of what had transpired since Charlie had more-or-less moved into his apartment uptown. It certainly wasn't nothing. They had been sharing a bed for a few days now and were attracted to each other. Nature had taken its logical course.

"Well," said Andrew. "Perhaps not too forcefully."

Charlie smiled. "Andrew, anything that has happened between us is something I chose. Do you know how much freedom you have given me? You got me this job and I'm making money enough to support myself. I don't have to work for Julie anymore or service men unless I choose to. That is such a gift. You can't know how much it means to me."

"You could have quit at anytime."

"Yes, but no one wants to hire a washed-up working boy. I've tried getting other jobs. I'm too weak to build houses. I'm not smart enough to work in an office. I don't read well. There's not much I can do. But now I can work at the police department. Because of you."

"As a runner."

"I don't need a glamorous job. This is work I can do."

Andrew thought the work was beneath him and Charlie could do better, but perhaps his perceptions were not quite accurate. Charlie *was* smart, and could be taught to read better in order to get an even better job within the police department. Then again, as long as he wasn't working in Club Bulgaria or making money by letting men use his body, he was doing well enough for Andrew.

"What are your plans, now the heat seems to be breaking?" Andrew asked. They crossed the street and had to dodge a wayward pushcart that smelled of rotten fish.

Charlie paused. "Do you want me to leave your apartment?"

"What? No. Stay as long as you want. But aren't your things still at your boarding house?"

Charlie squirmed uncomfortably, twisting his hands together. "Well, it has been so long since I've been there the landlord has likely thrown away my things and rented my room to somebody else. I didn't have much there beyond some clothes. I had a uniform when I worked at Bulgaria, you know? But I suppose I don't need those clothes anymore."

"Hopefully you have enough income from the police department to buy all new clothes."

"Are you sure I am not imposing on you. I could find another boarding house, or make other arrangements, or—"

"No. Stay with me as long as you like." Andrew's voice came out sounding more harsh than intended. "That is, if you want to find another housing arrangement, I shall not stop you, but if you want to live with me, you may stay for as long as you feel comfortable there."

"You are a good man, Andrew Ritchley. Far better than I deserve."

"Stop saying things like that." Andrew felt the heat come to his face again.

"I shall be honored to be your guest for as long as you'll have me, and I promise to work hard at my job at the police department. I will earn my keep, I swear."

Andrew trusted Charlie would. "Than I shall continue to enjoy your company."

Charlie smiled, and it was innocent and bashful in a way that broke Andrew's heart. "I want to be with you in every way possible," he said.

"I as well."

Charlie practically beamed. "In all my years, I never expected—"

"Neither did I, and I've lived an entirely different sort of life from you. Let us not linger on the impossibility of what we've found and merely enjoy it."

Charlie laughed. It was a sound like a burst of joy.

Of all the decisions Nicky had ever had to make, the one to give up his apartment to Brigid and move in with Hank was among the easiest, but the one regarding keeping his job at Bulgaria was the hardest. He was thrilled Hank understood his odd need to keep performing as Paulina, but Paulina didn't need to be exclusive to Club Bulgaria.

Staying inside Hank's house felt safe, but Nicky knew he needed to at least determine if he still had a job. It seemed likely Julie would make the decision for him.

Shortly after Hank left for his meeting, before even unpacking much, Nicky dressed in a neatly-pressed gray suit, donned his favorite red scarf, and walked east to Club Bulgaria.

It was a relief to find it was not so hot outside as it had been. That at least meant the walk was not physically taxing, though Nicky still worried his heart would beat out of his chest. Something had changed during the ten days since Hank had entered his life, and it wasn't just that he'd fallen in love; something inside him had changed as well.

Perhaps that was why the grand entrance to Club Bulgaria seemed tawdry now instead of sexy and exciting the way it had when Nicky had first gone to work there. The lobby floor was scuffed, the red rug that led to the ballroom worn and threadbare, the walls peppered with fingerprints and what were likely shoe polish stains. In the daylight, it was filthy and smelled vaguely of rotten food and urine. It wasn't exciting and illicit the way it once was, but Nicky suspected it had always looked just like this—he'd been too thrilled to be a part of it to notice.

He found Julie in his office, poring over ledgers.

"Ah, Mr. Sharp. Nice of you to finally join us again."

"I can only offer my sincerest apologies. I've been detained the last few days." Nicky debated how much to tell Julie. "I imagine some parts of my tale will surface in the papers, in fact."

"Bah," said Julie, shaking his hands in Nicky's direction. "When you didn't show up two nights ago, I had to find other entertainment. You must know by now, men who wear dresses are not as hard to come by as you'd think. This fellow calls himself Claudia, though his voice is not nearly as good as yours. Still, he was here and you were not, so I promised him the evening show for the rest of the week."

"For the times when I would usually sing, I presume."

"Precisely. I like you Nicky, but I need to keep my business open. You understand."

Nicky nodded, because he understood how this world worked. "Well, like I said, I do apologize. I would like to resume my position if you'll have me." Though Nicky was no longer certain that was true. After walking through the lobby, he wondered how many times he'd be able to repeat the act. Bulgaria had always been a bit seedy, but now it seemed particularly uncouth and perhaps unsafe.

A shiver went through him. How many more Brigham Knights would there be out there? Knight was hardly the first man to come slumming at a place like Bulgaria and he would not be the last, not as long as the city's wealthy elite considered it sporting to see how the other half lived, as if attending a night club on the Bowery was some kind of cheap thrill. Knight was likely not the first or the last with more nefarious intent.

For the first time since Hank had rescued him, Nicky began to shake, but he wanted to at least keep his wits about him in front of Julie, so instead he held his breath and waited.

"Come back in a week if you still want the job," Julie said. "I can't make you any promises. The boys like Claudia."

"I understand, of course, darling," Nicky said. "Paulina will sing again, though."

"We'll see."

Nicky left a few minutes later. As he walked out onto the Bowery, an elevated train rattled above. The tracks blocked the sunlight, so this bit of street never got much light, which may have been why Nicky had never quite noticed just how disgusting it was.

Paulina *would* sing again if Nicky had anything to say about it, but whether it would be at Bulgaria was less certain. He could likely persuade Julie to give him his old gig back—he was too much of an asset to the club—but suddenly Nicky was not so sure he wanted it. He wanted to perform, but not to a room full of men about to get their cocks sucked by pretty working boys who escorted them to the backrooms.

Nicky knew he was not without talent. There had to be other opportunities out there. He just had to find them.

Chapter 21

Chaos burst on the main floor of Police Headquarters where the secretarial pool sat. A wave of activity passed from the far end of the room, opposite Andrew's desk, and it came back toward Andrew with an intensity that had him waiting, braced for impact.

"A fight broke out at the Tombs!" someone said excitedly.

"A fight?" said Andrew.

"In one of the cells!" The nearest secretary—Jenkins was his name—hopped to his feet and bustled over to Andrew's desk. "The report is there was some sodomite in a cell down at the Tombs, and he got into a fight with another inmate in his cell, and one or both of them were injured. Someone was stabbed, I think. Wait, what did you say?" He turned around. Everyone was talking at once and there was an air of excitement.

Andrew groaned. It wasn't uncommon for fights to break out at the Tombs, nor were the secretaries at Police Headquarters strangers to violence and death, especially not this week, but he supposed the sodomite detail added an extra bit of scandal.

And that brought Andrew up short.

"Has anyone heard the victim's names?" Andrew shouted above the fray.

No one seemed to.

Andrew grabbed his jacket and headed toward the door.

He ran most of the way and had worked up a good sweat by the time he arrived at the Tombs. Even though it wasn't nearly as hot today as it had been, it was still August in New York. He pulled his handkerchief from his pocket as he walked into the prison, where everything was still chaos. Several uniformed officers were yelling and one of the police surgeons was milling about in front as if waiting to be summoned. Andrew pushed through the crowd to the main desk.

"Excuse me. I'm Andrew Ritchley from the police department. Special Assistant to Commissioner Roosevelt." He had to shout to be heard because everyone seemed to be talking at once. "I've been sent to find out the details of what is happening here." A white lie, but Andrew had a sinking feeling he knew which sodomite had been caught up in the most recent altercation.

A harried looking clerk looked at him and nodded. "I imagine you heard about the incident of this morning."

"Yes. Police Headquarters is buzzing about it. Look, a few officers working on a case I have been overseeing brought a man in here yesterday under arrest. I wondered if he might have been one of the parties tied up in the chaos of the morning. Can you tell me the names of anyone injured? Or give me details?"

"I'm afraid I don't know their names," said the clerk. "But I'll tell you what I know." The clerk also shouted, and he was still hard to hear.

Frustrated, Andrew turned around. He clapped his hands together hard a few times and then cupped them around his mouth. "Would everyone keep quiet for just a moment! Keep your voices down!" His cries fell on deaf ears, apparently, because everyone still shouted.

The clerk sighed and then climbed up on the desk. He shouted, "Quiet! Quiet all of you!"

He managed to achieve a volume that snared everyone's attention, and while it wasn't quite silent, the volume of talking diminished significantly.

"Thank you!" shouted the clerk. "I've a man here from Police Headquarters who intends to investigate the incident of this morning. If you are a reporter, wait outside. We will pass details to you in a moment. If you are a surgeon, I understand your help is needed in the infirmary, which is just down that hallway." He pointed. "And if you have no business here but are just an onlooker, please leave. I am certain there will be a thorough and vivid report in the papers tomorrow."

"My thanks," Andrew said to the clerk as he climbed back off his desk.

The clerk grunted. They both waited for some of those gathered to exit the room.

"Look, here is what happened," said the clerk. "Or as much as I know. At around ten o'clock this morning or a little after, there was some kind of altercation between two inmates who were sharing a cell. One was a man who was arrested by police yesterday on charges I'm not sure of, but they weren't violent, so he was sharing his cell with a drunk who was sleeping off his intoxication. I do not know the circumstances under which the fight broke out, but the two of them got into a bit of a shouting match, and before the guards could get there, the drunk man pulled a piece of glass out of his pocket. He lashed out at the other man in the cell and cut him pretty severely. Both are currently in the infirmary."

"May I see them?"

The clerk looked around the room instead of answering. "Officer Skinner!"

Andrew turned to see who the clerk spoke to. A tall man with a thin mustache wearing a police uniform stepped forward.

"Would you please escort Mr. Ritchley to the infirmary?" said the clerk.

Officer Skinner led Andrew down the hall, barking at prisoners in their cells as they passed, until they arrived at the infirmary. It wasn't the first time Andrew had walked the halls of cells in the Tombs, but he never enjoyed it.

Andrew wished he had Hank with him, because he'd only ever seen the engravings of Knight in the paper he'd shown Charlie. He had been in the neighbor's house while Hank, Sherwood, and Polk had apprehended him the day before. He wasn't sure he could positively identify Knight, and he wasn't sure now why he'd rushed down here. It was too late to turn back now, though.

Inside the infirmary, there were a dozen occupied beds. Probably the Tombs had inmates suffering from the heat just as much as everyone else. And perhaps the injured man was not Knight; there were probably a few dozen men arrested each day who were cooling their heels in a cell while they waited for arraignment. The man who'd been cut could have been arrested for any number of non-violent offenses. If he was rumored to be a sodomite, he could easily have been a working boy and not Mr. Knight.

Andrew cursed his rashness.

One prisoner was strapped to his bed and rattled against his restraints.

"Do you know the names of the men involved in the altercation?" Andrew asked Skinner.

Skinner walked over to the bed. "What's your name, prisoner?" he barked at the man strapped to his bed.

The man growled and pulled at his restraints.

"Name!" said Skinner.

"Barnes," said the prisoner. "John Barnes."

Andrew looked at the surgeon. "Is this one of the men involved in the violence this morning?"

"He is," said the surgeon, who had a bit of an accent, maybe German. "This man pulled a piece of glass from a bottle or something from his pocket and brandished it at the other man in his cell. He seems mostly without injury aside from a few bruises and some minor cuts on his hands."

"And the other man?" asked Andrew.

The surgeon frowned. "Well, he's over here."

The surgeon walked over to a bed that had been covered with a sheet. Clearly, someone dead was beneath it. Andrew didn't want to see it, but he didn't think he had a choice. The corpse was already starting to smell. The surgeon lifted the sheet to reveal the pale body of a middle-aged man with dark hair.

"That filthy sodomite," growled the prisoner Barnes. "Do you know why he was arrested? He kidnapped a man for . . . immoral purposes."

Andrew closed his eyes and took a deep breath.

"He wanted to bugger me," Barnes shouted. "I could see it in his eyes."

When Andrew opened his eyes again, he saw that the man on the table had a big cut at his neck, big enough to at least have nicked an artery, and other cuts on his arms and chest. So Barnes hadn't just lashed out once, but repeatedly. Heaven forbid he share space with a known sodomite.

The dead man on the table bore some resemblance to Andrew's knowledge of Knight and was certainly too old to be a working boy.

"His name?" Andrew asked.

The surgeon walked over and picked up the toe tag. "Uh, this is a Mr. Brigham Knight."

That was decisive, at least. "All right," said Andrew. "Thank you, sir. Er, do you have a water closet nearby that I may use?"

The surgeon directed him to one just outside the infirmary. Andrew rushed inside and promptly vomited everything he'd eaten all day.

Hank wasn't altogether thrilled as he walked out of his meeting. The meeting itself had been mostly bureaucratic nonsense, which was for the good because Hank found it impossible to pay attention. He'd instead spent the time fretting about the future.

He couldn't prove his case.

It might be better to resign before the truth of his relationship with Nicky was exposed.

It was the latter that most scared him, because he loved being a police officer and enjoyed the detective work that went along with his current position, but he also had no desire to have his affairs aired to the whole police commission should there be an investigation into his private life. As Stephens spent a good portion of his morning skulking about, smiling as if he had a secret, Hank couldn't help but wonder if the days he could keep his secrets were numbered.

Hank had been called into Roosevelt's office for a chat about something after the meeting, which was awe-inspiring and terrifying all at once. He'd only met Roosevelt on a handful of occasions, and it had been Roosevelt himself who had recommended Hank for his promotion to inspector, but the timing of this meeting did not bode well. Hank dreaded this "chat" as he made his way through the main floor toward Roosevelt's office. A quick glance toward Andrew's desk revealed Andrew himself was absent, which was a shame because Hank could have used a friend or at least a few words of encouragement right then.

"Well, Inspector Brandt. I want to start by saying you have been an exemplary police officer," Roosevelt said as Hank took a seat after the customary greetings. "You were recommended for promotion to inspector even before I came to occupy this office. As I have done with all candidates for promotion, I reviewed your records. I supported such a promotion and spoke highly of you to the other members of the Board. You do not always adhere strictly to the rules of conduct, but your tenacity in investigating is to be commended."

"Thank you, sir."

"As you are likely also aware, the delay in changing your rank from acting inspector to full inspector was caused by some conflict within the police board."

Hank knew that, too; the rumor throughout the department was

Parker voted against any recommended by Roosevelt, apparently for spite.

"Yes, sir," said Hank.

"Having met you only briefly, I judged you to be a man of some character, despite your failure to adhere to some of the tenets of police business."

"Is this regarding the uniform, sir? I will resume dressing however you deem appropriate first thing tomorrow, if that is the case."

Roosevelt shook his head. "It is not your promotion I wish to discuss today. That matter may take some time to resolve, and you have my sincerest apologies for it. Such is the nature of politics, unfortunately." Roosevelt frowned briefly. "No, I have another matter. Some information regarding your work on your most recent case has prompted me to call you in. Your partner in this matter, Detective Stephens, had some concerns."

Hank waited.

"As you know, it is of great importance to me that each of the men on this police force must comport themselves with a great deal of respectability."

"Yes, sir."

Hank wondered if this would be the end for him. Stephens had probably found some bit of evidence that proved Hank was carrying on with a witness, despite Hank's best efforts to conceal the real truth of his relationship with Nicky. Or Stephens had come to Roosevelt with what he thought he knew, which might have been accurate but could not have been backed up with any real evidence. Or Stephens had made something up in order to get Hank expelled from the force. There were a lot of possibilities that all added up to Roosevelt very likely deeming Hank to be someone lacking in the moral character required of an officer within the New York City Police Department.

"I like Detective Stephens," Roosevelt said. "Reminds me of myself in my younger days. Ambitious, responsible, a good manager. Wouldn't you say?"

"He's a fine man," said Hank, not willing to be argumentative.

"Indeed. The captain of the Seventeenth Precinct also recently put him forward as a candidate for promotion. He strikes me as just the sort of man this department needs among its leadership ranks. I intend to fully back his promotion and advocate for him with the police board."

"Yes. He deserves it."

"I'm glad you think so." Roosevelt shot Hank a toothy grin. "I'd like to advocate for you as well, but now I've had some time to consider your record and the information passed to me from Detective Stephens, I wonder if you wouldn't be better suited for a different position."

Hank sat up. Perhaps he was not being fired after all. "What do you mean, sir?"

Roosevelt put both of his hands on his desk. "Let us face fact. Detective Stephens is the sort of man who excels at politics. Having met with him for a good long while yesterday afternoon and this morning, I do believe he intends to have my job one day. Let him have it, I say."

Hank sat with his hands folded in his lap, waiting for the real purpose of this meeting to present itself.

"You, Inspector Brandt, would be an asset to any investigative team, and as such, I'd like to keep you working cases. I understand you cracked an important kidnapping case yesterday."

"I did, yes."

"Everyone was safe and accounted for."

"Yes, sir. The kidnapper is currently awaiting legal intervention at the Tombs."

"Splendid. That is the kind of work you are best suited for. I'd like to keep you on this sort of detective work. Let Mr. Stephens play at politics and ambition. As you seem to not have much in the way of political ambitions?" Roosevelt paused.

"No, sir," Hank said. "In fact, I generally try to stay far away from politics."

"I gathered that, yes. Well, in that case, I do believe you would do well at detective work, so I will keep you in your position in the Seventeenth Precinct, and then I intend to promote Detective Stephens to a loftier position. I may even discuss an appointment with Mayor Strong."

Hank's disappointment at not earning his promotion was mild; he was sad not to have his work appreciated, but he agreed that he was better suited to detective work and not the bureaucratic nonsense that accompanied the inspector position. And more, to have Stephens out of his hair was something Hank greatly desired. "I think that sounds capital, sir."

Roosevelt grinned again. "I am dee-lighted you think so." Then he became serious. "Do put a little more effort into your appearance and keep on the straight and narrow. There are a few unsavory rumors floating around about you. No evidence to back them up, mind you, and I expect they are mostly hogwash, but just the same, keep your nose clean. I'd hate to have to launch any sort of investigation. And let us hope your current case results in a conviction, because Detective Stephens implied it took perhaps more of your time than it necessarily warranted."

"Yes, sir. I believe I may have been a bit overzealous in my pursuit, but as you know, it paid off in the end. I have the perpetrator behind bars. I believe he may have been responsible for the murders of at least five men."

"Then it is good you got him off the streets! Excellent work, Inspector. I won't take up any more of your time."

Hank walked out of Roosevelt's office a moment later not altogether sure he understood what had just happened.

On his way back out of Headquarters, Andrew intercepted him. "Hank, thank God," Andrew said.

"What is it?"

"Brigham Knight is dead. Another inmate killed him during an altercation."

"The devil you say." Knight was dead? How could that be possible? "What in God's name happened?"

Andrew took a deep breath and then related the story of the inmate with the glass shard.

"The surgeon said he bled a great deal and very quickly. The glass was sharp enough to cut the artery at Knight's throat. Had the guards intervened faster, the man with the glass might not have inflicted other cuts, which included another at his chest from which he bled profusely. He lost so much blood so quickly that by the time the guards did get to him, he was half-delirious. He expired in the infirmary within the hour."

"My God." Hank still had a hard time understanding what had transpired. Knight had been killed by an inmate? "What prompted the attack?"

"No one is certain, but when I got to the infirmary, the inmate with the glass raved about Knight being a sodomite. Rumor around police headquarters indicated the same, so I suspect news of the nature of the crimes of which Knight had been accused had made its way through the inmate population, and this man imagined some behavior in Knight that prompted him to attack."

Hank took in and let out a breath. "What a day! I just met with Commissioner Roosevelt and it seems not only am I not being fired, but Roosevelt wants to promote Stephens such that Stephens and I will no longer work together."

Andrew's eyes popped wide. "That is an unexpected turn of events."

"I think Roosevelt intended to tell me I will likely not earn the promotion from acting inspector to inspector, but it doesn't matter because he prefers to keep me doing actual police work, not working at a desk."

"Perhaps that is the best possible outcome."

For the first time since he'd left his house that morning, Hank smiled. "Yes, I agree."

"Do you have the time to accompany me to my desk to deal with the small matter of wrapping up this case before you adjourn for your precinct house?"

"Indeed I do."

"Then come on. I think you'll agree with me that we'd all like to put the past two weeks behind us."

Hank thought of Nicky. "Well, not all of it has been terrible."

A wistful expression briefly flashed over Andrew's face. "No. I suppose you're right."

Epilogue

Friday, November 13

Temperature: 48°F

The theater on Twenty-sixth Street was small and cramped and not altogether reputable, but Hank made his way to a seat in the middle row of the audience and settled into it. The audience was only about half-full, but it hardly seemed to matter. The show was the thing. The amount of attention it received was beside the point. Well, that, and Hank hoped the reputation of the show would spread quickly and draw more people to the seats, at least for the sake of the producer who owned the stage.

The house lights dimmed after a few minutes and somewhere off stage, someone shouted, "Ladies and gentlemen! May I present to you the newest sensation at the Townhouse Theater, Miss Paulina Clodhopper!"

The curtain rose on a man seated at a piano. He started banging out the opening bars of "The Sidewalks of New York," and it was clear to Hank the piano was out of tune, but he knew that was beside the point. The *raison d'etre* of this whole production sauntered onto the stage a moment later. She was a woman dressed in head-to-toe emerald green with a matching parasol she twirled into hands. When she at last began to sing, it was the sweetest sound Hank had ever heard.

It was Nicky.

Perhaps this was still not the most reputable of places. There were men skulking about in the back of the small theater, any of them likely willing to take Hank somewhere private. Hank wanted no part of it, given the most spectacular person Hank knew was right up there on stage. All other men would pale in comparison.

Speaking of people skulking about, Charlie ducked his head and hurried down the row to sit next to Hank. He nodded to acknowledge Hank and then watched Nicky sing for a moment. When the song ended and Nicky paused to consult with the pianist about the next song, Charlie said, "I apologize. I feel dreadful for having missed the beginning of the show."

"He just started."

"Andrew sends his regrets, but he's been detained at headquarters with the planning work for the election. He thought he'd be able to get away, but apparently one of the Tammany politicians is making a lot of noise about election fraud and security."

"A Tammany politician is concerned about fraud?" Hank asked.

"That was what I said. More likely he's perpetrating fraud and creating a smokescreen." Charlie motioned toward the stage. "He's about to sing again."

This time, Nicky broke into a rousing version of "Hot Time in the Old Town Tonight." Nicky's repertoire of popular songs was somewhat limited, but it didn't matter. Hank imagined Nicky could sing police reports and Hank would still be as captivated.

Nicky finished out the set by announcing, "I'd like to dedicate this one to my own dearest love, who I'm sure is somewhere in the audience, though I can see nothing past these infernal stage lights." He grinned and twirled his parasol. The audience whistled and hooted appreciatively. Then Nicky said, "My man is more of a chocolate brown than a strawberry blond, but you get the idea, I imagine." He began to sing "The Band Played On," changing all instances of "girl" in the lyrics to "boy," which had everyone in the audience laughing.

Much later, Hank and Charlie snuck backstage to see Nicky. Nicky greeted Hank with a quick kiss and Charlie with a brief hug. "Well, darlings, what did you think of my debut?"

Hank reached for Nicky and put an arm around him. "You were magnificent."

Nicky tittered a bit, mostly an act from what Hank could tell, but then said, "I was rather magnificent, wasn't I?"

"I'm glad you were able to find this place," Charlie said. "It's much nicer than Club Bulgaria."

Nicky nodded. "Did I tell you, Charlie? The owner is someone I knew from my Armory Hall days. He used to be one of the painted girls roaming the floors there. He recognized me when I came in to audition and gave me this job on the spot. And it's *perfect*. I only wish the seats in the audience had been more occupied."

"They will be," said Charlie. "Once word gets out."

Nicky ran a hand down the front of his gown, smoothing out the wrinkles. "I certainly intend to enjoy this for as long as it lasts. Mr. Graham, he's the owner, he thinks I might have a shot at singing at a fancier theater someday. Who knows? They're opening up all those places near Longacre Square. What's the name of the big theater Mr. Hammerstein opened?"

"The Olympia," Hank said. "I don't know what business he has opening a theater on Forty-fourth Street. It's so far from everything."

Nicky laughed. "You are so short-sighted, my love. As long as people move here and women have babies, this city will continue to expand, and where is there to go but up the island?"

"Unless this consolidation plan happens," Charlie said. "Can you imagine, if New York merged with Queens and Brooklyn? What a huge city we'd be then!"

"More police departments for me to fight with," Hank said.

"Oh, I thought you were satisfied with the direction your career had taken of late," said Nicky.

"I am, just ... I don't know. It's a lot of change being visited on the city all at once. You get used to it being one way, and then suddenly it's something else entirely."

Nicky patted Hank on the chest. "Change is good, Hank. It's progress!"

"It's a headache, is what it is."

Nicky laughed. "My dearest love, will you unlace me? I'd like to get out of this corset."

Charlie and Hank worked together to get Nicky out of his gown and into his street clothes, a simple gray suit with a white shirt. Hank knew Nicky hoped this theater job would last long enough for him to earn money for new clothes, but as it was, money was tight. There had been a long few weeks in which Nicky was certain he'd never get another job, but then at Hank's suggestion, he started auditioning for song-and-dance opportunities at concert saloons and small theaters. He'd acted in a terrible play in September, which hadn't lasted long once the papers started publishing reviews, and then he'd gone to an audition he'd seen advertised in the paper, and suddenly he had this job. Hank didn't mind supporting him while he pursued his dream, but Nicky insisted he continue to support Brigid and his father without Hank's help.

Hank didn't know if this current theater job would really last, but it felt like the beginning of something important, so he chose to remain optimistic.

"Do we still have that bottle of wine?" Nicky asked Hank.

"I believe so, yes."

"Good. Take me home. I want to celebrate with you."

And Hank wanted to celebrate. "Will you be all right to get home, Charlie?"

"Yes. It's a nice night. I think I'll walk. Andrew should be home soon."

"Good. Be careful."

"I always am."

Nicky gave Charlie a hug. Then he turned the full force of his charm on Hank. "Come, my love. The celebration awaits."

Hank laughed and followed Nicky out of the dressing room.

If you enjoyed *Ten Days in August*, don't miss Kate McMurray's
Such a Dance, available now!

**When a vaudeville dancer meets a sexy mobster in a speakeasy
for men, the sparks fly, the gin flows, the jazz sizzles—and the
heat is on...**

New York City, 1927. Eddie Cotton is a talented song-and-dance man
with a sassy sidekick, a crowd-pleasing act, and a promising future
on Broadway. What he doesn't have is someone to love. Being gay
in an era of Prohibition and police raids, Eddie doesn't have many
opportunities to meet men like himself—until he discovers a hot
new jazz club for gentlemen of a certain bent... and sets eyes on
the most seductive, and dangerous, man he's ever seen.

Lane Carillo is a handsome young Sicilian who looks like
Valentino—and works for the Mob. He's never hidden his sexuality
from his boss, which is why he was chosen to run a private night
club for men. When Lane spots Eddie at the bar, it's lust at first
sight. Soon, the unlikely pair is falling hard and fast—in love. But
when their whirlwind romance starts raising eyebrows all across
town, Lane and Eddie have to decide if their relationship is doomed
... or something special worth fighting for.

In the Jazz Age, anything
goes—except their love...

KATE McMURRAY

SUCH A DANCE

A Novel

Chapter 1

"Are You Lonesome Tonight?"

New York City, 1927

Left, right, left. Left, left, right, right, hop. Step forward, step back, hop, tip hat, blow the lady a kiss.

The steps were easy enough, the routine so committed to memory that Eddie could let a dozen other things swim through his mind without missing a beat.

He tossed his cane in the air and let it twirl. Light bounced off the polished silver shaft of it as the audience murmured appreciatively. Eddie caught it deftly, bowed a little, and moved his feet to the left, right, right, left, left, hop. He grinned at Marian, who stretched her arms above her head with grace, betraying her ballet training. Then she shuffled over to him, evidence of her years spent on the vaude-ville circuit. She sang her lines in her trademark style, which sounded a bit like a goose honking, and the audience roared with laughter. She smiled and winked at him, and he grinned back and sang the end of the song. Left, right, forward, together, a flourish from the horn section of the orchestra. Then there were deep bows before the curtain fell. Applause erupted throughout the James Theater. Eddie and Mar-ian did their goofy curtain call before retreating backstage.

Thus ended Eddie Cotton and Marian France's act in *Le Tumulte de Broadway*, more informally Jimmy Blanchard's Doozies of 1927, the variety act that was competing with George White and Flo Ziegfeld for ticket dollars and popularity. The song-and-dance team of Cotton and France was among the more popular acts. They were a comedy duo who told jokes, danced their way through physical comedy, and sang funny songs in funny voices. That year, they preceded the Doozy Dolls, fourteen barely-dressed chorines hired more for their looks than their dancing or singing skills.

While the Dolls paraded around on stage, Eddie walked back to his dressing room, Marian trailing behind him. She was already pulling off her shoes, and she padded past Eddie in stockinged feet. "I cannot wait to get out of here tonight," she said.

"Hot date?" Eddie asked.

"Hardly." Marian rolled her eyes, and then paused near the door of her dressing room. "I'm exhausted and my tootsies are killing me. I'd cut my feet off if it didn't mean Mr. Blanchard would fire me." She looked at Eddie, who chuckled. "What about you?"

"Nothing planned for tonight. Figure I'll just go home and sleep so we can do all this again tomorrow."

Marian smiled and kissed his cheek. "Good night, Eddie." Then she retreated into her dressing room and slammed her door in his face.

Eddie went to his room to change. He wasn't the least bit tired. No, his ailment was much worse: he was horny.

His restlessness had been building for days, starting as an itch and progressing to an all-out yearning, an uneasiness that wouldn't be quenched by Eddie pushing his needs aside.

He considered his options as he changed out of his costume and slid into a pair of brown trousers and a white cotton shirt. He could go home and forget about it. He could keep his regular appointment with his right hand. Or he could find someone who would help him take the edge off.

He washed the stage makeup off his face and examined his reflection in the mirror. He hadn't shaved in a couple of days, something Mr. Blanchard had taken exception to before showtime that day. The stubble looked like bronze dust on his otherwise pale jaw. His eyes looked tired. Eddie let his fingers dance over the black powder he kept on hand for the occasions when Blanchard wanted him to do blackface—thankfully, rare these days—and then dusted some over his eyes. He liked the effect, which created rings around his eyes and made him look a little less rosy and innocent, as he tended to present in his normal life. He grabbed his fedora from the shelf in the corner and plopped it on his head. He pulled the brim down so it hid his eyes. He thought himself hard to recognize as he posed in the mirror, his eyes hidden, his chin shadowed.

Mind made up, he slipped out of his dressing room and then out of the stage door, onto 41st Street. The cool spring air bit his exposed skin, but he liked it, liked the contrast to the sweltering lights of the stage. He adjusted the brim of his hat and walked.

He fingered the money clip in his pocket, tried to remember how much cash he had on hand. Behind him, he could hear a roar of applause from one of the theaters, though whether it was from the Doozies or one of the productions in the four other theaters nearby, Eddie couldn't tell. It didn't much matter. He was about to leave that world—the dancers, the lights, the laughter, the applause, the cute little families out for a night of entertainment—to go to a much darker place.

He walked east. The lights of Times Square seemed to fade as he left them behind, and then he was standing on one side of Sixth Avenue, the elevated train platform separating him from Bryant Park. He pulled the brim of his hat down a little farther and looked around. There was a man standing against a pillar, the train platform above casting striped shadows over his body. He was tall and thin with an elegant stance. A cigarette dangled from his long fingers, and he would occasionally lift it up to his lips and take a drag. He wore a dark coat and had a bright red scarf tied around his neck.

Julian, Eddie thought. *Maybe this will be easier than I expected.*

He approached slowly. Julian was looking at something in the distance, but he turned his head when Eddie got close. There was something wary in his eyes. Eddie lifted his hat so Julian could see his face, and something like relief showed over those delicate features before a wide grin spread across Julian's face.

"Dearest Edward. Funny meeting you here."

"How are you, Julian?"

"Marvelous." He took a long drag from his cigarette before dropping it and smothering it with the tip of his shoe. "You looking for something?"

"I am."

Julian nodded. "There's a new boy in my employ. He fancies himself my apprentice. He's over by the library. I can fetch him, if you like."

"I don't want a boy," Eddie said.

Julian smiled. "I know, darling. I was just offering." He reached over and stroked Eddie's arm.

Up close, Eddie could see the makeup caked on Julian's face, designed to make him look much younger than he really was. Eddie had known Julian for a while, but had never been able to ascertain his actual age. If he had to guess, he'd put Julian in his late thirties. Under the makeup, Eddie knew, there were crow's feet and frown lines. Strands of silver ran through his body hair, though the hair on his head was, of course, bleached blond.

Eddie looked at the aging fairy and saw that he was tired and underdressed for the weather. "You want a warm place to sleep tonight, Julian?"

"I would, yes," Julian said quietly.

Eddie crooked his finger so that Julian would follow. Julian pushed off the pillar and fell into step next to Eddie, who walked back toward Times Square along 40th Street.

"Dinner?" Eddie asked.

"No, darling, I already ate. An older gentleman named Roberto takes me to Sardi's every Thursday and buys me dinner just for the pleasure of watching me eat."

Eddie glanced at Julian. He could imagine that watching him eat would be quite a pleasure. He thought Julian beautiful, but of course couldn't say that. Men were not beautiful. Julian would probably joke that he was something else, but Eddie thought him a man in all the ways that counted, in all the ways that he needed to ease the tension and longing that had built up in his body.

"You're still at the Knickerbocker?" Julian asked.

"Yes. I'd prefer to go in through the Broadway entrance." Which was not through the main lobby where everyone could see what Eddie was up to.

"Of course." Julian fiddled with his scarf. "Fancy digs or not, my usual fee still applies. Don't stiff me." Julian paused and then chuckled. "Well, not monetarily, anyway."

Later, as Eddie lay awake in bed, contemplating the décor in his relatively modest room with Julian sound asleep and snoring softly beside him, he reflected on how he felt physically satisfied but empty at the same time.

The loneliness was familiar, was a comfort in its way. The knowledge that Julian would be gone in a few hours, that this room and its silence would be waiting for Eddie after the noise of the theater the next night, that life would carry on as it had been, these were all things he could trust and rely on, and a thousand days played out before him in his mind, days of the same. Eddie liked routine, thrived within the confines of it, but could he really go so long without change?

Julian stirred in his sleep. Eddie shuffled over in the bed and pulled the quilt up to his chin, careful not to let their bodies touch.

He chastised himself for his own fear of change. He glanced over at Julian's sleeping form and let himself imagine what it would be like if they forged some kind of partnership. He'd met other men like himself over the years, men who lived together or had some kind of permanent relationship. He even knew a few husbands. Having worked in the theater for a number of years, he encountered homosexual men almost daily, and often they acknowledged each other without much fanfare, which was just as well. Eddie wanted people to notice him for his dancing or his comedic chops; he didn't want them to notice after whom he lusted.

So he kept his little secret tucked away in the hidden corners of the city.

Julian stirred again. He woke and looked at Eddie. "You're awake."

"Just thinking."

"Such heavy thoughts you must have to be wearing such a serious expression." Julian leaned over and ran a hand down Eddie's chest. "Maybe I can help unburden you."

Eddie sighed. He gently moved Julian's hand back to the other side of the bed. "Thanks, but not right now."

Julian rolled onto his back. "You should know, I might have to move."

"What?"

"I adore you, you know that I do. I'm always glad when you wander over to the park. But I'm not sure how much longer you'll be able to find me there. Some club on Sixth didn't pay off their local law enforcement, so a raiding party got themselves worked up into a good frenzy a couple of days ago. They came to the park and arrested everyone who wasn't dressed like he was on the way to a funeral."

"You too?"

"No, I was visiting with a gentleman at the Hotel Astor, but my dear friend Jesse told me all about it. You'll know Jesse, of course. He's the fellow with the proclivity for violet."

Eddie had no idea to whom Julian referred, but he nodded.

"Not that I haven't been arrested before," Julian added.

"So where are you moving to?"

"I don't know yet, darling. And it may not even be a problem. But should you come to the park looking for something, you may not find it there for much longer." Julian rubbed a hand over his face. "Can I leave word for you somewhere?"

That seemed like a terrible idea. "No. I'll find you, I'm sure." But even if he didn't, Eddie was surprised that the prospect of not seeing Julian again was not too dire.

And what did that say about Eddie?

"Maybe I should go," Julian said, sitting up.

In the moonlight streaming through the window, Julian appeared to be an entirely different creature, less an effeminate affectation and more an actual man in his late thirties, a man who worked for a living, who had dreams deferred and given up on, who had come here tonight to do a job. Eddie wondered how much of Julian was real and how much was an act. As a rule, Eddie had long been fascinated by the fairy men who occupied the streets of New York, the queens who talked like women and dressed like them sometimes, too. He had never found them especially attractive—in fact, looking at a fairy sometimes brought shame, because Eddie, behind all other things, was a man who lusted after men the way he was supposed to lust after women. But here was Julian, thin and willowy, but with short blond hair on his head, and long limbs and broad shoulders. He had a pattern of blond hair on his flat chest that was unrelentingly masculine, and a large cock, of course, which was part of his appeal to Eddie just to begin with.

And Eddie found himself lusting again.

"You don't have to go," he told Julian, and he reached over and ran a hand over Julian's shoulder. "I'm sorry, I don't mean to be mean, I just have a reputation . . ."

"I understand, darling. Of course I understand. I didn't mean to imply . . ."

"I just . . ."

"I know."

Eddie frowned. "I need to keep my job. I've worked so hard."

"I need to keep mine, too."

Eddie sighed. "If you have to leave the park, I will find you. Or you can find me. I go to the club at the Astor sometimes."

"Where the sailors hang out."

"Yes."

Julian smirked. "I suppose that you are a man of sophistication. You like the trade. The big brawny men, the soldiers of fortune."

Eddie couldn't deny that. "I like to look at them, yes."

"And fuck them. I like to, too."

Eddie sighed. It was hard to believe he was having this conversation.

"But you don't want me to find you," Julian said. "It doesn't matter, I just thought . . . well, I figured you liked me."

"I do like you, Julian." Or Julian was a good companion for tonight. For any night. He had a working knowledge of men's bodies that could not be rivaled, and he could make Eddie forget his problems and his loneliness.

But was there anything more lonely than lying in bed next to a man who would take your money and leave in the morning?

Eddie sat up and pulled his legs up to his chest. He knew, too, that part of Julian's seeming affection now was borne of the fact that, when their encounters were over, Eddie didn't beat the shit out of Julian. In the thin white light that flooded the room, Eddie could see the bruises on Julian's torso from the last john who'd felt the need to prove his masculinity by pounding his fists into the effete object of his affection. Eddie wasn't sure if he should feel reassured by that, if it was a good thing that he made Julian feel safe.

"I'm sorry," Julian said softly, as if maybe he wasn't sure about that, either. "I do care about you. I won't come after you. If after tonight we don't see each other, I hope that things go well for you. Maybe I'll come see that show of yours sometime."

"Sure. It's very good. Or so I've been told." Eddie wasn't sure how the usual crowd at the James Theater would deal with a man like Julian.

"I'm sure that you are perfectly marvelous in it." Julian reached over and caressed Eddie's hair. He smiled affectionately. "But if I don't see you, good luck."

"You too."

"I don't need luck. I make my own." Julian grinned. "Perhaps you would like one last tussle with me. Free of charge."

When Julian reached for Eddie, Eddie let himself be pulled into those long arms. He wasn't feeling especially affectionate. If anything, the encounter felt more than anything like a good-bye. Would he ever see Julian again? He wondered as they moved and moaned and sweated together, and when Julian cried out at the end, something in Eddie's heart closed off.

Eddie got up afterward and went to the restroom. On his way, he left Julian's fee on the dresser. When he returned to the bedroom, Julian was gone and so was the money. Just as well, Eddie thought, returning to bed. The sheets smelled like sex and Julian, and it was enough to let Eddie sink into sleep.

Kate McMurray has published several best-selling male/male novels, including Rainbow Award winner *Show and Tell* and *Across the East River Bridge*. She has been writing stories since she could hold a pen. She started writing gay romance after reading a book and thinking there should be more love stories with gay characters. Her first published novel, *In Hot Pursuit*, came out in February 2010, and she's been writing feverishly ever since.

When she's not writing, Kate works as a nonfiction editor. She also reads a lot, plays the violin, knits and crochets, drools over expensive handbags, and is a tiny bit obsessed with baseball. She lives in Brooklyn, New York, and is active in the Romance Writers of America.